Celq

THE REGENCY LORDS & LADIES COLLECTION

**Glittering Regency Love Affairs
from your favourite historical authors.**

THE REGENCY LORDS & LADIES COLLECTION

Available from the
Regency Lords & Ladies Large Print Collection

MIRANDA'S MASQUERADE

Meg Alexander

First published in Great Britain 1997
Large Print Edition 2009
Harlequin Mills & Boon Limited,
Eton House, 18-24 Paradise Road, Richmond, Surrey TW9 1SR

© Meg Alexander 1997

ISBN: 978 0 263 21052 1

Set in Times Roman 15¾ on 18½ pt.
083-1209-71593

Harlequin Mills & Boon policy is to use papers that are natural,
renewable and recyclable products and made from wood grown in
sustainable forests. The logging and manufacturing process conform to
the legal environmental regulations of the country of origin.

Printed and bound in Great Britain
by CPI Antony Rowe, Chippenham, Wiltshire

Chapter One

"I'll make him sorry he ever offered for me!" With a cry of anguish, Frances Gaysford threw herself upon her bed and burst into a storm of tears.

"That shouldn't be too difficult, Fanny," her twin observed dispassionately. "Just let Lord Heston see you now and he'll cry off at once. The end of your nose is as red as your eyes…"

"Oh! Oh! Unfeeling! I might have known you'd make a joke of it…my own *sister!* You don't care in the least, Miranda."

"I might if I believed in this Cheltenham tragedy. Come to your senses, love. Harry Lakenham will never marry you. Even if he were of age, he won't wed to disoblige his family."

"We are promised to each other…" Fanny raised her head, the drowned blue eyes looking enormous in the delicate oval of her face. "His heart will not change, and nor will mine…"

"But yours has changed three times in the last three months! I have lost count of the men to whom you've sworn undying devotion."

"This time it's different. In the past…well…it was but an illusion. Now I know the meaning of true love."

"Perhaps so. In the meantime, you had best get up and bathe your face. Heston will be here at noon. You have less than an hour to change your dress, which, I may say, is sadly crumpled…"

"I won't see him. I can't. I am not well enough." Fanny's wails increased. "Uncle shall make my excuses…"

"He won't do so for a third time. Both Mr Mordaunt and Sir Patrick Caswell were insulted when you claimed the headache, and then they saw you later at the Opera."

"Could I help it if I felt a little better later in the day? I should not have taken either, in any case…a widower on the one hand, and a middle-aged country squire? I can't think what Uncle was about to allow them to address me."

"He hopes to see us comfortably settled, Fanny.

Was that not his object in giving us this Season? Mama could not afford it—"

"I know! Pray do not go on about it. He has been kind, but doubtless he has his reasons…"

"What can you mean?" There was a note of anger in Miranda's voice, and Fanny looked uncomfortable.

"Don't get upon your high ropes!" she said defiantly. "With Father gone, Uncle will not care to have our family foisted upon him. He would marry us to anyone."

"That is both ungenerous and untrue! You might at least see Heston. Uncle does not insist that you accept him…only that you listen to his offer."

"How can I? My heart is broken…" With a gesture worthy of a tragedy queen, Fanny raised herself upon one elbow and covered her eyes with a drooping hand.

Miranda recognised the scene at once. It was part of the repertoire of the latest actress to take the town by storm.

"What do I care for money or position?" her sister mourned. "I should be happy in a cottage with my darling."

"Stuff and nonsense!" Miranda said decisively. "Sometimes you put me out of all patience with you. You in a cottage? I can just see you feeding chickens and cleaning out the pigs. Remember how you hated life in Yorkshire...the plain food, no new clothes, an outside privy, and the cold? Have you forgot the cold?"

"No, of course not, but it will not come to that. Harry has expectations. All we need is a little time... He will see his grandfather—"

"Do be sensible, Fanny! It will not serve, you know."

"You have always been against him. How can you be so cruel? Why must I be sacrificed to that ugly dotard? Heston is a freak...a mountain...a positive Alp! He has neither manners nor wit to recommend him. Oh, why could he not take you?"

This suggestion was too much for Miranda. Her sense of humour bubbled to the surface. "Fanny, you will be the end of me! Do you believe that this...this monster, as you call him, would make me an ideal husband?"

"Of course not!" Fanny sniffed. "And you need not laugh. I doubt if any man would suit you. You treat them all as if their compliments are meaningless."

"Most of them are, and I won't be taken in by flattery."

"It isn't all false. We are not ill-looking, you and I. When a gentleman expresses admiration it is not kind in you to put him out of countenance by speaking out so plain. You frighten them away, you know."

"I'll try to mend my ways," Miranda promised. "Now, dearest, do get dressed. Much as I should like to help you, Lord Heston has not offered for me. He has asked to see Miss Gaysford, and you are the elder…"

"Only by twenty minutes. It isn't fair!" Fanny gazed at her twin, a look of speculation in her eyes. "He would not know the difference," she said thoughtfully. "We might play a trick on him, if you were to take my place."

Miranda stared at her. "I wonder that you could suggest it," she said in dismay.

"But we have exchanged places all our lives. It cannot signify for a mere half-hour. It could do no harm."

"I doubt if Lord Heston would see it so. It would be insulting, Fanny. Think of the scandal if we were to be found out? This is no childish game. The scandal would be unbearable—" She stopped. Fanny had given way to a series of hiccuping sobs. They were a certain prelude to an attack of hysteria. She looked up helplessly as her aunt came into the room.

"Why, what is this, my dears?" Mrs Shere gathered Fanny to her ample bosom. "There, my love, pray don't distress yourself. When your sister marries, she will not be lost to you, and you will be wed yourself before the year is out." She stroked her niece's copper curls with a gentle hand.

"I…I'm sorry, Aunt." Fanny lifted a drooping head. "I do not mean to be a watering-pot." The glance she threw at Miranda was one of triumph. Mrs Shere had mistaken one twin for the other, as she had often done before.

Miranda was about to correct her when Fanny caught at her hand. "You will come back at once and tell us what Lord Heston has to say?" she pleaded.

"Of course she will." Mrs Shere beamed upon the twins. "His lordship has arrived, and we must not keep him waiting." She took Miranda's arm and led her from the room.

"Aunt, please wait! I have something to say to you."

"Not now, my love. It must wait until later. This is not the time…" She hurried ahead, along the corridor and down the staircase, pausing only when they reached the door to the salon.

"You were right to wear the white sprigged muslin." She considered Miranda with a critical eye. "It is most becoming. I could wish that these short hairstyles were not so much the vogue, but there, we must be in the fashion. Be kind to Lord

Heston," she whispered finally. "Gentlemen, too, can be nervous on these occasions."

She opened the door and led her niece towards the man who stood by the window.

He turned as they entered and came towards her, bowing first to her aunt and then to herself.

Miranda felt a slight twinge of amusement. Anyone less nervous she had yet to see. A sharp glance from beneath his black brows had assured her of that.

She held her breath as she waited for his first words. Would he see through her deception? Then it became apparent that he too had mistaken her for Fanny. As he exchanged civilities with Mrs Shere, Miranda kept her eyes upon the carpet.

At last she nerved herself to look at him more closely. Immensely tall and built in proportion the perfect tailoring of his coat and breeches could not disguise his heavily muscled shoulders and thighs. He moved with the easy grace of an athlete.

Even the most partial would not have termed him handsome. Crowned by a mass of thick black hair, cut in the fashionable "Brutus" style, his face had a vitality of its own. The heavy jaw and a slightly crooked nose merely added character to his expression.

At this moment, that expression was unfathomable as his eyes met hers. She was startled. Hard and bleak as the grey of a winter sea, they roved over her with indifference.

It must be her imagination. She had seen him before, of course. His height alone made him conspicuous in any gathering. His lordship did not dance, and seemed to find no pleasure in feminine company.

"Who is that man?" she had asked her friend, Charlotte Fairfax. She had been half-piqued and half-amused when he had thrown her a single glance and, clearly unimpressed, had turned away.

"Heston? He is one of the richest men in London. Don't cast your handkerchief in his direction, my dear. You would be wasting your time."

"Why is that? Has he a reputation?"

"Not that I can discover, but he is a mis—a mis—well, one of those men who has not time for women. He thinks only of gaming, horses, and curricle racing."

"How very dull of him!" Miranda had watched as his lordship had strolled idly through the chattering throng and had made his way to the card tables in the adjoining room.

"Miranda, never let anyone hear you say so! Heston is a Corinthian and quite at the top of the tree. He is the idol of the younger set and a member of the Four-Horse Club."

"Remarkable! Are we supposed to admire him because he wears a Belcher handkerchief, a nosegay in his driving coat, and a spotted cravat? How ridiculous! It seems more like fancy-dress to me."

"Please, I beg of you…" Charlotte had drawn her friend into the shelter of an alcove, and had cast an anxious look about her. "Do guard your tongue, Miranda. You must not speak your mind so openly. Someone will overhear you. Gentlemen have their odd notions, and we must accept them."

"I suppose so…" Miranda had given her hand to the gallant who had come to claim her for the quadrille and had promptly forgotten Lord Heston's existence.

It was strange to see him again under these circumstances. She had been as puzzled as Fanny by his sudden decision to call upon their uncle. Fanny had met him once, when he was introduced to her by Harry Lakenham, and had taken him in instant dislike. Why, then, did he wish to offer for her hand? She was deep in thought when her aunt recalled her to the matter in hand.

Mrs Shere rose to her feet. Ignoring Miranda's imploring look, she murmured something about leaving the two young people to get to know each other and left the room.

A silence fell, which his lordship made no attempt to break.

"Won't you sit down, my lord?" Miranda asked in desperation. Standing over her as he did, Lord Heston seemed to fill the room.

"Certainly, madam." Heston took a seat on the other side of the fireplace. "I imagine you can guess why I am here?"

Miranda coloured. "My uncle said that you had asked to speak to me in private. I confess I was surprised…"

She heard an ugly laugh. "Were you? You do not suppose that Lakenham's friends would allow him to contract a *mésalliance* without making some attempt to save him?"

Miranda gazed at him in stupefaction.

"Come, now! Don't play the innocent with me. Will you deny that the boy has been fool enough to promise marriage?"

Miranda found her voice at last. "What has that to do with you?" she demanded. "You are not his guardian."

"True, but I am connected with the family. The details need not concern you. It is enough for you to know that I am here on behalf of Harry's grand-father, Lord Rudyard."

The cool effrontery of this statement made Miranda burn with rage. Heston was insolence personified.

"The decision must rest with Lord Lakenham," she snapped.

"On the contrary, it rests with you. Harry has refused to give you up. Nothing his grandfather could say will alter his resolution…"

"Then, sir, you are wasting your time!"

"I think not. It is up to you to make the break. You must cry off at once. It is contemptible to take advantage of a young man's inexperience. I must appeal to your better nature…"

Miranda gave him a limpid look. "What makes you think I have one? On the contrary, I have a fancy for a title and a fortune." Anger had betrayed her into indiscretion, but she did not care. Who did this pompous creature think he was, issuing demands and insulting her with every word?

"I see!" His voice was soft, but there was an underlying note of menace. "Well…let us get down to cases…how much?"

Fury threatened to choke Miranda, but she kept her eyes upon the carpet. "La, sir, I don't see an objection to the match," she simpered. "My family is perfectly respectable—"

"I know your background," Heston snapped. "You are penniless and your uncle is in trade."

"The money cannot matter. Harry will have a handsome fortune when he comes of age." The great blue eyes peeped up at him through long dark lashes. "As to the trade…well…no one need find out. When Harry and I are wed, I shall not spread it abroad."

"Strumpet! Make no mistake, ma'am, you shall not marry him."

"Who is to stop me, sir? When Harry knows of your visit here, he may insist on elopement."

"Such a marriage would be annulled."

"But think of the scandal, my lord! And then, you know, I might present his family with an heir."

Heston did not mince his words. "The child would be a bastard. Will you saddle yourself with a burden such as that for life? I ask you again… how much?"

"I could not think of such a sordid bargain," Miranda said demurely. "With every tender hope dashed, I might go into a decline… No amount of money would be of use to me if that should happen."

"It might soothe your final moments, madam.

They are like to be upon you more quickly than you realise if you do not stop this trifling."

"Threats, sir? I might have known it!" Miranda raised a hand to her brow in one of Fanny's more theatrical gestures. "Your reputation is not unknown to me, my lord. You are said to be the hardest of men, even in your dealing with the fair sex,"

"You may believe it. I have had dealings with your sort before. Every harpy in the country converges upon London in the Season, hoping to entrap some innocent boy. This time you won't succeed."

"No!" She favoured him with her sweetest smile. "You are mistaken, sir. Harry's letters have made his sentiments clear…"

She heard a muttered curse. "Letters, too? I wonder that the lad escaped his leading-strings. You have kept them all, I take it?"

"Naturally. How could I find it in my heart to part with them? Harry is so poetical. My eyes, so he says, are like the brightest stars in the heavens, and he compares my skin with that of the softest peach."

She heard a snort of disgust.

"Hardly original, madam!"

"But most sincere!" Miranda peeped up at him again, and then wished that she had not done so. His face was dark with anger, and there was a strange glitter in his eyes. For a moment she wondered if she had gone too far, but his lordship's insults had made her reckless.

"We are wasting time," he announced. "Tell me what price you set upon your charms. Shall we say five thousand pounds?"

She managed a coquettish laugh. "Does Lord Rudyard set so little store upon his family honour?"

She was unprepared for what happened next. Heston was out of his chair in a single lithe movement. Her chin was gripped in an iron hand and the harsh dark face came close to hers.

"Amazing!" he said softly. "The face of an angel, and a heart as hard as that of any common doxy. Aye, you're a beauty, you little vixen. I suppose you must peddle your wares."

Miranda struck out sharply and caught him full across the face. The imprint of her fingers showed up clearly on his cheek, but he merely laughed. She lifted her hand again, but this time he caught her wrist with such force that she gave a cry of pain.

"Temper!" he reproved. "Let us not turn this interview into a common brawl. You would have the worst of it, I promise you. Now, madam, pray consider. Lakenham is not the only catch in London. With money you might buy a house in which you and your sister might…er…entertain without the trouble of a husband."

As the implications of his speech came home to her, Miranda flushed to the roots of her hair. She reached out blindly and caught up a heavy vase, but he was too quick for her. The pressure of his fingers forced her to put it down.

"Insulted, my dear? I had not supposed it possible. Pray do not feel obliged to throw this delightful object. Your uncle would find your behaviour somewhat eccentric."

"You are despicable," Miranda cried. "You came here under false pretences. My uncle would never have received you or allowed you to be alone with me had he not believed that you intended to make me an offer."

"Have I not just done so?" His face was bland as he resumed his seat.

"You worm! You Corinthian! How dare you suggest that way of life to my sister and myself? Words cannot express what I should like to say to you."

"True! The title of Corinthian is, you know, regarded as a compliment. Perhaps your vocabulary is a little lacking in force?" He was very much at his ease as he lounged back in his chair.

Miranda longed to wipe the sneer from his lips. "I wonder that you did not make your offer to my uncle," she said in icy tones. "You may regard him as a counterjumper, but he would soon have disabused you of the idea that I am a—"

"A lightskirt?" he supplied helpfully. "I had considered such a course, Miss Gaysford, but I had not met you then. I decided to give you the benefit of the doubt, not knowing if your uncle was aware of Lakenham's entanglement. For all I knew, you might have been some simple country miss who fancied herself in love with him."

"You do not think so now?" There was a dangerous sparkle in her eyes.

"Not for a moment." Again she heard the ugly laugh. "It is more likely that you are all in this together…your aunt…your uncle…and your sister."

Miranda felt that she must explode with rage. How she longed to crush him…to grind her heel into that mocking face. She wanted to strike at him, to wound him as he had wounded her. He would pay for these insults, no matter what the cost.

"Silent, my dear? Am I to suppose you robbed of speech? A temporary condition only, I feel sure. I am prepared to give you a little time to consider my proposition."

He rose then and strolled over to the window, apparently convinced that the outcome of this meeting would be as he wished.

Miranda's mind was racing. She should have ordered him out of the house, but she longed to pay him back in his own coin. Yet how was she to do it? Oh, if she could but see this proud and arrogant creature grovelling at her feet.

Suddenly, the solution flashed into her mind. It would be dangerous, but it was worth it just to see him squirm. For once this haughty member of the nobility would find himself at a loss. A little smile lifted the corners of her mouth, but when she looked at him her face was composed.

"You are mistaken, sir," she told him. "My aunt and uncle know nothing of this matter. They do not accompany us into Polite Society."

"I had supposed as much." Heston's sneer grew more apparent. "I wondered how you got the entrée, but I supposed there are enough impoverished gentlefolk about to introduce you at a price."

"Quite so! Alas, when one is of indifferent breeding, it is necessary to make shift as best one can." Something in her voice made him eye her with suspicion, but her expression told him nothing. "Only my sister knows of Harry's attachment to me."

"Hmm! Well, that is of little consequence. You may change your mind, I suppose."

"My sister will wonder at it. You were right in thinking that we are penniless, she and I, and it is true that our mama hopes that we shall marry well enough to restore the family fortunes."

"That, at least, is honest," he said grudgingly. "Your ambitions are no worse than those of many another in the marriage market."

"Oh, you do understand. I felt sure you would when I explained." Any member of Miranda's family could have warned Lord Heston of the danger in that charming smile, but his lordship fell into the trap.

"I may have been a little hard on you," he admitted. "My remarks were not those of a gentleman, and for that I crave your pardon."

"They are forgotten." Miranda beamed at him. "I could not take the money, sir, even had I wished to do so. How might I have come into possession of such a large sum?"

"I see that it might have been a problem." He smiled at her, and Miranda was satisfied. He would not smile for long.

Heston resumed his seat. "Give up Lakenham," he pleaded. "With your beauty, half the men in London will offer for your hand."

Miranda dimpled. "Are you referring to my starry eyes and my peach-like skin, my lord?"

"Now you are making sport of me. Harry was a fool to put his sentiments in writing. If these young sprigs would learn to avoid the pen, much trouble might be avoided."

"How right you are! Perhaps the letters should be burned…?"

"That would be generous, indeed! Now, I do not mean to be offensive, but if you will oblige Lord Rudyard in this matter you may consider me your servant, ma'am. I will do my best to further your…er…"

"My career?" she said innocently.

"I was about to say your ambitions. I am not without influence—"

"Pray say no more!" Miranda waved his words aside with an airy gesture. "You have persuaded me. I shall give up Harry Lakenham."

He came to her then and raised her fingers to his lips. His relief was apparent.

"I had hoped that you would see the good sense of such a course," he told her warmly. "Harry will mourn his loss for a time, but the young are resilient. I shall invite him to my place in Warwickshire—"

"Before our wedding, my lord? There will not be much time."

Heston frowned. "Have you not this moment assured me that you will give him up?"

"I have, and I meant it. I was not speaking of Harry, my lord. I have decided to make you the happiest man alive…I accept your offer of marriage." Modestly she kept her eyes upon her folded hands.

He was silent for so long that she thought he had misunderstood her. Then he spoke.

"I made you no such offer," he said quietly.

"That is not my understanding, nor my uncle's. You said all that was proper to him, I believe, when you asked his permission to address me. I must suppose that you gave him some indication of your circumstances and went into the matter of a proper settlement?"

"I see that I have underestimated you, Miss Gaysford. In answer to your question, I did not explain my circumstances to your worthy relative. There seemed to be no need—"

"Of course not! How very stupid of me! Your wealth is common knowledge, is it not? How foolish I should be to pin my hopes upon a young man not yet in possession of his fortune when I might have the use of yours. I daresay you could buy and sell Lord Rudyard. Is that not correct?"

Heston bowed. "There is one small point which you may have overlooked. How are you to coerce me into making you my bride, or is that an indelicate question? Will you tear your gown and accuse me of rape, or have you some other plan in mind?"

"There will be no need for such dramatics, sir. We have made an excellent start. This household is at present agog to know the results of our tête-à-tête."

"I see! I might have had second thoughts, upon reflection. Had you considered that?"

"You, my lord? I think not! You are known to be a man of firm resolution. Alas, so is my uncle. He is an Alderman, as you must know. I fear he would advise me to sue for breach of promise."

Miranda felt a little breathless even as she spoke those hasty words. Heston had goaded her beyond endurance, and now she had gone much further than she had intended. She had hoped only to shatter his composure, to crack that icy mask of hauteur, and to pay him out for his offensive remarks. She felt a twinge of panic. To threaten such a man was the height of folly and she knew it. She waited for the explosion which must follow.

"Breach of promise? That would never do!" Somehow his calm words frightened her more than if he had shouted at her.

She looked up to find that he was smiling. It was more terrifying than anything she could have imagined. Though his lips were curved in a wolfish grin, there was no amusement in his eyes. They were as hard as stone. He reached out and pulled the bell-rope. Then he issued a swift order to the servant who came in answer to his summons.

"Ask Miss Gaysford's family to join us," he said briefly. Then he strode over to Miranda and pulled her to her feet.

"So you would try a fall with me, would you? Don't say you haven't been warned. I'll teach you a lesson you won't forget…"

His arms slid about he and he kissed her with such force that the breath was driven from her body. Miranda struggled wildly, but she was powerless against his strength. She clenched her teeth as he tried to force her lips apart, arching away from him until she thought her spine must crack.

He released her only as the door opened to admit her aunt, her uncle, and a startled Fanny.

Clamping her to his side with an arm that felt like a band of iron, he turned to face them.

"You may wish us happy," he said pleasantly. "May I present the future Lady Heston?"

Chapter Two

Amid the babel of congratulations, Miranda was conscious only of Fanny's stricken face. An imperceptible shake of her head brought her sister to her side. On the pretext of kissing her, Fanny drew her to the window-seat.

"Miranda, how could you?" she murmured brokenly. "You know I cannot marry him."

"Nor shall you! It is a fate I would not wish upon my worst enemy. Don't look so startled. I'll explain later."

Her mouth was bruised and swollen, but she managed a crooked smile as Heston came towards them with two glasses of champagne. He accepted a third from a nearby servant and turned to Alderman Shere.

That gentleman advanced towards Miranda, his

rubicund face glowing with pleasure. He took her hand and drew her to her feet. Then he raised his glass.

"To the betrothed couple! My dear young people, we wish you all the happiness in the world!"

Miranda swayed. This could not be happening. Events had moved with the speed of some dreadful nightmare from which she must awaken.

Then Heston slipped a hand beneath her elbow, holding her upright by main force. "Until tomorrow, dearest," he said tenderly. "Your uncle and I have much to discuss…settlements…the announcements in the morning papers…"

Miranda gazed at him in horror. He could not mean to continue with this farce. Her eyes pleaded with him to release her…to make some excuse… but his expression was impassive.

What had she done? She must have been mad to think that she could worst him. She felt that she had opened Pandora's box, only to let out all the evils in the world. She had put herself in Heston's power, and she could think of no way to escape.

"Dearest, you look a little pale," he murmured with exaggerated concern. "It is the excitement, I expect. I shall leave you in the care of your aunt…" He pressed a chaste kiss upon her cheek.

His lips seemed to burn her skin, but she did not flinch, although she longed to jerk her head away. Heston's smile was jovial as he took her uncle by the arm and left the room.

"My dear love, what a match for you!" Mrs Shere embraced her niece.

It was all too much. Miranda burst into tears.

"There…his lordship was quite right. How thoughtful he is! You are overwrought and it is not to be wondered at. The future Lady Heston? Your mama will be beside herself with joy. It is more than even she had hoped for you."

Miranda could not speak, and her aunt began to look a little anxious. "Will you not lie upon your bed for an hour or two? Perhaps a tisane…and a hot brick for your feet?"

"Thank you…I am being foolish, I expect, but I do feel a little strangely." Miranda dabbed at her eyes.

Fanny, too, appeared to be suffering from shock. She put her arm about her sister's waist and hugged her.

"Let us go upstairs and then you may rest," she said.

"What a pair you are!" Mrs Shere regarded her nieces with a benevolent eye. "This is an occasion for rejoicing, not for tears. Ah, well, I know how close you are. You will not care to be separated, even by marriage. Off you go! I will send up your luncheon on a tray, and you shall not stir from your room until this evening."

"Miranda, what has happened?" Fanny swung round upon her twin as soon as they were alone. "I was never so shocked in all my life when I heard that you had accepted Heston. How could you betray me so?"

"I didn't," Miranda told her dully. She ached all over and was convinced that when she slipped out of her gown her arms and shoulders would be black and blue. "That brutal creature! He should be whipped at the cart's tail!"

"But…but…you are betrothed to him."

"No, I am not," Miranda snapped. "He tricked me…at least I think he did. Oh, Fanny, I am so confused…I don't know what happened. I was hoping to frighten him, you see."

Fanny gasped. "You must be mad! What did you say to him? What have you done? You lost you temper, didn't you? When you fly into alt, you never guard your tongue!"

"Nor does he. If you must know, he did not come to make you an offer at all."

"Then why did he ask to see me alone?"

"He came to buy you off. Harry has been to see his grandfather, who will have nothing to say to the connection. Heston is Lord Rudyard's envoy, come to save his grandson from a fortune-hunting harpy who is tainted by the smell of trade."

Fanny's face grew scarlet. "Cruel!" she whispered in a failing voice. "Has he persuaded my darling to give me up?"

"No, he has not." The sight of her sister's distress fuelled Miranda's sense of outrage. "You had best hear the whole of it, Fanny. You won't like it, but I feel you should know what Heston was about."

Her recital was interrupted at frequent intervals by Fanny's moans and sobs. It was not until the letters were mentioned that she raised her head.

"There are no letters," she wailed. "Harry has never written to me. When he picks up a pen, he cannot think of anything to say."

"It is of no importance. I offered to burn the letters in any case when I offered to give him up."

"You did that? Then my life is over..." Fanny buried her head in the pillow and gave way to despair.

"At nineteen? Really, Fanny, where is your spirit? You cannot think I meant it?"

"Heston must have been delighted!"

"He was, but his delight lasted for no more than thirty seconds."

"I don't understand you. How could that be?"

"His rapture was short-lived when I said that I would marry him instead—"

Fanny screamed. She was on the verge of a strong attack of hysterics, but Miranda held her hands.

"No, listen to me. I meant it only as a joke. Well, not perhaps a joke, but I could not bear his insults. I wanted to pay him back, to shock him out of his smug complacency."

"Oh, do not say so! I cannot bear it. What folly to defy a man like that! He had not even offered for you…for me, I mean."

"I pretended I thought he had. I even—"

"Even what? There cannot be more!"

"I'm afraid there is. I mentioned…er…an action for breach of promise."

Fanny lay still. Her face was white to the lips. "Then we are ruined. Have you no sense at all? Heston is the most ruthless creature alive. Have you not heard what is said of him? A threat is merely a challenge."

"I know it now. It was a stupid thing to do, but I had no idea that he would take me at my word and move so fast. You were all in the room before I had time to think."

"What did you expect?" Fanny's voice was bitter. "Did you imagine that he would flee the house with his tail between his legs? You do not know him. He will be revenged on all of us. And when the announcement appears in the *Gazette,* Harry is sure to call him out."

Miranda was dismayed. "I hadn't considered that. Can you get a message to him?"

"What can I say? He will think me faithless…and all we needed was a little time."

"Ask him to call this evening. If we can contrive to leave you alone, you could explain—"

"Explain what? That I am to marry a dotard?"

"Heston isn't exactly a dotard, Fanny. He can't be more than thirty, but that is beside the point. You are not going to marry him. Can Harry keep a secret? You might tell him what has happened."

"Tell him the whole, you mean?" Fanny grew thoughtful. Then her eyes began to sparkle. "He would think it a famous jest, and it would throw Lord Heston off the scent. If only he may not discover that he is betrothed to the wrong person. When Harry comes of age in December he may do as he pleases…it would give us the time we need."

"You must warn him to be careful. He must appear to be broken-hearted. Still, loving you as he does, he must wish only for your happiness."

The twins exchanged a glance of pure mischief. Then Fanny's face clouded.

"What of you?" she asked. "Can you support Lord Heston's company for a time?"

"I intend to do so. For the moment he believes that he holds the upper hand, but I shall find some way to crush his…his pretensions."

Miranda had recovered her composure and now she began to dwell with pleasure upon the delightful prospect of seeing Lord Heston grovelling at her feet, begging for mercy.

Quite how this desirable state of affairs was to be achieved she had no idea, but she would think of something.

"Do be careful, dearest," Fanny pleaded. "You are so reckless when you fly into the boughs, and Heston is a dangerous man. There is a sort of black glitter about him…about his eyes, I mean."

"His eyes are grey," Miranda said shortly. "He thinks himself a god, you know. A Corinthian, forsooth! What has that to say to anything? He may be a famous whip, and the idol of a pack of silly boys because he boxes at Gentleman Jackson's saloon, and can afford to buy his clothes from Schweitzer and Davidson. I have seen no evidence of honour or of a pleasing character in him."

"That is what I mean. He is unscrupulous. Oh, love, I fear he means to harm you."

"He won't so do," Miranda told her stoutly. "Now you must write to Harry without delay. Ellen will take it for you. There is not much time if you wish to avoid a duel."

This terrifying thought was enough to send Fanny to her desk at once. When Ellen came up with a tray she was told to slip out with the message during the afternoon.

"I do feel hungry." Miranda lifted the lid from a tureen of asparagus soup and began to serve her sister.

"I don't know how you can eat." Fanny pushed her plate away. "This is all such a tangle. Heston cannot mean to marry you."

"Of course not! He intends to frighten me. Would he wed the niece of a mere Alderman…a nobody? His pride would not allow it. Well, he will learn. This nobody will prick the bubble of his conceit. These chicken patties are delicious…won't you try one?"

Fanny was persuaded to nibble at a little of the food and to take a glass of wine. Then, worn out by the events of the last few hours, she fell asleep.

Miranda took up her book, but she could not read. Heston's lightning reaction to her attempt to worst him had shaken her to the core of her being.

She drew a hand across her swollen mouth, as if by doing so she could wipe out the memory of that brutal kiss.

She had never been handled so roughly in her life. The man was a monster. He must have known that she was merely teasing him, but he had not spared her.

She slipped out of bed and walked over to the mirror. Dark bruises showed up clearly on her milky skin. He would be made to pay for each one of those marks, and pay in full.

She wondered if he would go ahead with his plan to announce the betrothal in the morning papers. If so, the world would take him for a fool if he mistook the name of his bride-to-be. Then she frowned. That solution would not serve at all. She and Fanny shared the same initials.

Fanny had been christened Melissa Frances, whilst she had been named Miranda Ferne. Not for the first time she wondered what had possessed their mother to indulge in such flights of fancy.

It could not be helped. Miss M. F. Gaysford

might be either of them when the name appeared in the *Morning Post* and the *Gazette.*

In any case, it was important that Heston should continue to believe that he was betrothed to Fanny. She would play out his charade for the present. Meantime, Fanny might grow out of her infatuation with Harry Lakenham. That would be the ideal solution. Then she herself could cry off from her supposed engagement, and let the world believe that she had jilted Heston.

Even so, she felt dispirited. Nothing had worked out as she had hoped.

She and Fanny had been in transports when their uncle had offered them a Season. It was true that they had enjoyed the balls, the drums, the routs, visits to the Tower to see the King's Beasts, the Grand Firework Displays and the Balloon Ascents, yet not all the efforts of Lady Medlicott, the faded gentlewoman who was their chaperon, had served to produce the type of offer upon which their mama had set her heart.

If only Mrs Gaysford had not been so taken with the story of those Gunning girls. The famous Irish beauties had taken London by storm more than fifty years earlier. Elizabeth Gunning had married the Duke of Hamilton, and Maria Gunning had become the bride of the Earl of Coventry. Mrs Gaysford could think of no reason why her own girls should not enjoy similar success.

Instead, Fanny had fallen in and out of love with a succession of young officers, dazzled by their splendid appearance in their regimentals, and not one of them a suitable match for her.

Her own heart had remained untouched. Such offers as had come their way had been from middle-aged worthies, warm enough in the pocket to overlook a lack of dowry, but scarcely calculated to arouse the interest of two lively nineteen-year-olds.

She laid aside her book as her aunt entered the room.

"That's better." Mrs Shere looked with approval at Fanny's sleeping figure. "Your sister will be more herself when she awakens. The excitement was too much for her, and it is not to be wondered at. Who could have supposed that Lord Heston would offer for her?"

Miranda managed a faint smile. "It was surprising," she agreed. "Ma'am, may I ask you something?"

"What is it, my dear?"

"Would you object if Lord Lakenham were to speak to Fanny alone…that is, if he calls upon us?"

Mrs Shere looked mystified.

"The thing is that he has conceived a *tendre* for Fanny. It is but calf-love, yet it would be kind if you could allow her to tell him herself of her betrothal."

Miranda felt ashamed of herself. It was not at all the thing to be deceiving this gentle woman who had been so kind to them.

"I don't know, Miranda. I cannot think that Lord Heston would agree to such an interview..." Mrs Shere was clearly troubled.

"Ma'am, he need not know. If Lakenham were to call, you would not turn him away?"

Mrs Shere smiled. "You know your uncle better than that, my dear. No military man is ever refused admittance to this house. Shere is only too well aware of what we owe to Wellington's armies."

Miranda kissed her aunt's cheek. "How good you are," she said warmly.

Her kiss was returned, and Mrs Shere patted her cheek. "It will be your turn next," she announced. "Then how happy your mama will be. Your uncle has sent off to her already with the news, but Fanny must write too."

"So soon?" Miranda was startled. Events were moving so fast that they were overtaking her.

"Of course, my love. She must not read it first in the *Gazette*. That would be most improper. We shall not make the announcement until she has given Fanny her blessing. You had best wake her. Were you not to go to the play tonight?"

"I think we should cry off," Miranda told her. "I doubt if Fanny will be up to it."

"You are right. A quiet evening at home would be best. I will send a message to Lady Medlicott, and your uncle will be pleased. He wishes to speak to Fanny about arrangements for her marriage."

Her parting words did nothing to reassure Miranda. She was becoming entangled in a web from which it was growing more and more difficult to free herself. At least she had ensured that Fanny would be at home if Harry came in answer to her summons.

Later that evening she and Fanny walked into the dining-room, dressed alike in pale blue muslin. Alderman Shere greeted them with a beaming smile.

"You are both in looks tonight," he announced. "Alike as two peas in a pod! I'm blessed if I know how Lord Heston could tell you one from the other."

Miranda stiffened. It was merely one of their uncle's endearing jokes, but it was uncomfortably close to the truth.

"Well, well," he continued. "Come and sit you

down. We have much to celebrate. Fanny, you are a lucky girl. I confess you might have knocked me down with a feather when his lordship called on me. The finest catch in London, and he has offered for you."

Fanny's enchanting smile peeped out. She dimpled as he chucked her under the chin.

"That's a good girl," he said approvingly. "Those sparkling eyes tell me all I need to know. Swept off his feet, was he? My dear, I hope he will make you happy. I was a little worried at first, if the truth be known. I had heard him spoken of as high in the instep and a cold fish, but you have not found him so, I imagine."

His eyes twinkled as a blush rose to Fanny's cheeks.

"Nay, I won't tease you further. Now you shall take a glass of wine." He signalled to the footman and sat down.

Though not as wealthy as many of his friends, the Alderman kept a good table, and prided himself upon the excellence of his cook.

He made short work of a dish of mushroom fritters, followed by a slice or two of tongue braised in Madeira wine. This was followed by a serpent of mutton with green peas. A succulent pigeon pie was waved aside in favour of a curd pudding.

To Miranda, the meal seemed endless. She looked across at Fanny and frowned a warning. Her twin was trying without success to hide a feeling of suppressed excitement. Miranda hoped that her aunt and uncle would put it down to the supposed betrothal.

She took a little of the delicately flavoured Floating Island pudding. It was one of her favourites, but tonight she found it tasteless. She sighed with relief when Mrs Shere withdrew, leaving the Alderman to his port.

"Aunt, the drawing-room feels so warm. May I open the windows?"

"Certainly, my dear. On a night like this we shall not take a chill."

Miranda threw open the long French doors and walked on to the terrace with Fanny by her side.

"Will Harry come tonight?" she murmured in an undertone.

Fanny nodded. "He told Ellen that he would. Oh, this is famous!"

"Is it? I don't like to deceive our aunt and uncle."

Fanny pouted. "You haven't changed your mind already? You will go ahead with our plan?"

"I won't fail you," Miranda said with some asperity. "There is the door-knocker. It must be Harry."

As Fanny disappeared into the drawing-room, Miranda pressed her fingers to her burning cheeks. What on earth was she to do?

For a moment she was tempted to make a clean breast of the whole, in spite of her promise to her sister. Yet it could serve no useful purpose. Reproaches would be heaped upon the twins from their mama, to say nothing of the humiliation which must fall upon her relatives. She was forced to admit it…she was caught in a trap of her own making.

When the door opened to admit Harry Lakenham and his friend, John Helmsley, both girls made their curtsies. Then Miranda walked over to the spinet. "Aunt, shall I play for you?" she asked.

"Would you dearest? That would be pleasant, and if Mr Helmsley would be kind enough to turn the music for you…? Lord Lakenham, I fear I am sitting in a draught. Might I ask you to close the window a little? Fanny will explain the catch."

Miranda threw her aunt a look of gratitude as Fanny and her lover moved out to the terrace. They were gone for so long that Mrs Shere grew agitated.

Miranda looked up at John Helmsley. "Will you forgive me, sir?" she said. "I am a little tired tonight."

She closed the instrument and walked towards the window. As she peered into the night she caught a glimpse of Fanny's gown, pale against the darkness of the shrubbery. Harry Lakenham and her sister were locked in each other's arms.

Miranda walked towards them. "Are you quite mad?" she hissed. "You will ruin everything."

Harry seized her hand and kissed it. "Thank you!" he said in fervent tones. "You have saved us!"

"I shall not be able to do so if you continue to behave so foolishly. For heaven's sake, take care, my lord. Don't forget that you have your part to play in this."

Miranda grasped Fanny's arm and led her sister back indoors. They were followed by Harry who was striving to give the appearance of a rejected lover.

"Dear boy!" Mrs Shere said fondly. "You will not desert us, even though Fanny is to wed? You are always welcome here, you know."

Harry sighed, but his eyes were dancing, and Miranda took him to task at once.

"Do you take your leave," she urged in an aside. "You look like the cat with its paw in a pot of cream."

Obediently he signalled to John Helmsley and they moved towards the door. There he blew her a kiss behind her aunt's back, laughing as she frowned at him.

"Have I missed our guests?" The Alderman

walked through from the dining-room. "You should have called me, wife."

"They could not stay, my love."

The Alderman beckoned Fanny to his side. "Lord Heston agrees that we must wait to hear from your mama before the announcement appears, but the world will learn of your good fortune before the week is out. Don't trouble your head about settlements and so forth. I have undertaken to discuss those with him. You will not find him ungenerous, I believe."

Fanny nodded as he beamed at her. Then he settled himself more comfortably in his chair, legs planted firmly apart, with his plump little hands resting on his knees.

"There is one other thing," he continued. "You are not to trouble your head about the cost of bride-clothes and the other female fripperies which you'll need. Those shall be my gift to you. We shall send you off in style."

Fanny looked uncomfortable, but she murmured her thanks and kissed him, colouring as she did so.

"No need to be embarrassed about it," he told her kindly. "I could wish I might do more, but sadly, dowries are beyond my means—"

"Sir, you have been more than generous," Miranda

broke in swiftly. "You have your own boys to consider. Is not George to transfer from a line regiment?"

Her uncle nodded. "I must set up Frederick, too, when he is done with Oxford…"

"You must be very proud of them."

"Aye! I want to give them a better start than I had myself." He looked across at her aunt. "Still, we haven't done so badly, Emma, have we?" A look of affection passed between them, and Miranda sprang up to kiss them both.

How unjust it was of Heston to sneer at these good people. They were more honourable than he would ever be. Her determination to humiliate him grew even stronger as she looked at their two lined faces.

She said as much to Fanny when they were alone.

"I hope you know what you are about," her twin said doubtfully. "Harry was delighted. He says that Heston needs a set-down, but I cannot help but fear for you. I wish that you may not get yourself into a scrape."

Miranda stared at her in disbelief. "I am already in a scrape," she cried. "I should never have agreed to take your place."

"Thank heavens you did so. Had Heston insulted me as he did you, I should have fainted on the spot.

I did not tell Harry the whole of it, but he was already planning an elopement."

"Fanny, you would not! Think of the scandal… the disgrace! It would break Mama's heart, and my uncle would blame himself for not taking better care of you."

"Well, it need not come to that if you will but keep Heston occupied." Fanny drew her bedgown over her head and began to tie the ribbons of her nightcap. "He must not know the truth until we are safely wed, so do take care not to betray yourself."

"Heston cannot wish for my company," Miranda said with decision. "I doubt if he would consider it amusing to take me about." In that she was mistaken.

Both girls were sitting by the window on the following morning when a high-perch phaeton drew up at their door. Heston threw the reins to his tiger, and ran lightly up the steps.

Miranda felt sick with apprehension, but apart from her heightened colour there was little to betray that emotion when Heston was shown into the room.

She took her sister's hand as they rose to greet him. She and her twin were dressed alike in white sprigged muslin with blue ribands in their hair. This was the test. Would he be able to tell them apart?

To her astonishment, he did not hesitate. He strode straight towards her and took her hand.

"My love!" he uttered in throbbing accents. "An hour apart from you seems like a lifetime..." He drew her to him, kissed her fingers, and pressed a chaste salute upon her cheek.

She longed to free herself, but with Mrs Shere's indulgent eyes upon her she was forced to submit to his caresses.

"Make haste, my love," her aunt urged gently. "If Lord Heston hopes to take you for a drive, he will not wish to keep his horses standing."

"Quite right, ma'am!" Heston bowed to indicate his pleasure at her understanding. "Sadly, the phaeton is unsuitable for more than one passenger, but you have no objection to my taking your niece to the Park?"

"Of course not! We have promised ourselves a shopping trip to Bond Street." She glanced at Fanny. "You will enjoy that, will you not, my dear?"

Fanny's smile of agreement was unconvincing. She had nothing to say either to her aunt or to Lord Heston.

"Miss Gaysford, have you seen the Elgin Marbles? They are very fine, I assure you. Perhaps on another occasion you may care to accompany us to the British Museum?"

Fanny murmured an inarticulate reply, which caused her aunt to stare, but she was saved from further embarrassment when Miranda reappeared.

"Charming! Quite charming!" His lordship put up his quizzing-glass to inspect the neat little figure who stood before him. "How well that shade of bronze becomes you! The bonnet, too! It is quite a triumph! I shall be the envy of every man in town."

"You are too kind, my lord." Miranda gritted out the words through clenched teeth, feeling rather as if she were a slave on sale in an Arab market.

"Not at all! My words come from the heart!" With a bow to the two ladies, Heston gripped her elbow and ushered her from the room.

He handed Miranda up into the phaeton, and dismissed his tiger. "I shall not need you, Jem."

Miranda was at a loss to account for the astonishment on the lad's face, but Heston did not appear to notice it. He took the reins and turned the splendid pair of chestnuts south in the direction of Piccadilly.

That thoroughfare was crowded, but, as Miranda soon realised, his lordship was capable of driving to an inch. With careless ease he avoided the press of hackney carriages, a stately landaulet, and a smart barouche.

He stopped for a crossing-sweeper, moved on and then was forced to swerve as a curricle, clearly in inexperienced hands, shot out from the southern end of Bond Street.

Heston did not hesitate. He was past the plunging horses in an instant as Miranda gasped.

"My apologies, ma'am. I trust I did not frighten you. The town is overfull with the arrival of the Allies for the Gala Celebrations."

"You did not," Miranda told him with more dignity than truth. Her knuckles were white as she gripped the side of the vehicle.

"Liar!" he said smoothly.

"Did you seek my company merely to insult me?" Miranda's face was pale. The day was warm and the stench in the streets was overpowering. She began to wish that she had provided herself with a nosegay to counteract the vile odours, but she had not done so. The near-collision had disturbed her, and suddenly she felt sick.

"You will feel better when we reach the Park," Heston predicted. "London can be trying on a hot day. Bear up, my dear. When we are settled in Warwickshire, I shall not insist that you come to town again."

"Warwickshire?" Miranda was perplexed.

"My country seat. Had you forgot? With your children about you, you will not yearn for the pleasures of the capital."

"My children?"

"Naturally. Why do you look surprised? I am hoping for a full quiver, as the saying goes. At least four boys and perhaps a girl or two. I won't promise to keep you company in the Season, but you will not mind that."

Miranda eyed him with acute dislike.

Chapter Three

"My love, must you give me dagger-looks?" Heston continued smoothly. "Have I said something to offend you?"

Miranda did not answer him.

"Lost your tongue? You surprise me! Yesterday you had so much to say. Must I crave your pardon for being so indelicate as to mention the main purpose of our marriage? I had not thought your sensibilities quite so nice. You are not, I must hope, of a frigid disposition?"

"No, I am not! How dare you speak of such things to me?" Miranda cried hotly.

"There must be no misunderstanding between husband and wife." Heston's tone was sententious. "The physical side is, after all, an important part of marriage." He looked down at her then, assessing her from head to toe, and Miranda flushed to the roots of her hair, feeling naked beneath his gaze.

"There! I have put you to the blush. How unforgivable of me!" With a cynical grin his lordship drove his phaeton into Hyde Park. "Do you think you could manage a smile or two, my dear? My friends must not be led to believe that we have quarrelled at this early stage in our relationship."

Miranda tried to compose herself. Anger threatened to overwhelm her, but her voice was calm as she replied, "I shall play my part, my lord."

"Of course you will, and very prettily, too." Heston bowed and smiled as he slowed the horses to a walking pace, and threaded his way past other carriages.

Thankful to find his attention diverted from herself, Miranda looked about her. She was not too green to realise that the passers-by included the cream of Polite Society. She saw a look of surprise on several faces, and wondered why everyone was staring so. She was not long kept in ignorance.

A cavalier reined in beside them and swept off his hat.

"Adam, you sly dog! I might have known…"

"Might have known what?" his lordship answered mildly.

"That you are not the misogynist we suspected. Here you are, with the loveliest girl in London—"

"Ah, yes. May I present my cousin to you, my dear? This is Thomas Frant."

Miranda was disarmed by the cheerful smile with which the young man greeted her. He was short and stocky, but he had a pleasant open face. A dusting of freckles across his snub nose emphasised a pair of bright blue eyes.

Miranda gave him her hand.

"I won't say I'm surprised," Thomas told her gaily. "Who could resist you, ma'am?"

"Who, indeed? My love, you have made yet another conquest." Heston gathered up the reins and prepared to move on, apparently oblivious of the effect of his tender words upon his cousin.

Thomas caught him by the arm. "Adam, you ain't thrown the handkerchief at last?" he said in awed tones.

"You may believe it!" Heston replied. "As you said yourself, my dear Thomas, who could resist such beauty?" He gazed down fondly at Miranda as he spoke.

"Good God, Adam!" Thomas was brought to his senses by the cool expression in his cousin's eyes. "Beg pardon, ma'am. I meant no offence…

but Adam ain't in the petticoat line, not as a rule, I mean."

"You have said quite enough. In confidence, Thomas, Miss Gayford and I are recently betrothed. You will keep it to yourself for the moment…?"

"Of course! Of course!" Thomas was so astonished that he grabbed sharply at his reins, causing his mount to jib. "Not a word! You may rely on me." He moved away.

"I hope we may," Miranda said in scathing tones. "Did we not agree, my lord, that no one was to know of our betrothal, until my mother had been informed?"

"You feel she may object? Oh dear, I hope not. You see, Thomas, charming though he is, is possibly the worst gabster in London. He is incapable of keeping a secret."

"You knew that, and yet you told him?"

"A lamentable oversight on my part…due, perhaps, to my longing to acquaint the world of our happiness. Will you forgive me, dearest?"

Miranda's anger threatened to overcome her. Heston was taunting her, utterly sure of himself. He would soon learn that he had met his match.

"Of course!" She smiled up at him. "I am so

happy to know that you care nothing for the opinion of the *ton.*'

Heston raised an eyebrow. "Would you care to explain yourself?"

"I was thinking only of the possible consequences to you, of such a connection, sir. I'm sure you understand me. The betrothal of such a notable Corinthian as yourself to a mere nobody, moreover one who is related to a cit? I fear it may have a sad effect on your position in society."

Heston laughed aloud. "If you believe that, you will believe anything. My credit will survive the worst *mésalliance.* I am known to be eccentric, and I do as I please, as I hope to prove to you."

Miranda turned her head away. Yet again this unpleasant creature had managed to have the last word. She was still fuming when they were hailed by a well-known voice.

"Lakenham, by all that's holy!" Heston drew his carriage to a halt. "How are you, my dear boy? What a surprise to find you here! I had not thought that you rose till noon."

"I could not sleep." Viscount Lakenham was much in danger of overacting, Miranda thought to herself. She wished him elsewhere with fervour as he looked at her with a mournful expression.

The boy was a fool, and Heston must be sure to see through his pretence of abject despair. She stole a fleeting glance at her companion, to find him all concern.

"Liverish this morning, are you?" Heston said cheerfully. "Take my advice, my lad, and change your wine merchant."

Lakenham threw him an angry look and was about to address Miranda.

"No, you shall not delay us," Heston protested. "Miss Gaysford finds the heat oppressive. I have promised to take her home. My regards to your mother." He whipped up his horses and left the Park by the West Gate.

"Harry looks somewhat subdued," he remarked idly as they rejoined the traffic in Piccadilly.

"Are you surprised, my lord?"

"I had not thought to see him so dejected merely because you are in my company. You have not found his jealousy excessive?"

"Sir, he knows the truth. My aunt allowed me to tell him of our…of our betrothal."

"You assured me yesterday that she was unaware of Harry's infatuation."

"She was…but my sister explained to her that it was but calf-love, scarce worth a mention.

We…I thought it best that he should learn the news from me."

"Hoping to save his skin, my dear? You may be easy in your mind. I shall not allow him to call me out. In any case, I doubt if he would be so foolish."

"You are a marksman too, Lord Heston? How very splendid! You put all my acquaintance in the shade…"

"Ah, yes, but then your acquaintance is not large, and, dare I say it, a little questionable?"

Miranda did not rise to the bait, though it took a supreme effort not to do so. She gave him an innocent look, thinking as she did so that if she were a man she would have called him out herself for that remark.

"Quite so!" she murmured. "But now that I am to rise in the world, your friends will be mine, I trust. It can only be an improvement." Her tone left him in no doubt that she did not think so for a moment.

To her fury he laughed again.

"Well done!" he said. "A palpable hit, my dear. I must learn not to lead with my chin when sparring with you."

Miranda did not trouble to reply. Instead, she gazed at the passing scene which never failed to fascinate her. Piemen shouting their wares, flower-sellers and a group of quarrelling jarveys striking out at the beggars who barred their way, all contrasted sharply with the fashionable exquisites who lounged along the pavements. Women dressed in the height of fashion lounged in their barouches, accompanied in many cases by their beaux, riding alongside.

Heston was hailed again and again, and Miranda found herself subjected to many a hard stare, both from the occupants of the carriages and their companions.

"You seem to be creating something of a stir today, my lord," she murmured wickedly.

"I cannot claim the credit for that. Much of it is due to you. Did I not say that every man in London must envy me? Think what a furore you will arouse at the play tonight."

"I do not intend to visit the play this evening," she told him stiffly.

"No? What a disappointment for your sister and your aunt! They were looking forward to it."

"You asked my aunt?" Miranda was astonished. She had not supposed that Lord Heston would care to be seen with someone so far beneath him in status.

"Naturally…and your uncle, too. You must not think me lacking in courtesy, my dearest. Sadly the

Alderman has another engagement, but your aunt felt free to accept my invitation."

Miranda's mouth set in a mutinous line.

"I do not care to go."

"But you will, my dear, you will. That is, unless you decide to plead the headache. That would be unworthy of you. I had not supposed you capable of cowardice."

Miranda's eyes flashed and her chin went up, but they had arrived at their destination, and she had no opportunity to utter the angry words which sprang to her lips.

Heston handed his reins to the groom who came down the steps towards them and handed Miranda down from the phaeton with great solicitude.

"Until tonight, then?" Oblivious of the passers-by he saluted her with a tender kiss upon her cheek and sprang back into the carriage.

Miranda stalked indoors without a backward glance, to find that Fanny and Mrs Shere had returned from their shopping expedition. The hall was littered with bandboxes and parcels.

"Did you enjoy your drive, my dear?" Mrs Shere did not wait for an answer. "We have been so busy you would scarce believe it! Pray come upstairs and see what we have bought for you. How fortunate that you and your sister are the same size and colouring. What becomes one of you must suit the other…"

Still chattering, she led the girls upstairs.

"See now, is this not delightful?" She held up a gown of sea-green gauze over an underslip of satin.

"It looks expensive," Miranda said doubtfully.

"It was, but your uncle will not care for that. He is not a penny-pincher, and we must consider what is due to Lord Heston." She began to rifle through the other boxes, drawing out filmy undergarments, long kid gloves, silk stockings and handkerchiefs trimmed with Valenciennes lace.

Fanny was in raptures when she found herself the proud possessor of a matching gown. She flung her arms about her aunt and kissed her.

"There, it is little enough, my dear girl. It will cheer you up, I hope, and your uncle likes to see you dressed alike. You both look so charmingly together…"

Miranda tried to smile, but such generosity served only to depress her spirits further. She longed to end the deception, but she could not find the courage to do so.

Fanny was quick to sense her mood.

"Was it very bad?" she asked when Mrs Shere had left them. "Surely Heston did not continue to insult you?"

"What makes you suppose that he will give up now? His lordship is enjoying himself, knowing that I cannot escape."

"Harry said that he had seen you. We met him in Bond Street."

"Fanny, you must speak to him. He should not have sought us out. You are fond of telling me that Heston is a dotard, but he is far from being feeble-minded, I assure you. Harry's manner was such as to make him question me later, and should he ever suspect that we have changed places…"

"Harry thought he gave a very good performance as a rejected lover," Fanny said defensively.

"Perhaps he should be on the stage! It would be better if he returned to his grandfather for a time. He is sure to give us away."

"No, I won't be parted from him!"

"Very well, but you must both be more discreet. You can't be seen together. Lord Heston intends that Harry shall sever all connection with our family. It won't serve if he thinks that you are now the object of his attentions."

"I suppose I may meet him in company?" Fanny sulked.

"If you do so, pray take care! Last evening, for example, if anyone but myself had found you in the garden, all would have been lost. I won't go on with this charade if you don't play your part."

"I thought you wanted to punish Heston."

"I do, but you must help me. The insults were addressed to you, you know."

"Oh, very well!" Fanny dismissed the matter from her mind, and began to peacock round the room with a shawl of Norwich silk thrown about her shoulders.

"There is another thing," Miranda added quietly. "I cannot like all this expense. Uncle cannot well afford it."

"Of course he can! Did he not insist? And Aunt Emma enjoyed herself so much this morning. She tells me that she has always longed for a daughter. I don't see how you can stop her."

"We might mention that Mama would wish to be consulted."

Fanny stared. "Have you written to her?"

"I have not," Miranda said with a heavy heart. "I don't know what to say."

"Well, Uncle will think it strange of you. You might mention that Heston has offered, and that you hope for her blessing. You may be sure it will be given. Nothing could be more certain."

"And what then?"

"Why ask me? You were so set on getting back at Heston. Surely you have some plan?"

"I have not, and well you know it. As far as I can tell I am simply getting deeper into the mire."

"You'll think of something," Fanny told her comfortably. "After all, you always do. We have been in scrapes before and you have got us out of them."

Miranda was not attending. "Fanny, don't you find it strange that Heston never mistakes us one for the other?" she said thoughtfully. "He came to me at once this morning."

"Nor does Harry," her sister replied. "Have we not always found it so in men who care for us? Oh, I see what you mean..." Fanny looked startled.

"Exactly so! Heston must be the exception. Do you suppose that he can have noticed the mole behind my ear? It is the only difference."

"He must have done. He seems to see everything. I must confess he frightens me. His eyes are so penetrating...they seem to look into my mind."

"I hope you are wrong. I would not have him know what is in my mind."

"Let us forget him," Fanny cried impatiently. "Shall we wear our new gowns tonight?"

"That is Aunt's intention, I believe."

"She was pleased to be included in the invitation.

She refused at first, you know, but Lord Heston can be most persuasive. He insisted…"

"And why not, pray? The world may consider that Aunt Emma married beneath her, but her birth, like our own, is unexceptionable."

Fanny began to giggle. "I love you when you get upon your high ropes, dearest. Have you told Lord Heston of our worthy connections?"

"No, I have not!" Miranda snapped. "I intend to make him squirm. Let us see if he can carry off this affront to his consequence."

She looked at her sister and dimpled. "If I thought that Aunt Emma would permit it, I should try to look as vulgar as possible, with plumes, and feathers, and gauds. I should even paint my face…"

"Miranda, you wouldn't?" Fanny was shocked. "Aunt would send you to wash it off."

"I know." It was with regret that Miranda abandoned the idea. "But Heston need not think that he will find me biddable, hanging upon his every word as if it were…were the laws of the Medes and Persians…"

"I expect he has never heard of the Medes and Persians and nor have I. What have they to do with anything?"

"Nothing, love. Let us go down. We shall be late for luncheon."

She was thoughtful as she toyed with a dish of buttered eggs, and took so little of a proffered platter of cold meats and salad that her aunt was moved to protest.

"My dear, this will not do! If you go on in this way you will be naught but skin and bone, and that will not please his lordship."

Obediently, Miranda allowed herself to be helped to another slice of beef from the sirloin, and forced herself to take a little of the Celerata cream which followed.

At last Mrs Shere rose from the table, announcing that she planned to rest for an hour or two, and indicating that the twins should follow her example.

"But, Aunt, we intended to go to Richardson's, to change our library books," said Fanny. "That is, if you have no objection.

"Very well, but you shall take the carriage, and Ellen must go with you. Now do not dawdle about, my dears. I believe that you should lie upon your beds for at least an hour before you dress this evening."

Both girls kissed her and went upstairs to put on their bonnets.

"I could wish that Aunt did not treat us as a

couple of dowagers," Fanny grumbled. "Where is the harm in walking on such a pleasant day?"

"I expect she was thinking only of our comfort. In any case, it will give you more time to find another of those dreadful Gothic romances." Miranda's eyes twinkled. Fanny's passion for romantic fiction had made her the butt of their elder brother's jokes for years.

She was too preoccupied with her own search for something to read to pay much attention to Fanny when they reached the library. She had taken out much of the stock already, including *Evelina* by Fanny Burney, and the works of Samuel Richardson. Her eye fell upon a copy of *Tom Jones,* but then she decided against it. Aunt might not approve. The book was considered too explicit to be thought suitable reading for an unmarried girl, even though the author, Mr Fielding, was a magistrate.

Poetry? No, she was no admirer of Lord Byron, though his works were all the rage. *Ivanhoe* looked promising, and there could be no objection to any of the works of Sir Walter Scott. She would lose herself in the story, and it would help her to forget her present troubles.

"I will take this," she said decisively "Have you found anything, Fanny?"

There was no reply. Fanny had disappeared. Miranda was untroubled, thinking that her sister had wandered into another part of the shop. Then she saw Ellen. Their abigail was standing by a deep recess and her furtive expression warned Miranda that something was amiss.

As she approached she heard the murmur of voices. Anger threatened to consume her as she recognised that of Harry Lakenham.

"You may wait in the carriage, Ellen," she said sharply. As their maid scurried away, Miranda walked towards the lovers.

They were standing in the shadows, oblivious of all about them. Harry's arm was about her sister's waist and her head was resting on his shoulder.

"I see now why you were so anxious to change your library book, Fanny. When did you make this assignation?" Miranda's tone was so cold that Fanny fired up at once.

"It is not an assignation," she cried hotly.

"What else would you call a clandestine meeting? Did I not beg you most particularly to take care?"

"It is all my fault," Harry intervened. "I persuaded Fanny when we met this morning. Do not be cross with her. It is I who deserve your censure."

Miranda ignored him. "You had best return to the carriage, Fanny, but before you go I have something to say to both of you. If Lord Lakenham appears at the play tonight, I shall not help you further."

"You would go back upon your word?" Fanny stared at her in consternation.

"You have not kept yours. I mean it, Fanny. I will put an end to this ridiculous charade."

Pausing only at the counter to record the loan of her book, she marched out of the shop.

Aware of the coachman on the box, Miranda did not trust herself to say more until they reached the privacy of their bedchamber. Then she swung round upon her twin.

"How could you deceive me so?" she demanded. "Have you no sense at all? Suppose Lord Heston had seen you?"

"There was no danger of that." Fanny's face was sullen. "Harry said that he was gone to Tattersall's to look at bloodstock. You do not suppose that he spends his time in libraries, do you?"

"I have no idea how he spends his time, nor do I care, but he is not blind. You know how gossip travels among the *ton*. Any of his friends might have seen the pair of you together."

"It was unlikely," Fanny protested. "Harry is no reader, nor are his friends…"

"Then how strange that he should enter a library…it must give rise to comment."

"Suppose it did? I am supposed to be you. Heston could not take exception…"

Miranda eyed her twin in disbelief. "You think not? Heston would no more countenance a match with you than with me."

"He can't forbid a mere friendship. Harry might have sought me out to comfort him for his loss…"

"And we all know what that can lead to. You put me out of all patience with you. I meant what I said. If Harry appears tonight, you may say goodbye to all your hopes."

"He won't," Fanny sulked. "You made it clear that he must not, though I do not see how you can stop him."

"You don't? I could cry off from this supposed engagement, Fanny, having mistaken my own heart. It happens every day, and it must come to that in the end."

"Not yet, I beg of you!" Fanny began to whimper. "I will be good, you'll see."

"Very well, but don't be such a watering-pot." Miranda looked at the clock. "I shall take Aunt's advice and rest for an hour. You had best do the same. I suppose you had no time to choose another book?"

In silence Fanny held out *The Mysteries of Udolpo* for her sister's inspection.

Miranda smiled. "That will do very well," she said. "Better to frighten yourself with that than with thoughts of Heston's anger if he should discover how we have deceived him." She picked up her own book and was soon deep in the story.

Before she knew it, it was time to dress and not all her worries could quite destroy her pleasure in her new gown. It was a perfect fit, and over the slender column of the under-dress the pale green gauze whispered softly to the ground, caught at the bosom with matching ribbons.

She gazed at the mirror-image of herself as Fanny twisted and turned before the glass.

"Have you ever seen anything so beautiful?" Fanny whispered reverently. "We have never worn anything so expensive!"

Miranda grimaced. "We did not pay for the gowns, I must remind you."

"I know it, but may we not enjoy our finery just for tonight? Oh, if Harry could but see me now…"

"You must pray that he does not," her sister told her sternly. She frowned at Fanny and was about to repeat her warning when Mrs Shere came to find them.

"Why, Aunt, how fine you are this evening!" Fanny caught the older woman by the shoulders and turned her round. "You will put us in the shade…"

Mrs Shere shook her head in a disclaimer, though she was pleased. Her dark grey silk was trimmed at the neck with rows of French lace, and she carried a shawl of the same material. The garment was beautifully cut, and it did much to disguise the outlines of her ample figure.

"Nonsense, my dear, you are too kind. I admit that, before we married, your mama and I were used to have a fondness for the latest modes, but I have grown stout, I fear."

"No, ma'am, Fa—my sister does not exaggerate." Miranda caught herself before she made a fatal slip. "You look charmingly…that gown is so becoming…"

She felt that she was babbling in fright. She had come so close to giving herself away. Would Aunt Emma notice?

"Well, we owe it to Lord Heston to appear at our best," Mrs Shere told her. "Most certainly he cannot find fault with either of you, my dears. I have not seen you look so well before. The gowns were a good choice, were they not?"

"They were," Miranda kissed her warmly. "I hope that our uncle will be pleased with the results of his generosity."

"He is gone out to dine," her aunt announced. "Lord Heston invited him, you know, but he felt that he owed it to his lordship's consequence to refuse. I was a little undecided on my own account, but Heston insisted."

"And why should he not?" Miranda cried. "We may not be of noble birth, not persons of consequence, but we have some pretensions of gentility, and our family is respectable."

"Of course, my love! You must not think me insensible of our connections, though my family has cast me off…"

"More fool them!" Miranda cried inelegantly. "There are no better people alive than you and my uncle… To spurn you just because you married for love…? It is past all bearing."

"It is an old story, and we shall think no more about it at this present time," Mrs Shere said firmly. "Now, my dears, we must go down. We have not allowed ourselves much time to dine, and Lord Heston will be here at eight."

Again Miranda felt slight panic, but she crushed it firmly. Why should she be afraid of Heston? The afternoon had given her time for reflection, and all that was necessary was to treat him with the civility due to his position. Sadly, he had the most unfortunate habit of throwing her off balance with a word or the lift of an eyebrow. His spurious tenderness in the company of others was hateful to her. She knew his true opinion of her character.

He might have made a fortune on the boards, she thought scornfully. His acting rivalled that of Edmund Kean.

When he arrived she looked at him askance, though honesty compelled her to admit that no fault could be found with his appearance. He was dressed *de rigueur* in a black swallow-tailed coat and satin knee-breeches with silk stockings. A splendid waistcoat of watered silk softened the severity of his garb, but apparently he had no other modish leanings. The bosom of his shirt was unadorned by a frill.

Miranda stiffened as he bent to salute her cheek. She turned away, but he stayed her with a hand upon her arm.

"My darling, this betrothal gift is unworthy of your beauty, but I beg that you will accept it." He handed her a long flat box.

Miranda did not attempt to open it, so he took it from her and threw back the lid to reveal a fine string of perfectly matched pearls.

Mrs Shere gasped and Fanny's eyes grew round.

"I trust the necklace pleases you," his lordship murmured. "Will you wear it tonight?"

Miranda looked at the gleaming pearls. Their sheen was such that they seemed like living things, sending her a warning.

Chapter Four

Miranda closed the lid of the box with a snap.

"My lord, you are most generous," she said smoothly. "But I cannot wear the pearls. We are not yet officially betrothed. My mama has not given her consent."

"Dearest, you must not refine too much upon the matter." Mrs Shere looked startled. "Nothing is more certain than that she will give you her blessing…"

"Even so…" Miranda would not be swayed.

"Try them at least," his lordship pleaded. "Here, let me clasp them about your neck." He caught up the necklace and led her to a mirror, turning her to face it, his hands resting lightly on her shoulders.

"There!" He fastened the clasp, his fingers lingering upon her skin.

Miranda flushed as she looked at his dark face

beside her own. Although his hands were cool they seemed to burn her flesh. She shuddered. There was a curious expression in his heavy-lidded eyes, and it turned her knees to water. She caught her breath.

"Very pretty!" To her relief her voice sounded calm. "Another time perhaps, my lord?"

"As you wish, my dear." Heston returned the pearls to their box and laid it on the sofa-table.

He did not speak to her again until they reached the theatre, reserving his attention for her aunt. That lady answered him politely, but she was quick to admonish Miranda when his lordship spoke to Fanny, careful of her comfort as he led her to a seat with a good view of the stage.

"Dearest, that was not well done of you to refuse to wear his lordship's gift." Mrs Shere sounded re-proachful as she drew Miranda aside.

"I'm sorry, Aunt, but I could not think it right. It must have given rise to comment, and all eyes are upon us as it is."

Miranda spoke no more than the truth. The appearance of the twins with their aunt in Lord Heston's box had resulted in a buzz of speculation from all parts of the theatre. They were the cynosure of all eyes, and she felt ready to sink with embarrassment as lorgnettes were raised and quizzing glasses levelled in their direction.

Lord Heston seated himself beside her. In her opinion he was much too close, and for one awful moment she thought he intended to lay a casual arm along the back of her chair. Surely he could not be so lost to all sense of propriety?

"My darling, I trust that you are perfectly comfortable?" he enquired in a solicitous tone, which did not deceive her for a second.

A sharp retort rose to Miranda's lips, but she bit back the angry words, aware that her aunt must overhear her.

Heston smiled, knowing that he could taunt her with impunity, and that she was powerless to reply.

She turned her attention to the stage, but later she could recall neither the title of the piece, nor the names of the players. The presence of the man beside her filled her mind to the exclusion of all else. What had she done?

It was all very well to promise herself that she would pay him back for all his insults, but his reaction to her attempt to worst him had been both swift and unexpected.

What could he hope to gain by taking her at her word? She stole a glance at him to find his eyes upon her. His sardonic gaze held her own and she felt her colour rising.

"Puzzled, my dear?" he said gently.

"Not at all, my lord. The piece has a simple plot." She pretended to misunderstand him, but she saw the flash of white teeth in the semi-darkness as he laughed.

"Has it? You must tell me about it later…it is not perfectly clear to me." He lapsed into silence once more, leaving Miranda to her own thoughts.

They were not pleasant. Not for the first time she felt a stab of panic. Matters had gone much further than she had intended. It had not occurred to her that Heston would be so quick to call her bluff, but who could have supposed that this haughty creature would insist on a betrothal, however false his intentions? And then to appear with her in public, and to offer distinguishing attention to her sister and her aunt? It was not to be borne, but for the moment she could see no way to extricate herself from her predicament.

During the interval, her composure was severely tried as Heston's friends descended upon the box. Miranda knew one or two of them by sight, and also by reputation, but neither she nor her sister had been introduced to them.

His lordship was quick to remedy the omission, and Miranda found herself the subject of a number of speculative glances, especially from the ladies.

"Is she Heston's latest flirt, do you suppose?" The play was about to resume, and Miranda heard the careless words as the door to the box was closing.

Fiery colour stained her cheeks, and she felt ready to sink with embarrassment. The reply did nothing to restore her composure.

"What else? Heston isn't the marrying kind, and even he would not present a bird of paradise to you, my dear."

Miranda pressed her hands to her burning face. Thankfully, Heston was speaking to her aunt and had not heard the muttered exchange.

"Forgive me, ma'am, but are you quite well? May I bring you a glass of wine?"

Miranda looked up to find that she was being addressed by a gentleman in a military uniform which she did not recognise. There was a slight but attractive foreign accent in his voice.

Realising that she had been too preoccupied to notice him earlier in the press of introduction, she bent her gaze upon him, striving in vain to remember his name.

The young man brought his heels together and bowed.

"Alexei Toumanov at your service, Miss Gaysford. You may not have caught my name. I am with the Tsar of Russia's entourage. May I be of service to you?" A pair of gentle brown eyes looked down at her with an expression of concern.

"You are very kind, but it is nothing," Miranda said quickly. "I found the heat a little oppressive, that is all, Count Toumanov." She sipped gratefully at the proffered glass of wine, thankful that she had at least remembered his title.

As the curtain went up once more, he slipped into a chair beside her after a questioning look at Heston.

His lordship chuckled. "Alexei, you are a complete hand. Was it your intention to usurp my place?"

"Not at all, my dear Adam, though you did invite me to join you."

"So I did! Now, was it a mistake, I wonder?" Heston threw a pointed look at Miranda, which she ignored.

She found herself wondering at their obvious friendship. It was clear that the two men were on easy terms, and it puzzled her. In the Count's presence Heston had dropped his supercilious manner, and for the first time she saw something of his charm.

As the play resumed he stopped his banter and took a chair behind her, slightly to her left.

Miranda felt indignant. Did he intend to spy upon her? The look he had given her when he found the Count beside her had spoken volumes. Did he imagine that she intended to try her wiles upon his friend? It was apparent that she was not to be allowed to indulge in any conversation which he might not hear.

During the next interval she was glad to have the opportunity to confound him.

"Do you ladies care to walk about the corridor?" the Count enquired. "I believe that you would find it cooler there…"

Miranda rose at once and laid her hand upon his arm. With a mischievous smile at Heston the Count took Fanny upon his other side and left the box.

Mrs Shere had no opportunity to do more than look a little dismayed, for Heston was drawing back her chair and offering to escort her.

The crush in the passageway was excessive, but the Count was quick to lead them to a seat in a deserted alcove from where they were able to watch the fashionable crowd about them.

"I doubt if I have ever seen so many people," Fanny exclaimed. "Where have they all come from?"

"Many are foreigners, as I am myself," Count Toumanov explained. "The Allies intend to celebrate their victory over Napoleon in extravagant style. It is a little hard upon the inhabitants of this city."

"Oh, no, they will enjoy it, Count. There is not a seat to be had along the processional route, you know." Miranda gave him her enchanting smile.

"But you, at least, will see it, will you not? I cannot believe that Heston has not made arrangements."

"He has not told us of them," Miranda said demurely.

"Then you must allow me. There will be no difficulty, I assure you."

"Quite unnecessary, Alexei!" Heston had come up to them with Mrs Shere upon his arm. "You have spoilt my surprise, you villain!"

Unperturbed by Heston's reproof, the Count grinned at him. "You will not blame me for trying, Adam?"

"Not at all, but you will have enough to do, my friend, upon the great occasion. We shall look down upon you from the comfort of our seats as you clatter along behind your master's carriage. I shall feel for you, of course. It cannot be comfortable to wear all your finery for any length of time."

"You are speaking to a man of iron, my dear sir.

Later I hope to dance the night away. Ladies, may I beg that you will partner me?"

Fanny was thrown into confusion. "I do not know, Count Toumanov."

"As yet our plans are undecided," Miranda broke in firmly.

"Then I must beg Adam to decide them for you." The Count's enthusiasm was infectious. "Come, Adam, what do you say? May we not make up a party?"

"I see that I shall have no choice," his lordship murmured. "Leave it with me, and I shall get in touch with you."

With that the irrepressible Alexei had to be contented. With great good humour he led the ladies back to their box and stayed with them until the play was over.

"You are well acquainted with the Count, my lord?" Mrs Shere enquired as the carriage took them home.

"A boyhood friend, ma'am. We lived in Russia for some time. My father was attached to the Tsar's court."

"I see." Mrs Shere looked thoughtful, but she did not pursue the subject, although Miranda suspected that she was disturbed by the young man's evident admiration for the twins.

Her suspicions were confirmed when Mrs Shere made a point of leaving her alone with Heston when they reached the house.

Fanny was inclined to linger by her sister's side, unwilling to abandon her to his lordship's less-than-tender mercies, but Mrs Shere would have none of it. She took Fanny by the hand and led her from the room.

"Well, my dear, another triumph for you! Count Toumanov was smitten to the heart." Heston gave Miranda a lazy look. "I wish you might have heard his raptures when we were alone…something about eyes that a man could drown in… He cannot decide if they are blue or violet."

Miranda gave him an angry look.

"He was right, of course," his lordship continued. "For my own part, I am sure that they are violet. They darken when you are furious, did you know it? A pity that Alexei cannot see beneath that innocent appearance to the heart beneath."

"I wonder that you dared to expose him to my evil influence," Miranda retorted.

"I intend to dare much more than that." Heston moved to stand in front of her. "Now, my love, may I claim what is due to your prospective husband?"

Before she could protest he caught her to his

chest and his mouth came down on hers. Miranda felt a dizzying sensation. His lips were soft, warm, and most insistent as they found her own.

She had vowed earlier that if he ever tried to kiss her again she would not struggle. Her strength was useless against his own, and she had no wish to find herself once more covered in bruises. She let herself grow limp and unresponsive in his arms.

Heston held her away from him. "New tactics?" he said in a soft voice. "They will not serve, my dear. Let us try again…" He picked her up and carried her to a sofa. "I see that you demand finesse."

Miranda found herself upon his knee. "The servants…" she gasped. "Have you no sense of propriety, sir?"

"None whatever," he said equably. He lifted her hand to his lips, turned it over and kissed the palm. Then his mouth travelled upwards along the inside of her arm.

Miranda found the butterfly kisses strangely disturbing, and a new sensation possessed her as he began to caress the back of her neck with the fingers of one hand.

"Please!" She tried to push him away.

"Please what? You must tell me how to delight you, dearest."

To Miranda's horror his hand travelled from her waist until it cupped her breast. She tried to strike out at him and found herself helpless as both her wrists were gripped.

"No, no, my little termagant!" he reproved. "Pray do not struggle. To enjoy love, it is necessary to relax."

"Love?" she spat at him. "You call this love? How dare you insult me so? I might be no better than one of those creatures who were peddling their wares at the Opera House tonight!"

"You recognised them, did you? It was only to be expected. Tell me, my dear, how do their ambitions differ from your own?"

Miranda looked at the mocking face. If he kissed her again, she would bite through his upper lip. Sadly, he seemed to have no such intention. He set her upon her feet, and rose to take his leave.

"A word of warning, Miss Gaysford! Count Toumanov is not for you. In future, I must beg of you to save your charms for me."

He was gone before she could reply, but her anger knew no bounds.

Her temper was not improved when she was confronted by her aunt. Mrs Shere took one look at her face, and tried to heal the breach.

"You could not expect Lord Heston to be pleased, my love," she murmured. "Count Toumanov was most particular in his attentions. It was not wise to encourage him."

"I did not encourage him," Miranda snapped. "Heston invited him. You would not expect me to be less than civil to his friend."

"There are degrees of civility, dearest, and the young man seems volatile..."

"He was very kind to me and, Aunt, I am not yet betrothed, whatever you may think."

"Very well, I shall not interfere, but do take care. This is a splendid match for you. You must do nothing to overturn it."

Miranda kissed her aunt goodnight and sought the sanctuary of her bedchamber. There she found Fanny waiting for her.

"What is Heston about?" her twin demanded. "Did you see Aunt Emma's face when she saw the pearls? They must be worth a fortune!"

Miranda glared at her. "Do you suppose their cost would weigh with him? Doubtless he hands out similar trinkets to his lightskirts every week."

"That is hardly fair," her sister protested. "I have never seen him in the company of a woman, and nor have you. That is why our appearance in his box tonight created such a stir."

"Of course we have not seen him with a woman. The type of female he prefers would hardly be thought suitable to hang upon his arm at the Opera."

"You mean…you think he is a libertine? Oh, love, that can't be true. He is thought to be a cold fish."

"I assure you he is not." The colour rose to Miranda's cheeks. "And if he had kissed you you would know it."

"Oh, dear! I had not thought that he would press his attentions on you in that way…"

"Why not? He intends to punish me for daring to stand up to him. What better way than to take advantage of the fact that we are supposed to be betrothed?"

"That is not the action of a gentleman."

"Great heavens, Fanny, what kind of person do you suppose that we are dealing with? Heston is under the impression that he can walk on water, and I intend to disabuse him of that idea."

"You are grown very hard," Fanny ventured.

"Is it surprising? Heston would bring out the worst in anyone. He misses no opportunity to give me a setdown. Do you know that he actually warned me… warned me not to encourage Count Toumanov?"

"But, love, the Count was very attentive to you."

"To both of us, Fanny, and he meant no harm. It was a pleasure to speak to such a gentle and entertaining person. There was no need to keep up one's guard, as I am forced to do with Heston."

"It would be hard to find two people less alike than his lordship and the Count," her twin agreed. "Their friendship is surprising."

"Monsters are few and far between, thank goodness! There cannot be another such as Heston. Beside him anyone must seem charming."

"But he did give you the pearls, Miranda. Why would he do that if he dislikes you so?"

"It was simply another attempt to put me out of countenance. To frighten me, he will carry this deception as far as he dare go."

Fanny hesitated, twisting her handkerchief between her fingers. "And how far will he go?"

She looked so pale that Miranda stared at her.

"What do you mean?"

"I am afraid of him," Fanny said simply. Slow tears rolled down her cheeks. "Do you think that he intends to marry you? I could not bear it."

Miranda went to sit beside her and slipped an arm about her sister's waist. "What nonsense!" she said in a rallying tone. "Would his lordship wed a nonentity? He would not give the idea a moment's consideration. Oh, I know he thinks his position unassailable, but he would not care for the humiliation. He has no such thought in mind. In any case, not even he could marry without his bride's consent."

"I hope you may be right." Fanny dabbed at her eyes. "But I fear you are mistaken in him. He does not care for the opinion of the world, else he would not have spoken to Uncle, or agreed to the announcement being made."

"There is that, of course." Miranda looked thoughtful. "But he thinks himself safe enough. He knows that I shall cry off, but I shan't do it yet. This is a test of nerves, my love, and I intend to win it."

Fanny shuddered. "Heston is playing some deep game, I know it. Suppose you have misjudged him? He must intend to marry before he is much older...there is the question of an heir, you know. For all we are aware, he may decide to wed you simply for that purpose."

"Stuff!" Miranda was out of all patience. "Have I not explained that he cannot force me into marriage?"

"He thinks that he need not do so. Does he not believe that you want a title and his fortune? How will he guess that you plan to cry off?"

Miranda felt dismayed as the truth of her

sister's words came home to her, but she forced herself to smile.

"He must intend to cry off himself, possibly at the last moment. Come, Fanny, in your wildest dreams you can't think that he would care to wed me. Mutual dislike is no basis for marriage. His life would be hell, and he must know it."

"So would yours," her sister said dolefully. "He could shut you away in the country, and I should never see you again." She began to wail.

"For heaven's sake, do stop!" Miranda cried. "What would you have me do? Am I to confess the whole and take the consequences?"

Fanny raised her head. She looked shamefaced. "I'm sorry," she murmured. "I must suppose that you know what you are doing, and Harry and I are so grateful for your help. Perhaps it will all work out as you would wish."

"Of course it will! Now, Fanny, we must go to bed. It's very late and I have no wish to look hagged tomorrow. Heston must not think that he is robbing me of my sleep."

It was a sensible suggestion, but sleep did not come as easily as Miranda hoped. Fanny's words had disturbed her more than she would admit, and it was not only her sister's remark about being shut away in the country, which echoed Heston's threats, made earlier in the day.

What was it Fanny had said? Something about his lordship playing a deep game? Try as she might she could not guess what it might be. Fanny must surely be mistaken, and yet a tiny doubt remained.

What had started as a simple hoax had now turned into something very different, and not only her sister and herself were involved in it. Their mama, their aunt and uncle, Harry Lakenham and Heston himself were all entangled in the deception.

Miranda's face burned. She could never lift her head again when the truth came out. She must have been mad to let matters go so far, but it was no use repining or wishing the events of the last few days undone. There was no going back. The only time she might have told the truth was at the end of that first ugly interview with Heston, and that would have put the cat among the pigeons with a vengeance.

She must go on, but how was she to support this dreadful farce for what might be several months? Her only hope lay in Fanny's volatile temperament. Fickle in her affections, it was more than likely that her twin would discover a passion for someone who pleased her more than Lakenham, before that young man attained his majority.

London was crowded for the coming celebrations, and Heston had made it clear that they were to mingle in the highest circles. Surely there was someone who might take her sister's fancy. With that hopeful thought, Miranda fell asleep.

The following day she was tempted to plead exhaustion as a means of keeping to her room, but Heston's taunt of cowardice had stung. He should never be allowed to think that of her. She dressed quickly and accompanied Fanny to the breakfast-room.

As she sat down she cast an anxious look at the pile of letters beside her uncle's plate. It was only when he had finished reading them that she allowed herself a sigh of relief.

"Uncle, is there nothing from Mama?" she murmured.

"Nay, love, we cannot hope for an answer yet. It is too soon, but do not be fretting yourself. Your match with Heston must be all that she has hoped for…more, in fact. You will have her blessing, I am sure of it."

Miranda gave him a feeble smile, feeling relieved that she was to be spared from the announcement for one more day. Her hopes were not to be realised.

Later that morning her uncle burst into the room, with a young man close behind him. He was waving a missive, and as she looked at him her heart sank. His beaming face confirmed her worst fears.

"There now! You may set your mind at rest, my dear. Here is your mother's letter, brought to us by your brother's friend."

Miranda nodded to Richard Young, wishing him still in Yorkshire. He was a neighbour and she knew him well, but what was he doing in London? It was sheer bad luck that he had been on hand to act as her mother's messenger.

"How kind!" The irony in her tone was not lost upon her twin and Fanny threw Miranda a warning glance as she moved to greet their visitor.

"It was indeed! Very civil, sir, I must admit," said Alderman Shere. "Now you shall meet my wife, and you will join us, I hope, for luncheon?"

Richard blushed, but he was easily persuaded. He came towards Miranda and handed her another billet.

"This one is for you, Miss Gaysford." He looked from one twin to the other, an anxious frown upon his face. "I have it right, I hope?"

"Thank you, Richard." Miranda held out her hand for the letter. It was not mere courtesy which stopped her from begging leave to read it there and then. She could guess what it contained, and the thought of her mother's inevitable raptures filled her with despair.

Her aunt was quick to urge her not to stand on ceremony. "Mr Richard Young will excuse us if your uncle tells us what your mother has to say. He must be in her confidence already." She smiled and nodded at the young man. "We are so excited, my dear sir. Who could have hoped for such a match for Fanny?"

Richard smiled and bowed. "Ma'am, you are right. Mrs Gaysford is delighted for her daughter."

All eyes were on Miranda as she opened the letter. The single sheet of paper was covered on both sides with her mother's untidy scrawl, but she could not make out a word of it. The letter had been crossed and re-crossed so many times that it was undecipherable. Mrs Gaysford must have written it with the intention of sending it by the mails.

"I'm sorry, but it is a little difficult to read." She handed it to her uncle, who raised his eyebrows and gave it to her aunt.

"Now isn't that just like Letty?" Mrs Shere exclaimed. "She was hoping to save you money, George. What does she say to you?"

The Alderman's eyes twinkled. "Mine was written in less haste. Shall I read it to you?"

They sat in silence as he began to do so. Mrs Gaysford had been so overcome by the prospect of her elder daughter's brilliant match that the page was filled with superlatives. Her tears of happiness had blotted out several words, but he was able to assure Miranda that all the blessings in the world were called down upon her head.

Miranda squirmed inwardly, and her dismay increased tenfold when Lord Heston was announced.

"My lord, we have splendid news for you!" The Alderman hastened to greet him. "We have heard from my sister-in-law, who sends you every good wish for your future happiness. She has given her consent to your betrothal."

"Splendid news indeed!" Heston gripped the older man's hand, but his eyes were on Miranda's face. In their grey depths she detected a look of triumph. It was no more than the impression of a moment. Then he turned as Richard Young was introduced to him.

"My dear sir, we have much to thank you for. We had not hoped for such an early reply. My darling, your cup of happiness must be full." With an outstretched hand, he drew Miranda to his side.

As his lean fingers gripped her own, Miranda longed to draw away. He sensed it, and his grasp tightened.

"At last!" he murmured tenderly. "Now the announcement may be made, and the world shall know of our joy."

Chapter Five

Miranda coloured and her uncle began to tease her. He could not know that her rosy blush was due to anger rather than embarrassment. As Heston slipped an arm about her waist, kissing her hand before saluting her cheek, her rage increased.

"Now, now, there is no cause to be shy, my girl! We all understand his lordship's feelings, and we'll have no ceremony here. You will join us for luncheon, my lord? Quite informal, you know, and Mr Young is to join us."

"Sadly, I have another engagement," Heston told him smoothly. "I came merely to ask if Miss Gaysford will drive with me this afternoon?"

There was no way that Miranda could refuse, though she threw a desperate glance at Fanny.

"Aunt, were we not to drive along the processional route to the Guildhall?" Fanny broke in swiftly.

Mrs Shere looked startled. "No, no, you are mistaken. I cannot recall that I mentioned such a thing…"

"Nevertheless, it is a splendid idea! Perhaps the Elgin marbles first, and a drive through the city later? You will all accompany us, I hope."

"My lord, you cannot wish for such a large party on your drive?" Mrs Shere shook her head, but she was pleased.

Heston chuckled. "You are all consideration, ma'am, but lovers do not expect always to be alone—that is, until they are married."

"Then, if you are sure…?"

"Did you not tell me that your phaeton takes no more than two?" Miranda's tone was hostile.

"Very true, my love, but it is not my only carriage. You will be comfortable in the barouche."

Miranda did not argue further. Naturally, Heston would have more than one carriage. Most probably he has six, she thought bitterly.

"Shall we say four o'clock, then?" Heston was all courtesy as he consulted Mrs Shere.

Mrs Shere smiled her assent, but when he had gone she drew Miranda aside.

"My dear, you must try to be a little more amenable. Gentlemen prefer to see a smiling face, you know. Now I do not mean to scold. Let us go in to luncheon."

The reproof was gentle but Miranda felt disturbed. She had allowed her dislike of Heston to betray her into incivility. More worrying than that was her mother's swift acceptance of her supposed betrothal. She groaned inwardly, yet what else had she expected? A feeling of depression seized her, but she forced herself to take part in the conversation of the others, hoping that her low spirits would pass unnoticed.

As always her aunt had provided an excellent meal. Conscious of Mrs Shere's anxious scrutiny she took a little of the asparagus in butter sauce, and a slice or two of a fine York ham.

As one course followed another, she pushed the food about her plate, hiding it as best she could beneath an Italian salad.

Fanny was chattering happily to Richard Young, and from their conversation Miranda learned that her mother and her brothers and sisters were in good health, and looking forward to her marriage.

"Shall you be wed in Yorkshire?" Richard asked. "Your mother wishes to know."

"I have no idea," Miranda told him helplessly.

"Of course not!" The Alderman broke in at once.

"How could that be? Lord Heston will wish the ceremony to take place in London, as befits his consequence. My sister-in-law will come to us, together with her family."

"We have not yet decided on a date," Miranda faltered.

"If I don't misjudge his lordship, it will be sooner rather than later." Alderman Shere gave his niece a mischievous smile. "Heston is head over heels in love with you, my dear, and he does not strike me as a man who is prepared to wait for his happiness."

Miranda felt an uncomfortable churning in the pit of her stomach. "There is no hurry," she protested.

"Perhaps not for you, my dear child, but gentlemen have different ideas…" He left it there, but her aunt was not so tactful.

When the meal was over and Richard Young had left them she came into the drawing-room. A glance sent Fanny hurrying away.

"Now, dearest, I must speak to you," Mrs Shere said firmly. "You have surprised me. One might think that you did not care to fix Lord Heston's interest. The match is not distasteful to you, is it?"

Miranda hesitated. She longed to tell her aunt of her deception, but the words would not come. She shook her head.

"Very well, then. You know us well enough, I hope, to believe that we should not wish you to engage yourself to someone you dislike. Is that not so?"

Too stricken to speak, Miranda nodded.

"My dear, you are very young, and you have led a sheltered life in Yorkshire. I doubt if you understand the full extent of your good fortune. Heston is the finest catch in London…" She paused as Miranda frowned.

"Well, perhaps that is an unfortunate expression. I should not wish you to think me mercenary, dearest, but the comfort of a fortune is not to be denied."

Miranda looked at her with swimming eyes.

"There now, you shall not be distressed, but we must face the facts. Consider your mama, my love. She was cast off by her family, as I was myself, for marrying beneath her."

"Papa was not beneath her. He was a scholar…"

"Of course, but he had no money. I was more fortunate. George is comfortable, if not wealthy. However, that is not what I intended to say. Do you not see that if you do not go on with this betrothal…if you were so foolish as to give Lord Heston a dislike of you…well then…you would face a second Season?"

"We could not ask that of uncle," Miranda muttered.

"He would do it gladly, but it rarely serves. There is a certain stigma attached to young women who do not 'take', as the saying goes. Too many hopeful maidens are keen to step into their shoes."

Miranda felt unable to reply.

"Well, there it is." A comforting arm stole about Miranda's shoulders. "Do not take my words amiss, my child. I think only of your happiness, and I would a thousand times see you shy rather than unbecomingly bold, but perhaps you should be a little kinder to his lordship."

Miranda promised to do her best. She dressed with care that afternoon, in an effort to please her aunt.

When Heston arrived she greeted him with every appearance of pleasure which, though assumed, caused him to regard her with suspicion.

She dimpled at him, realising suddenly that to play the part of a loving bride-to-be would baffle him more than covert hostility. If he could play the fond lover, so could she. She would beat him at his own game.

As they drove towards Bloomsbury, Miranda

hung upon his lordship's every word, simpering and smiling in what she hoped was a perfect imitation of a shy but excited maiden charmed by the attentions of her lover.

Fanny's face was a study in perplexity, but Mrs Shere looked with approval at Miranda, pleased to think that her words of censure had been heeded.

With the easy address of a man of fashion Heston drew both Fanny and her aunt into conversation. He seemed to know everyone of note in London, including the Prince Regent.

"Have you visited Carlton House?" he asked.

Miranda suspected him of offering them a setdown. He knew as well as she did that an invitation from the Prince would be unlikely to reach the home of Alderman Shere.

"Alas, we do not move in such exalted circles," she said demurely. "Nor have we been to Almack's."

It was an effort to forestall what she imagined would be his next question, and she would not have her aunt distressed.

Mrs Shere had suffered a bitter disappointment when she was informed that not even Lady Medlicott could obtain the coveted vouchers for her nieces. The highborn Patronesses of that august establishment had not looked kindly upon the hopes of her penniless relations, without even a title to recommend them.

"You haven't missed much," Heston said indifferently. "It's a barn of a place without a shred of comfort. Why everyone flocks to King Street to eat stale bread and butter and drink orgeat and lemonade, I can't imagine."

Mrs Shere could have told him. Almack's was the recognised marriage mart for members of the *haut ton*. Lord Heston might despise it, but for lesser mortals the possession of an entry voucher was prized more than gold. Those unfortunates who were excluded might only consider themselves upon the fringes of society.

"Is it true that they dance only country dances?" Fanny murmured.

"They are moving with the times at last," his lordship said with heavy irony. "Quadrilles and waltzes have been approved, so I understand."

"But that would not affect you, my lord." Miranda gave him her most enchanting smile. "You do not dance, I think?"

The heavy-lidded eyes looked down at her, and then his harsh face softened into an expression of what she recognised as spurious tenderness.

"Dearest, I could be persuaded to waltz," he told

her in a sentimental tone. "The thought of holding you in my arms…"

"La, sir, you will put me to the blush." Miranda opened her fan and hid behind it. "We are not alone." She was careful to avoid Fanny's eye.

It was not until they were standing amidst the statuary brought from Greece a few years earlier that Fanny managed a word alone with her.

"Sister, what are you about?" she asked. "You are so unlike yourself that even Aunt must notice, and as for Heston…"

"I'm trying to annoy him," Miranda chuckled. "At least he is confused."

"So am I. You will give him a strange impression, and Aunt must wonder at your odd behaviour."

"Aunt will be pleased. She told me only this morning that I should be more…er…forthcoming."

"Oh, you make me so cross!"

"Do I, love? You must try to bear it. I'd planned to spray myself with the cheapest, most obnoxious perfume I could find, but sadly there wasn't anything suitable in the house."

Fanny threw up her eyes to heaven and went to join the others.

Heston was pointing out the features of the sculptures to her aunt, and in spite of herself Miranda was drawn to listen to his story of the difficulties involved in bringing them to England.

"And they were shipwrecked, do you say? Lord Elgin must have been distraught. We heard that he gave an enormous sum for them."

"Something in the region of seventy-four thousand pounds, ma'am, but look at the crafts-manship. These wine-bearers are from the north frieze of the Parthenon in Athens. They are the work of Pheidias."

Miranda was enthralled as they strolled from one group of figures to another.

"They are very fine, are they not?"

She had moved away from the others, and was startled to find that Heston was beside her.

"They are quite wonderful," she breathed. "The marble almost looks like living flesh, and see how the draperies flow about the figures. Pheidias must have been the finest sculptor in the world."

"They are not all his work, so it is believed." The grey eyes gave her a penetrating glance. "Other splendid artists worked upon the Parthenon and the temple of Nike Apteros, but their names are lost to us."

"It seems such a pity that they should have been torn away from their original sites…"

"You think it wanton destruction?"

She nodded.

"So do I." For once the mocking note was absent from his voice. "But since we have them here, we must make the most of the pleasure that they give us. There is some talk of buying them for the nation."

"Will that happen, do you suppose? I do hope so. At least they would be preserved."

"I am happy to hear that you approve." His eyes were warm as he looked at her, and Miranda gave him an answering smile before she remembered that she was acting out of character for the part which she intended to play.

"La, sir, I can have no opinion on the subject," she simpered.

Heston took her arm and led her behind an enormous group of charioteers.

"Let us have no more of that," he chided softly. "You are so much more entrancing when you are yourself, Miss Gaysford. For a time you had me believing that your mother's blessing had brought about a change of heart, but I realise that it is not so."

Miranda crimsoned, too mortified to answer him, and furious when she heard a low laugh.

"A good try, but unconvincing," he announced. "To play a part successfully, one must be consistent."

"As you would know, my lord."

"You think I am playing a part," he said in mock surprise. "Dearest, my heart is at your feet…"

She was spared the need to answer when Fanny came to find them.

"Aunt is a little tired of standing, Lord Heston. She is sorry…"

"Not at all! It is I who should apologise. I have been remiss in not considering the length of time we have been here." He went at once to order the barouche.

"Shall you wish to go directly home, ma'am?" he asked when they were seated in the carriage. "We may take our drive on another day, you know."

"No, no, I would not spoil your pleasure for the world," Mrs Shere protested. "It is just that my feet are inclined to swell…" She paused, uncomfortably aware that the great Lord Heston could have no possible interest in her complaints.

"That can be a trial, ma'am. My own mother suffered in a similar way. She found that lying flat, with her feet raised at an angle, was of the greatest help to her."

Miranda was astounded. Clearly there was an unsuspected side to his lordship's character. She could not have supposed it possible that he could be so kind in his concern for her aunt. She was forced to admit that his sympathy was unfeigned. What a mystery he was. This man who was said to have no interests other than in horses and in gaming had also surprised her that day with his love of art, and his knowledge of history.

As they drove through the Park, she was conscious once again of the unwelcome interest of the fashionable exquisites who strolled along the footpath arm in arm. Other carriages slowed at their approach and she saw avid curiosity on the faces of their occupants. She shrank back into one corner of the barouche, praying that the ordeal would soon be over.

"I have never before seen such crowds in London," Mrs Shere said brightly. "But it was only to be expected. The end of the war with France is certainly a cause for celebration."

"Let us hope that the celebrations are not premature, ma'am." Heston's face was grim.

"What can you mean, my lord?" Miranda was startled into speech. "Napoleon has abdicated and is in exile."

"On Elba?" Heston laughed. "If you suppose that the man who has conquered most of Europe will relinquish power so easily, you are more of an optimist than I."

"But what can he do? He was stripped of everything. His titles, his possessions, his armies…"

"The man is a genius…a magician, if you like. He was an idol to his men. He has only to land in France again, and the Little Corporal will have an army at his back."

"Pray do not say so!" Mrs Shere grew pale. "My eldest son is with Wellington, my lord. I could not bear to think of him in danger yet again."

"Aunt, it will not come to that." Miranda threw an angry look at Heston. "Napoleon is well guarded. How could he escape?"

Her words of comfort cheered her aunt a little and she began to draw Fanny's attention to the passing parade of fashion. Miranda seized the opportunity to speak to Heston.

"Pray do not frighten my aunt with your ridiculous notions," she said in a cool tone. "How could you be so tactless?"

He gave her a penetrating look in which there was more than a hint of sadness.

"Tactless, perhaps," he said in a quiet voice, "but the notion of an escape is not ridiculous, my dear. Elba is close to the southern coast of France, and the Emperor still has many adherents. For twenty years, as you know, he was accounted the saviour of his country."

"I can't think why," she retorted sharply. "Unless it is considered admirable to lose so many men in battle."

"Have you forgotten the Napoleonic Code?"

"No, I have not." Miranda was about to launch into a spirited discussion when she caught her aunt's eye and subsided.

"An interesting subject," Heston observed. "Perhaps we might continue with it later?"

Miranda nodded, though the look of astonishment on Mrs Shere's face was mingled with disapproval. In her view, ladies left all discussions of political matters to their menfolk, who were so much better able to understand them.

It was some comfort to think that Heston had not patronised her. He had not told her not to bother her pretty head about such things, which was the usual reaction from the gentlemen she knew. But then, he was no gentleman. Her lips curved in a tiny smile. For once she found herself in charity with him. He had seemed to be quite interested in her point of view.

This did not save her from another lecture from her aunt later that day.

"My dear, I did not like to see you pick up Lord Heston in that hey-go-mad way when he spoke of Napoleon," she scolded. "Such matters are not for ladies to understand. You would not have him think you a blue-stocking?"

"I doubt if he thinks that, Aunt Emma."

"He cannot have been pleased to hear you speaking out so boldly. I thought he must have given you a setdown, and you would have deserved it."

"He seemed quite interested in my views," Miranda told her mildly. "But I shall not speak of such things again unless he should desire it." She changed the subject with a coaxing smile. "In any case, I do not think he will attend the Grand Masquerade at Vauxhall. We were to go with Lady Medlicott, if you recall."

"But not without a male escort, my love." Mrs Shere looked shocked. "You must give up that plan. I can't think that his lordship would approve."

Miranda was tempted to announce that his lordship did not own her, but she bit back the hasty words.

"Richard Young has offered to accompany us. He is come to London to see the sights, Aunt, and we have known him all our lives. Mama would not object…"

Mrs Shere shook her head. "It is to be hoped that

you know what you are doing, dearest." It was a dismal echo of Fanny's words. "I cannot like your manner with Lord Heston. You do not appear to realise the extent of your good fortune."

Miranda kissed her cheek. "Lord Heston is not an ordinary man," she said with perfect truth. "I am learning to understand him. Believe me, he will not cry off." She crossed her fingers behind her back.

"You may be right, but it is easy to push good nature too far." Mrs Shere sighed, and then a thought struck her. "Your mama approves of Richard Young, you say? Has she hopes of him for your sister? What is his background?"

"Richard is just a country gentleman. He is the eldest son of the local squire and our good neighbour." She smiled. "But you shall not raise your hopes, Aunt Emma. Mama aims higher than Richard for my twin."

"Your sister makes no push to fix any gentleman's interest," Mrs Shere said sadly. "And, with the Season well advanced, most of the eligible gentlemen are committed. Will you have a word with her, my dear? Any advice would come better from you and be more readily acceptable. As I say, a second Season is never so successful. The novelty of a new face is gone, and other girls are more admired."

"I'll do my best," Miranda promised.

"That's right, my love. You, at least, have exceeded your mother's fondest hopes."

Miranda went to fetch her twin, thankful that she had escaped with only the mildest of scoldings. To hear Heston described as good-natured had shaken her a little, but she could not deny that he had been charming to her aunt.

"Thank heavens you had the sense to ask Richard to escort us to the Masquerade," she told Fanny. "Aunt was about to forbid us to go. Of course, Lady Medlicott must accompany us."

"Even that will be better than today." Fanny's face was sullen. "I can't think what possessed Heston to drag us off to look at a heap of broken stones. I thought I must die of boredom... How Harry would have stared to see us there!"

"I expect he would. Sculpture is not to everyone's taste, but I enjoyed the visit."

"Did you? I thought that you were still acting for Heston's benefit. I thought I should burst out laughing."

Miranda was silent.

"And then all that dreary talk about Napoleon! So dull! In Heston's company you have more to bear than I imagined. He has no conversation..."

"He doesn't gossip, Fanny, if that's what you mean. I suppose if he had entertained us with the latest crim. cons. you would have approved?"

"He moves in the Regent's circles. He might have told us the truth about the Princess Charlotte's broken engagement to the Prince of Orange, or if the Regent really is a bigamist. I confess I'd like to know if he had married Maria Fitzherbert before he was wed to Caroline of Brunswick."

"You put me out of patience with you, Fanny. It would be most improper of Heston to discuss such matters when he is in a privileged position to know the truth of them."

Fanny stared at her. "I thought you hated him? Why do you defend him now?"

"I am not defending him. I am defending the principle that it is wrong to discuss confidential matters, especially when they refer to a friend."

Fanny was not satisfied. "Are you beginning to think better of him? I didn't think you'd change your mind so quickly. Have you forgot his insults?"

"No, I have not! For heaven's sake, Fanny, let it rest! I have enough to trouble me. I can't think what I am to do if the announcement should appear in the *Gazette* tomorrow..." Her words served to silence Fanny.

* * *

But the next edition of the *Gazette* did not carry the news of the supposed betrothal, and Miranda could not disguise her relief. The announcement must have arrived too late to be included, but Mrs Shere was disappointed.

"Perhaps it is for the best," Miranda soothed. "Now there can be no objection to our going to the Masquerade with Richard."

Her aunt looked doubtful. "Dearest, I am persuaded that his lordship would not like it. You should ask his permission first."

Miranda kept her opinion of this suggestion to herself.

"Lord Heston is at Carlton House today," she pointed out. "And, Aunt, we shall wear our dominoes as well as our velvet masks. No one will recognise us."

"Very well then." Mrs Shere gave her permission for the outing with some reluctance. "But you must not stay too long."

"We shall be home by midnight," Miranda promised. "And with Richard to take care of us, we cannot come to any harm."

This prophetic statement proved to be untrue. The crowds at the Vauxhall Gardens were immense and it was difficult for the four members of their party to stay together. Lady Medlicott, an incorrigible gossip, insisted upon chatting to those persons whom she recognised, whilst Richard was diverted by the Grand Display of Fireworks.

"Oh, there is Harry!" Fanny cried out in delight. "Will he know me, do you think?"

Miranda threw her a glance filled with deep suspicion and Fanny pouted.

"I did not know he would be here," she insisted. "Don't glare at me, Miranda! This is a chance meeting."

"Obviously!" Miranda looked at Harry's companions. In addition to one or two gentlemen, there were a couple of well-known Incognitas.

Fanny's face grew pale. She had been about to rush over to her lover, but the sight of the high-flyers had stopped her instantly. A hand flew to her mouth.

"Oh no, he could not…" she whispered. Then she swayed and seemed about to faint.

"Don't you dare!" Miranda hissed. "Do you wish to make a spectacle of yourself and me? Those women may have nothing to do with Harry. You must forget that you have seen him in their company."

"How could I? Miranda, I must know." Before Miranda could stop her, she rushed to Harry's side.

It was the height of folly, but worse was to come. Fanny tore off her mask and confronted her lover with accusing eyes. His look of surprise changed to one of dismay, and he led her away from the others into a side turning, off the main promenade.

Miranda plunged after them, but the impetus of the crowd carried her far beyond the little group as it surged towards the Water Spectacle which was about to begin.

"All alone, little lady? You must not lose your footing." To Miranda's horror, an arm slid about her waist, and she caught a glimpse of gleaming teeth beneath a mask.

"Let me go!" she cried. "How dare you?"

"Unhand the lady, sir!" Suddenly Richard was by her side. His face was flushed, and his eyes were bright with anger.

"Out of it, stripling! This prize is mine." Her captor shouldered Richard aside as he tightened his grip upon Miranda's waist. Then he swung round. Richard had gripped his shoulder, and a bunched fist gave notice of his intentions. Next moment a blow from her attacker's cane felled Richard to the ground.

"Now let me see your face, my pretty!" A rough hand swept Miranda's hood from her hair and began to untie the strings of her mask.

As she fought him, Richard shook his spinning head, gathered himself and launched another attack upon the man who held her.

This time he was tripped and landed on his back. Miranda screamed as she saw the flash of light upon a gleaming blade. The innocent-looking cane was a swordstick and its tip was now against Richard's throat.

"You are in need of a lesson, my friend. A scar upon each cheek will remind you of this night—"

"He is unarmed!" Miranda cried wildly.

A circle had cleared about them as the crowd moved back. For a frozen moment Miranda stared at the spectators.

"Will no one help me?" she begged. A murmur of disgust was the only reply. No one was prepared to face the swordsman, much as they disapproved of his actions. She could see Fanny's ashen face on the outskirts of the group, and beside her Lady Medlicott was on the verge of collapse.

"Cowards, all of you!" Miranda shrieked. She took a step backwards and kicked her attacker sharply behind the knee. Her silken sandals were too soft to injure him, but he swung round with a curse.

"Hell-cat!" he growled. Then his face changed as his raised arm was caught in a bone-crushing grip.

He gave a yelp of agony, and the weapon clattered to the ground.

"You! I might have known!" The contempt in Heston's voice brought an ugly flush to the man's face. He scurried away, helped along by a kick to the seat of his breeches.

Chapter Six

Heston looked at Miranda. "All right?" he asked.

Miranda nodded. She was shaking so violently that she thought her legs would not support her, and she felt incapable of speech.

Heston reached down to help Richard to his feet.

"My lord, I'm sorry!" The younger man was white to the lips. "What must you think of me? I made the poorest showing as an escort for the ladies."

"You did very well." Heston's harsh, dark face softened for a moment as he smiled. "An unarmed man has no defence against a weapon such as this." He picked up the discarded sword, and then he turned to Miranda.

"I think we should leave, my dear," he said mildly. "We have provided quite enough entertainment for these bystanders. Where is your sister?"

"I saw her over there with Lady Medlicott." Miranda pointed with a trembling finger.

"Ah, yes!" His lordship took her arm and led her through the rapidly dispersing crowd.

Lady Medlicott had been supported to a nearby seat. She looked very ill. Fanny was chafing her hands, but there was no sign of Harry Lakenham.

"Mr Young, will you be good enough to take her ladyship home? I will bring her to the carriage…"

"A pleasure, sir!" Richard was eager to make amends for his previous failure to take care of them. "Shall I take Fanny and Miranda, too?"

"That will not be necessary. Count Toumanov and I will see them home."

"Oh, I did not see you." Miranda turned to find Alexei Toumanov by her side.

"Hardly surprising, ma'am. You had more than enough to occupy you." The Count smiled, but Miranda felt ashamed. What must Heston and his friend think of her? To be discovered in such circumstances was the outside of enough. She looked up at Heston, but his face was inscrutable.

"How…how did you find us, my lord?" she murmured.

Heston took her arm and led her ahead of the others, supporting Lady Medlicott upon one arm.

"Later, my love." With exquisite courtesy he handed her ladyship into the carriage with his wishes for her swift recovery, and the express hope that she would soon forget the ugly incident.

Lady Medlicott was no fool. She nodded, aware of his wish that she should not speak of it.

Fanny had regained her colour. As the carriage drove away, she smiled up prettily at Heston.

"How fortunate that you were here tonight," she cried. "I had not supposed you to like masquerades, my lord."

His penetrating eyes scanned her face. "I don't," he told her bluntly. "Mrs Shere advised us that you were come to the Vauxhall Gardens."

"We had thought you occupied at Carlton House," Miranda faltered. "I did not expect that you would call on us this evening."

"Obviously not!" It was clear that he was furious. "Have you no sense, madam? How came you to be separated from your party?"

"Don't speak to me in that tone, if you please! If you must know, I was carried along in the crush."

"Really? Without your sister?" Miranda knew that he did not believe her. "On our way in we passed Lakenham. Had you an assignation with him?"

"No, I had not! I am surprised that you could

think it. He knows of our…of our betrothal." She was speaking the truth, but a blush rose to her cheeks.

"Don't play games with me, my dear. If I find that you have been deceiving me, you will regret it. You asked how I found you? It was simple. When we saw the disturbance, I guessed that you would be at the centre of it."

"No, no, Adam, that is coming it too strong! Ignore him, Miss Gaysford! Adam is so tall. He looked above the crowd and saw your hair." Count Toumanov had come up to them and was attempting to heal the breach. "He is angry because you were in danger."

Heston glared at him, and then he began to laugh. "There is some truth in that," he admitted ruefully. "But I meant what I said. Trouble has an unerring way of finding you, my love. It is a sobering thought."

Miranda would not be mollified. She turned to the Count. "I hope we have not spoiled your evening," she said. "This has all been most unpleasant for you. It will give you a sad opinion of London."

"Not at all!" Alexei bowed. "Our only disappointment was in not finding you at home. That is one reason for Adam's sour expression. We had hoped to take you to the Piazza for some supper."

"Famous!" Fanny clapped her hands. "I should like that above anything."

"But you cannot wish to go after such an experience?" Heston's eyes were on Miranda. "I believe we should take you home. It must have been a shock…?"

"It was, but I am quite recovered." Blue eyes locked with grey. "You need have no fears for me, my lord. I do not plan to faint."

"As you wish." His tone was casual, but she saw the spark of something like admiration in his look. "The carriage is by the gates." Again he took her arm and led the way, leaving Fanny and the Count to follow.

"Tell me, where did you learn your street-fighting, dearest? It came as a surprise to me, though I have always been aware that you have unsuspected talents."

"I can't think what you mean." Miranda said stiffly.

"Must I explain?" He looked down at her dainty silken sandals. "Let me give you a word of advice. That kick to the back of the knee is more effective when you are wearing stouter shoes, but it served its purpose. Foolish, of course. If he had struck you, you might have been badly injured. I think I must teach you rather better. Your previous tutor left much to be desired…"

"My brother did not think that I should ever be in such a situation," she cried hotly.

"Then I must suppose that he does not know you very well. Personally I have no such sanguine hopes."

Miranda did not trouble to reply to this gibe. A thought had struck her.

"That man. You know him, do you not?"

"I know of him," he corrected. "An ugly customer, my dear, with a string of scandals behind him. It was no surprise to find him here, hoping to find a companion for the night."

Miranda flushed to the roots of her hair.

"Surely he could not imagine that I…that I…?"

"That you were available? Why not? You were apparently unattended and he saw his chance. Men are not saints, you know, and you are a prize worth the taking. Your face is likely to be your downfall, madam, unless you take more care."

"I did not know that such things could happen," she protested. "No gentleman would thrust his attention upon a woman in that brutal way."

She heard an ugly laugh. "What an innocent you are! Do you know nothing of the reputation of this place? These gatherings in the Vauxhall Gardens offer opportunities for many a lightskirt to find a rich protector. Your aunt should have forbidden this expedition."

"How dare you criticise her? She could not have known the truth of what you say, and I…well, I insisted upon coming here."

"That does not surprise me in the least. I hope you have learned your lesson."

"I have learned what cowards people are. Not a man in the crowd would lift a finger to help us."

"You forget…the man was armed. Courage is of little use against a sword."

"It did not stop you, my lord." Miranda spoke without thinking. Then she coloured a little.

"Ah, yes, but then, you see, I took your assailant by surprise. You had diverted his attention."

"Even so, it was a brave thing to do, and I thank you for it. It was unforgivable to draw on Richard as he did…he threatened to scar his face, you know."

"He would have done so without a second thought. Stroud has something of a reputation as a sadist. Not only was he blackballed at Brooks and White's, but he is barred from many…er…houses of ill repute. A girl was killed upon one occasion, I understand."

Miranda shuddered.

"Now I have shocked you. You must forgive me, but I wished to make the danger clear to you."

"It is clear enough, my lord. I shall not visit this place again," Miranda said firmly, forgetting for the moment that had he forbidden her to do so she would most certainly have defied him. "It is hateful."

"Not altogether. The concerts and the entertainments can be delightful if one is in a party, and uses a little common sense."

Miranda flushed again, but she did not argue, although it was not entirely her fault that she had found herself isolated from the others.

"Even so, I hope that you will accept my thanks," she murmured.

"I could do no less for my beloved." The mocking note was back in his voice as he handed her into the carriage.

His lordship did not appear to notice her annoyance. He chatted amicably to Fanny and the Count as the carriage bore them towards the Piazza, and Alexei was quick to extol the excellence of the food.

Then Miranda's ears pricked up.

"Mr Richard Young is an old friend of yours?" Heston's question was apparently casual, but there was something in his tone which warned her of his interest.

"He is a neighbour of ours in Yorkshire, and an old friend of my brother," she said shortly.

"We have known him all our lives," Fanny intervened. "He is come to London for the celebrations."

"You are fortunate in your friend. He does not lack courage. Do you suppose that he would care to join us to see the Regent's procession?"

"That would be kind." Miranda turned to him, her face alight with pleasure, and surprised something in his expression which she had not expected to see there. She blinked, feeling that she must have been mistaken. It was almost a look of tenderness.

The twins had not previously visited the Piazza, and they were suitably impressed. Their supper was all that the Count had promised but, though Miranda joined in the light-hearted conversation, she felt troubled. The incident in the Vauxhall Gardens had shaken her, but it was not that.

Heston was beginning to fill her mind to the exclusion of all else. She strove in vain to remember how much she had disliked him, but honestly compelled her to admit that she might have been mistaken in his character.

A teasing remark from the Count recalled her wandering thoughts. Knowing of her impending betrothal he was accusing her of daydreaming and being lost in love.

"Adam, you are a lucky dog!" he announced.

"You have captured the heart of one of the two most beautiful girls in London." As he spoke, he took Fanny's hand and raised it to his lips. His smile was full of mischief. "I must pin my hopes upon capturing the other."

Fanny coloured, but she was not displeased by the young Russian's evident admiration.

Miranda's spirits sank. Heston could only be annoyed by this flirtation, innocent though it was. To her surprise, his face was bland as he looked at the other couple.

"You may find it more difficult than you imagine," he said softly.

A moment of panic seized Miranda. It was a strange remark. Her discomfort was increased by the level look his lordship gave her. How much did he know? Surely he could not have guessed at the deception? It was impossible.

Later that night she tossed and turned as she lay in bed, unable to sleep. Heston did not trust her. He had made that clear. Yet he had warned her not to encourage the Count.

Why had he brought his friend along on that particular evening? Perhaps he imagined that Harry Lakenham would transfer his attentions to her sister. Alexei Toumanov must have been invited as a diversion, but she could not be sure. Suddenly she was tired of the whole ignominious business. She should never have become involved.

Heston was not the monster she had thought him. Common sense told her that. After all, it was not so dreadful for a man to wish to rescue a friend from a designing female. If the truth were to be told, it was admirable.

As for his insults, well, she had brought most of those upon herself. Not for the first time, she bemoaned her hasty tongue.

She was not entirely to blame, although she had been persuaded into this stupid hoax against her better judgement. The fact that she had sought to protect her sister was no excuse.

Lord Heston had been hasty, too. He had misjudged her from the start. Sadly, that was no comfort now. Somehow it seemed important that he should think better of her as their acquaintance grew.

In this last day or two she had seen him in a different light. He had been kind to her aunt and also to Lady Medlicott. She had been surprised, too, by the wide range of his interests. His conversation was stimulating, and on more than one occasion she had forgotten her dislike of him as they discussed particular topics.

Miranda tossed off her coverlet and turned her pillow, pressing her cheek against the cool linen. Yet still sleep would not come. Something deeper was disturbing her and at last she was forced to face the unpalatable truth. Tonight at the Vauxhall Gardens, her heart had jumped when she found that massive figure by her side, and it was not simply the fact that he had rescued both herself and Richard.

Later, as they supped at the Piazza, she had been aware of no one else. She could recall neither Count Toumanov's conversation nor that of her sister, and the other diners were merely a blur.

Only one thing stood out clearly in her mind, and that was the harsh, dark face of Adam Heston as his heavy-lidded eyes gazed down at her. She knew every detail of those features, the black brows, the acquiline nose, the clean line of his jaw, and the curve of his lips.

Her face grew hot as she recalled his kisses. His mouth had been warm upon her own as he held her to him, and the remembered scent of soap, sweet clean linen and the outdoors came back to haunt her.

She closed her eyes, pressing her palms against

them as if by doing so she could shut him out of her mind. It was ridiculous. The last thing she needed was to fall in love with that formidable creature. He despised her. She must remember that, holding on to the thought as if it were some kind of talisman.

All she needed was the firm resolution to keep him at a distance, but in her present situation that was impossible. If only Fanny would fall out of love with Harry Lakenham she might manage to extricate herself from her predicament. She could then announce that she had mistaken her own heart and cry off from her supposed betrothal.

She had meant to chide Fanny for leaving her to run to Harry's side in the Gardens. Now she realised that her sister had said nothing of that meeting. It was strange. In the usual way Fanny was so open.

Miranda had expected tears and sulks. Fanny, she knew, had been shocked to see her lover in the company of such birds of paradise, yet later she had not even seemed subdued. Her enjoyment of the rest of the evening had been obvious.

Miranda looked at the sleeping figure beside her with a mixture of love and exasperation. Then she sighed. Perhaps it was as well that her twin could sleep so soundly, untroubled by the chaotic state of their affairs. She would make a few discreet enquiries in the morning. Upon that thought she fell asleep herself.

She had no opportunity to carry out her plan to question Fanny. The arrival of their aunt with the *Gazette* drove any such idea out of Miranda's mind.

"See, my love. The announcement is here in black and white!" She brandished the paper under her niece's nose.

Miranda took it from her with a shaking hand. She had expected it, but somehow the words leapt out at her, larger, blacker, and more final than she could have dreamed. Heston had been given all his titles, but it was her own name which burned into her mind.

"Now at last we can make plans," Mrs Shere announced happily. "You must dress at once, my dearest. His lordship is sure to call within the hour. I'll send your maid. Will you wear the French sprigged muslin?"

Miranda nodded, but her heart was thumping in a most alarming way, and she felt a little sick. With an effort she controlled her nausea and slipped out of bed.

The news had awakened Fanny. As their aunt left the room she looked across at her twin.

"Are you all right?" she whispered. "You look so pale…"

Miranda took refuge in a sharp retort. "Why did you leave me in the Gardens?" she demanded. "You should not have gone to Harry, and well you know it. If you'd had any sense at all, you'd have pretended not to see him."

"I could not do it, Miranda. I had to know what he was doing with those awful women. You need not scold. You would have done the same yourself." Fanny began to sulk.

"No, I should not. We all know that gentlemen have convenients in their keeping, but we need not recognise them."

"I didn't speak to them. Harry took me away…he wished to explain that the…er…lightskirts were with his friends."

"That may be true, but you need not have taxed him with it there and then. Suppose Lord Heston had seen you? He did meet Harry later."

"But not when he was with me," Fanny told her in an injured tone.

"Even so, he asked if I had arranged an assignation. I said not, but I doubt if he believed me."

"Does it matter? You were with Richard when Heston found you."

"I was, indeed! And what he must have thought I can't imagine, with Richard lying on the ground and a swordsman standing over him."

"That was not my fault," Fanny pouted.

"You can't escape all blame. Had our party stayed together, the man would not have dared approach me."

"It seems I can do nothing right. Perhaps you have forgot that Lady Medlicott stayed behind, chatting to her friends, and Richard was watching the fireworks?"

"That isn't the point," Miranda cried impatiently. "The whole thing might have been avoided if you had shown a little more conduct."

Fanny shrugged her shoulders as she sipped her morning chocolate. "We came to no harm." Her face brightened. "Was it not splendid at the Piazza? I am so glad that the Count and Heston came to find us. I did enjoy our supper, and I was even in charity with his lordship. He was not angry, was he?"

"He was furious," Miranda told her shortly. "And with good reason."

"Why should you care?" Fanny gave her sister

a curious glance. "Was it not your intention to annoy him?"

"Not by risking Richard's neck, and making a spectacle of myself."

"Don't be such a crosspatch!" Fanny nibbled at a roll. "Alexei Toumanov is a character, isn't he? Do you like him?"

Miranda swung round on her.

"For heaven's sake, don't set your sights on him," she cried. "Heston has already warned me not to encourage the Count."

"Naturally, you may not, but the same cannot apply to me. They came to invite us both to supper. That was an odd start in Heston if he did not wish his friend to know us."

Miranda had thought much the same herself, but she was not prepared to discuss the matter.

"What of Harry?" she demanded. "Is your affection for him fading already?"

"Of course not!" Fanny looked uncomfortable. "Yet I may not see him. You said as much yourself, and I won't wear the willow else Aunt would notice my low spirits."

It was the most transparent of excuses for Fanny's clear delight in the Count's obvious admiration.

"Stuff!" her twin said rudely. "Fanny, if you

bring more trouble down upon our heads, I shall wash my hands of you." With that threat she swept out of the room.

For the rest of the morning the knocker went incessantly as notes were delivered to her uncle's door by hand. All bore good wishes for her future happiness.

Miranda was leafing through a pile of cards and invitations from members of the *ton* who had not previously acknowledged her existence when Heston was announced.

"You, too?" He grinned at her as he looked at the scattered pieces of pasteboard on the table. "Today we are the most popular pair of lovers in London."

Miranda turned her head away. Her lips were trembling, and for some unaccountable reason she was on the verge of tears.

"Come for a drive with me," his lordship suggested gently. "The air will do you good."

Miranda shook her head. Then his hand cupped her chin and forced her to look up at him.

"Courage, my love! Yesterday you faced a swordsman. You will not tell me now that you cannot bear the scrutiny of the Polite World?"

The great blue eyes looked too large for her pale face, and Heston dropped a kiss upon her nose.

"Get your bonnet!" he insisted. "My devotion will wear thin if you keep my horses waiting."

His teasing restored her spirits a little.

"Don't worry," he promised. "I shall not throw you to the wolves. All you need do is smile and bow and look delightfully as you always do. I will take care of the rest."

His kindness brought fresh tears to her eyes as she hurried away. She would never understand him. At one moment he could be hard and ruthless, so secure in his pride and arrogance that she found it easy to detest him. His concern to help her through the coming ordeal was far more difficult to bear. Fanny had suspected him of playing some deep game, but what it was she could not begin to guess, and nor could Fanny.

As she settled a gay little hat upon her copper curls, she began to regain her composure.

"Charming!" he announced as she rejoined him. "I like the jaunty feather."

Miranda felt far from jaunty as they drove into Hyde Park. Their appearance was the signal for a crowd to surround their carriage, and she found herself the centre of a large group of well-wishers.

Astonishment was plain on many faces, and she fell prey to acute embarrassment. Most probably these people imagined that Heston had run mad to offer for a bride so far beneath him.

"Cheer up, my love!" he whispered. "No one will say it to my face, but they are all happy to see a confirmed bachelor caught by the foot at last."

That was not true of all his lordship's acquaintance.

"We have not met before, I think." A matron in an ornate turban signalled to her coachman to pull up. She eyed Miranda with undisguised hostility. "Where have you been hiding your betrothed, my dear Heston?"

Miranda flushed to the ears. The cold words had made it sound as if there were something shameful in her which Heston had been at pains to hide.

The girl beside her was as scarlet as Miranda. She held out her hand. "I hope you will be very happy," she murmured in a voice choked with mortification.

"Thank you." Miranda smiled. "Is this your first Season?"

"It is!" The matron answered for her daughter, as she tried to stare Miranda down. "We do not see you at Almack's, Miss...er...Miss...?"

"Miss Gaysford," his lordship supplied helpfully. "My apologies, ma'am. I should have spoken more clearly. I had forgot your difficulty in hearing well."

It was a crushing setdown, and it had the result

which Heston had intended. An alarming purple flush stained the woman's face, and her several chins began to wobble as she sought for a reply. Words failed her. She poked her coachman in the back with the tip of her parasol, and with a last dagger-look at Heston she was borne away.

Miranda had difficulty in keeping her countenance. Her shoulders were shaking as she made an unsuccessful attempt to turn a chuckle into a cough.

"Something amuses you, my dear?" Her companion looked down at her. His expression was as bland as usual but his eyes were twinkling.

"I fear you have made an enemy for life, sir. The lady will not soon recover from such a snub."

"You may be right. It is a lowering thought, but I shall try to bear it. It would not do to fall into a fit of the dismals…"

His words were too much for Miranda, but she made a last attempt to hide her amusement.

"You were not kind," she reproached.

"Neither was she. An ill-natured creature, Lady Eddington, and well known for her vicious tongue."

"I liked her daughter," Miranda ventured.

"Amabel?" his lordship shrugged. "A pleasant girl with a heavy cross to bear in such a mother. I pity her future husband with a dragon for a mother-in-law."

Miranda was silent, but his next words filled her with dismay.

"Tell me about your own mama," he said. "Is she like you or like your sister?"

"My lord?"

"I wished merely to know what I am to expect, my dearest." His smile filled her with acute foreboding. He could not be serious. He intended no more than she to go through with the marriage. Miranda stiffened. It was just another attempt to frighten her.

"I don't quite understand you," she replied in a cool tone.

"I think you do. You and your sister are so unlike, are you not?"

Panic seized Miranda. Was Heston beginning to suspect that he had been deceived?

"We are thought to be identical," she babbled. "Few people can tell us one from the other."

"How odd!" he mused. "I do not find the slightest difficulty in doing so. It is something about the eyes, I think."

This was dangerous ground. Miranda cast about wildly in her mind for some way to change the subject.

"You have not answered my original question," he reminded her.

"Oh, you mean in her nature?" Miranda made a quick recover. "Mama is more like Fa—like my favourite sister."

Heston did not appear to have noticed the slip, but Miranda's blood ran cold. She had come so close to giving herself away.

"Then I have nothing to worry about." Her companion did not look at her, but his lips twitched.

"Do you mean that as an insult, sir? It is unworthy of you." Miranda spoke with some heat, hoping that a quarrel would divert his lordship's attention from this perilous topic.

Heston would not be drawn.

"It was meant as a compliment," he told her smoothly. "Your sister is of a sanguine temperament, I believe."

"You don't mean that at all! You think her silly and frivolous and flighty!" Miranda stopped in dismay. Swift in defence of her twin, she had allowed her annoyance to lead her into saying more than she intended.

"Don't you?" he asked mildly.

"How dare you! You do not know her in the least."

"Then I crave your pardon. I must get to know her better…" He stopped as a cavalier on horseback came up to their carriage to offer his congratulations.

Miranda sank back thankfully against the cush-
ioned seat. She had been reprieved, but for how
long? Was Heston playing with her as a cat might
play with a mouse before the kill?

That morning he had almost trapped her into
betraying herself, and she found his veiled remarks
deeply disturbing. If he should carry out his
promise to get to know Fanny better, she could
place no reliance upon her twin's ability to deceive
him. If he pushed Fanny far enough, the result
might be a hysterical outburst in which everything
would be revealed.

Her face showed nothing of her inner emotions.
She smiled prettily at the compliments offered to
her, and by the time the horseman moved away she
had regained much of her composure.

"Do you dine at Carlton House tonight, my
lord?" she asked.

"Unfortunately, yes. The Prince is giving a dinner
for the Tsar and the King of Prussia. To refuse the
invitation would be to give offence."

"You do not enjoy these gatherings, it would seem."

"The food is beyond reproach, and the music excellent." There was a cynical note in Heston's
voice. "That is, if one enjoys a 'descent into hell'."

"My lord?"

"A favourite saying of the Prince's guests, my dear. The heat throughout the house is suffocating."

"I had heard that the Prince is afraid of draughts, but surely the interior is very fine? A friend described one of the chandeliers as looking like a shower of diamonds."

"It was probably almost as costly. You will go there, naturally, and you may see for yourself. The Regent will wish to meet my bride-to-be."

Miranda heard his words with dread. This was the worst blow of all. How could she appear at Carlton House under false pretences? It would likely be considered treason and she would end up in the Tower.

A shaky laugh escaped her lips.

"I like the idea of going there no more than you do," she protested.

"You will find that you have no alternative," he told her lightly.

Chapter Seven

The thought of deceiving the heir to the throne effectively destroyed the last traces of Miranda's peace of mind. Her face whitened to the lips and she could not speak.

"Come now, pray do not look as if you have seen a ghost! Prinny is no ghost, in fact very much the opposite. You will find him charming. It is his greatest gift." Heston took her hand and raised it to his lips.

In the ordinary way Miranda would have snatched it away, but now she left it in his grasp, her fingers tightening instinctively. He responded to the pressure, and then he released her to take up the reins once more.

"Chin up!" he said. "All is not yet lost, I assure you."

It was an odd remark, and it struck her forcibly.

Distraught though she was, she could not let it go unchallenged.

"You speak in riddles, sir." She gave him a look of deep suspicion.

"Hedgehog!" he reproved. "I meant merely that you will enjoy a meeting with the Regent and his friends. He is a cultivated man, and a great patron of the arts, the best since Charles I."

As he had intended, Miranda's attention was diverted.

"But he is hissed and booed by the public whenever he appears, my lord."

"Are you surprised? The English distrust an intellectual. In the public mind, hunting is more to be admired than sculpture, gaming rather than an interest in literature, and the work of the finest artists is not to be compared with an afternoon at the races."

"But the Prince does all those things," Miranda pointed out.

"He did. He has not hunted for some years, and he was never more popular than when his colours appeared on the racetrack. The scandal was unfortunate...he gave up racing on the spot."

"Scandal? I had not heard of it."

"It happened more than twenty years ago. His horse, Escape, was said to be the finest on the turf.

It failed one day at Newmarket, and the odds against it shortened to five to one. Next day it won with ease, and both the Prince and his jockey, Chifney, were thought to have made large sums of money. The Prince was told that if Chifney rode for him again, no gentleman would start against him."

"But surely it was not true? The Prince would not stoop to cheating?"

"Of course not! It was just malicious gossip. Chifney published a vindication some time later, but the Prince had vowed that he would not race again."

Miranda gave him a curious glance. "You like him, don't you?"

"I do. Admittedly, he is his own worst enemy. The public sees him preoccupied with expensive trivia, his dress, his passion for building and redecoration, but how else is he to spend his time? He is excluded from the serious business of governing the country."

"He has a good friend in you, I think." Miranda smiled at her companion, quite forgetting her previous fears.

"I can give him little else but friendship," Heston murmured. "So much has gone amiss for him."

Miranda was silent. It would have been presumptuous to comment upon matters of which she knew so little.

"Much of it is due to his disastrous marriage to the Princess Caroline." Heston seemed to be speaking more to himself than to her. "One could wish that Mrs Fitzherbert had been born a Protestant princess."

"But the people sympathise with the Princess of Wales," Miranda protested. "She is cheered when the Prince is hissed and booed."

"The public do not know her." Heston's face was sombre. "Few of them can have considered what it must be like for a cultured and fastidious man to be wed to a hoyden who is not even clean in her person, and whose way of life is such that not even the most liberal-minded can condone it."

"She may not be entirely to blame," Miranda ventured. "It is said that she loved someone else before she was married to the Prince."

"So did he!" Heston looked down at her then, with a strange expression in his eyes. "What deep pits we dig for ourselves when in the grip of strong emotion. It is as well to guard oneself against such follies." His mocking tone annoyed her.

"You can be in no such danger, sir," she told him coolly.

"Very true, my dear. The more tender emotions are not quite in my style, or in yours, I believe."

"How well you are getting to know me, sir. You

have expressed my feelings perfectly." She turned away, so that he would not see the glitter in her eyes. He thought her hard and mercenary and she could not bear it.

"I'm happy to know that you won't suffer because I am forced to leave you for a day or two," Heston said lightly. "The Prince is to go to Oxford to receive a loyal address and I am invited to form part of his entourage."

Miranda looked her surprise.

"He has earned it," Heston replied to her unspoken question. "He is an honorary Doctor of Civil Law, and has founded two university readerships, among other things."

"How long will you be away?" Miranda's first feeling of relief was tempered by a sense of disappointment, which she did not care to examine too closely.

"Am I to suppose that you will miss me?" Heston's smile did not reach his eyes. "How touching!"

"I doubt if I shall go into a decline, my lord."

"I doubt it, too. Until our next meeting, then?" He had drawn up before her uncle's house, and sprang down from the phaeton to help her to alight.

She turned to bid him farewell, but he took her arm and accompanied her indoors.

"I must pay my respects to your aunt," he said.

That lady was descending the staircase as they entered the hall, and Heston greeted her with the utmost courtesy, explaining as he did so that he would be out of London for a day or two.

"I expect that you would like to take your leave of each other in private," Mrs Shere said kindly. "There is no one in the salon at this present time…"

Heston's eyes sparkled with amusement, but Miranda had no alternative but to accompany him. She stalked ahead of him and tossed aside her hat.

"That's right," he murmured. "Delightful confection though it is, the veil is something of an obstacle."

Next moment she was in his arms and his mouth came down on hers.

Miranda had promised herself that the next time he kissed her she would not respond. If she stood quite still, this demanding creature would soon grow tired of making love to a statue.

It was easier said than done. The touch of those warm lips was producing a most alarming sensation in the pit of her stomach and turning her limbs to jelly. Insensibly she relaxed within his arms.

"Let us sit down," he said. He slipped an arm about her waist and led her to a sofa. Miranda stiffened as he took a seat beside her. Then she turned her face away.

"Shy, my love? That will not do…" His lips grazed her cheek. "What a tease you are!" He began to kiss her eyelids, and then he pressed his mouth against the hollow of her neck. "Must you be so cold?"

"Please, my lord…you really must not…" She tried to fight a sudden urge to throw her arms about his neck and hold him to her. She wanted to press her cheek to his, to trace the curve of those smiling lips, and to stroke that thick dark hair.

Then he found her mouth again and the world was lost. Her pleasure was such that she felt powerless to resist him. She found herself responding with a passion that startled her.

When he released her, she could not look at him. Nothing in her experience had prepared her for the emotions which now threatened to overwhelm her.

She was trembling and made no effort to resist when he took her in his arms once more.

"So there is fire beneath the ice?" he murmured. "I had suspected it." There was no trace of mockery in his voice as he turned her face to his. "Blushing, my love? There is no need. It is nothing to be ashamed of, rather to be delighted in."

"Please go!" Miranda choked out the words. She felt ready to sink with mortification.

It was not until later when she was alone that his curious reaction struck her. It seemed that he had understood that this was her first experience of true passion. Yet that could not be true. Heston despised her as a mere adventuress…a fortune hunter. Was it likely that in that role she would be unversed in the ways of love?

She was still lost in thought when her aunt came to find her.

"Don't look so sad, my dear. Lord Heston will not be gone for long." Mrs Shere patted her hand.

Miranda managed a reluctant smile. "It is not that," she said.

"What then? Has something happened to disturb you?"

"Oh, Aunt, I feel so worried. Heston says that he will present me to the Regent."

"Is that all? Love, I must imagine, has driven all thought of protocol from his lordship's mind."

"What do you mean?"

"Dearest, you cannot appear in the presence of royalty before you have been formally presented at Court."

Her aunt's words went some way towards re-storing Miranda's peace of mind, but it was quickly shattered.

"I have been considering the matter," Mrs Shere said thoughtfully. "Lady Medlicott is not quite the person to sponsor you. Perhaps we should consult his lordship…"

"Yes, let us do it." Miranda was anxious to change the subject. "Richard has promised to call on us tomorrow. He has promised to take us to see the Balloon Ascent in Hyde Park…"

"Should you be going about so much without Lord Heston? I cannot think he would approve. If you had but seen his face when he called here last night and found you had gone to the Vauxhall Gardens…"

"His lordship can have no wish that I should stay indoors, Aunt Emma. In any case, I should not heed him if he had."

"My dear girl, think what you are saying!" Mrs Shere was scandalised. "In a few weeks time you will promise to obey him…"

"But not yet! In any case, he has not forbidden it. A pleasure outing in an afternoon is unexceptionable."

"Oh, dear, I suppose so, though I could wish that you were not so headstrong, dearest. You speak out so freely, and the way you take decisions in such a determined way is not quite—"

"Ladylike?" Miranda kissed the older woman with a rueful smile. "Aunt, I have had to make decisions all my life. Mama will not do so."

"I know it. Your mama is lost without a husband to guide her. She has had to rely so much upon her children, but now all will be changed. What a comfort it will be to her to be able to ask our dear Lord Heston for advice. Such a sensible man, and most good-natured, too!"

It was clear that his lordship had won the heart of at least one of Miranda's relatives.

"Do you think so?" she murmured.

"Of course, my love, and your uncle is much taken with him. Perhaps I should not say so, but we had heard that he was excessively proud and disagreeable. We both feared that you would find him so, and not even the prospect of a splendid match could be allowed to weigh against your future happiness."

Miranda was silent.

"You can't think what a relief it was to find that gossip had lied," her aunt continued. "I am per-suaded that jealousy has much to do with it. His lordship's manner is charming…so courteous! He must be a model for any gentleman. Only the most depraved could take against him!"

A smile touched the corner of Miranda's mouth. She had not previously considered herself a monster of depravity, and she had most certainly taken against him.

"Aunt Emma, I must believe that you think Lord Heston perfect," she teased.

"Don't you, my love?" Mrs Shere saw the amusement in Miranda's expression and she returned the smile. "Well, perhaps not perfect," she admitted. "A saint would be difficult to live with, but one can't fail to admire his character." She looked steadily at her niece. "You don't know him well, as yet, my love. I don't expect transports of affection, but you think well of him, I hope?"

"He puzzles me," Miranda said with perfect truth. "I wonder if anyone would grow to know him well." She saw her aunt's troubled expression and hastened to amend her words. "You are right, of course, the more I am in his lordship's company the more I realise that much of what is said of him is unjustified. He is not a mere gamester, with no interests beyond his horses."

Her aunt kissed her. "You are growing up, my dear. You will not take it amiss if I tell you that at first I thought you much more frivolous than your sister? Now I see that I was mistaken..." She patted Miranda's cheek. "Enjoy your outing with your friend."

Left alone, Miranda's thoughts were troubled. It was becoming more and more difficult to play the part of Fanny. The twins were so different in character, and Mrs Shere had noticed it. She herself had spoken without thinking when she had mentioned the need to make decisions for her mother. Fanny had never done so. She must make an effort to indulge in charming nonsense, to giggle, and to be light-hearted. She had never felt less like indulging in such behaviour.

A sense of relief swept over her as she stepped into the carriage the next day. Fanny knew the truth. There would be no need to dissemble with her twin.

As for Richard, he was too excited by the prospect of seeing his first Balloon Ascent to notice that Miranda was not her usual self.

"I have never enjoyed myself so much in all my life," he announced happily. "I wish you had been with me yesterday...the city was ablaze with light. It is the illuminations, you know...at night it looks a different place..."

"And so wonderful!" Fanny told him earnestly. "I could not go back to live in Yorkshire ever again. When one has lived in the capital the rest of England seems so…so provincial!"

"It's all very well to be here for a celebration," Richard said defensively. "But, Fanny, it does smell vile, and I can't say that I care much for the crowds."

"It isn't always like this." Fanny was in the mood to quarrel. "The foreigners are everywhere…"

"They won't be here for ever," Miranda intervened. "Richard, you are looking very fine today… quite the town beau, in fact."

"This rig?" Richard glanced down at his yellow pantaloons with assumed indifference. His brocade waistcoat was so brightly patterned that it was dazzling to the eye. Above it, his stiffly starched shirt-points rose almost to the middle of his cheeks, making it difficult for him to turn his head to left or right.

"It don't do to look the country cousin," he explained defensively. "I'd stand out like a sore thumb here in London."

"Whereas in that waistcoat you are all but invisible," Fanny giggled.

Richard's face fell. "Do you think it too much?"

he asked anxiously. "M'father said I might buy what I chose."

"It looks very well." Miranda frowned at her sister. "Quite the latest thing, in fact. I'm sure you looked about you to see what others are wearing before you visited the tailor."

"Oh, I did, and he told me that it was all the crack, you know."

"Then you may be easy in your mind." Miranda smiled at him. His garments were expensive, and she felt sure that he had been persuaded into parting with a great deal of money in his efforts to become a gentleman of fashion. She would not spoil his pleasure for the world, although she felt sure that the shirt-points in particular were causing him discomfort.

"Well, it would not do for Yorkshire." He grinned at her a little consciously. "But one must be in the correct way of things."

Miranda nodded her agreement. She had always been fond of him. Good-natured to a fault, he, more than any of her brother's friends, had been the one to take the twins' part in any of their scrapes. Scorned by the other boys, who refused to have mere females take part in their adventures, Richard had raised no objections. He bore the expostulations of his friends with great good humour, but he would not be swayed.

She looked at him with renewed affection. He was hung about with fobs and an expensive tie-pin gleamed in the folds of his cravat, but he did not quite achieve the appearance of a dandy, which was clearly his intention.

Miranda suspected that he had chosen his present rig knowing that he was to escort them, and wishing to do them credit.

"Are any of your friends in London?" she asked kindly.

"No, but I am putting up at Grillon's, and I made a new acquaintance. He is a famous fellow. We went to see the wild beasts in the Tower, and to Astley's Ampitheatre…" He did not think it prudent to mention the cock-fights to which his new friend had taken him, nor his visit to Gentleman Jackson's saloon to watch that gentleman sparring with other devotees of The Fancy. Ladies were not interested in such exciting sports.

He saw her worried look and smiled at her. "He is not an ivory-turner. You may have no fears on that score."

Miranda felt relieved. In the short time she had spent in London, she had heard stories of the men who lay in wait for gullible boys, leading them to ruin in the many gaming hells which had sprung up in the capital.

At that moment she was hailed by Charlotte Fairfax.

"Do you go to the Ascent?" her friend called out.

The twins nodded in unison.

"Then may we go together? We must walk from here, you know, and I want to talk to you." Charlotte's face was alive with curiosity as she dismissed her brother.

Young Fairfax needed no urging to be relieved of his charge. He handed his sister down from their carriage and, with a bow to Miranda's party, he went off to find his friends.

"Wretched boy!" Charlotte said with feeling. "I wish you might have heard the fuss he made when Mamma said that he must bring me."

"Brothers are all the same," Fanny agreed. "It was only Richard here who would ever allow us to go about with him when we were children."

Charlotte looked at their escort, a question in her eyes. "This gentleman is not your brother? I had supposed…"

"Richard is a family friend." Miranda made the necessary introductions. Under the cover of the ensuing civilities, Fanny tugged at her elbow.

"You will not fly into the boughs if we see Harry, I hope? He is quite likely to be here today."

"Of course not! We can't prevent him from going wherever he wishes, but pray do not slip away with him. It is a different thing if you meet him in company."

"You two are the outside of enough!" Charlotte teased. "Now which of you am I to congratulate upon your betrothal?" She turned to Richard. "Do you find the same difficulty, sir? If you have known Fanny and Miranda from childhood, perhaps you can tell them apart?"

Miranda froze, and beside her she felt her sister stiffen. It was true that Richard knew them as well as their own family.

She should have thought of it before. It was no more likely that they could deceive Richard than that they could deceive their own brother. Yet he had handed her the letter from her mother with no more than a moment's hesitation, clearly believing that she was Fanny. It was that which had lulled her into a sense of false security. She held her breath, waiting for the blow to fall.

"We have not been much in each other's company for these past few years," Richard said easily. "I was at Oxford, Miss Fairfax. Meantime, the twins have grown even more alike. Sometimes they confuse me, too."

Miranda looked at him with gratitude in her eyes. He met her own with a level gaze and only the faintest of smiles. It was enough. He knew of the deception, she was convinced of it.

Fanny took her arm. "You must wish my sister happy, Charlotte. She is the fortunate bride-to-be."

Charlotte threw her arms about Miranda. "Sly creature!" she chaffed. "We had not the least idea…why, I almost fainted when I read the announcement. I would not believe it! Lord Heston of all people! I thought it must be some mistake when you had both taken him in such dislike."

Miranda gave her an ironic look, and Charlotte's hand flew to her mouth. "Oh, my stupid tongue again… I should not have said that. Indeed, I wish you happy."

"I know you do." Miranda rescued her from her confusion. "We had best go, or we shall miss the ascent."

As they strolled through the crowds to get a better view, Miranda allowed Fanny and Charlotte to go ahead. She fell into step with Richard.

"Thank you," she said simply.

"For what?"

"I think you know quite well. When did you guess?"

"When I brought the letters."

"But you gave Mama's letter to me, and it was addressed to Fanny."

"Your uncle made it clear that he thought that you were Fanny. It was not up to me to correct him."

"You must be wondering…!"

"I wondered if you were in a scrape again. It wouldn't be the first time…"

She heard a low chuckle.

"This time it isn't so amusing, and it is all my fault. If I hadn't lost my temper and said things which I now regret, we should not be in this situation."

"You will not tell me that Fanny had no hand in it? I should not believe you."

Miranda hesitated.

"You need not tell me if you don't wish, you know, but if there is anything I can do…?"

"There is nothing anyone can do, I fear. Sometimes I long to turn tail and run back home."

"That isn't like you. You were always the one with the lion heart. Can you not think of a way to put matters right?"

"I wish I could. Meantime, I feel wretched to be

deceiving everyone in this way. Oh, Richard, I should not—"

"You should not worry so. Neither you nor Fanny would do anything really bad. I know you well enough for that. It will all come right, you'll see…"

With these words of comfort he took her arm and caught up with the others.

They had found a vantage point beside the roped-off enclosure from which the balloon ascent was to be made. The silken globe was already tugging at its moorings in the breeze, the brilliant colours gleaming in the sunlight. At each corner men held tightly to the mooring rope, whilst some argument seemed to be taking place beside the wicker basket which was to hold the occupants.

"How many will it hold?" asked Charlotte.

"Two, or possibly three, I should imagine." Richard eyed the proceedings with interest.

"Oh, no!" Fanny's eyes were upon one of the men at the centre of the argument. He was muffled to the eyes, but she had no difficulty in recognising Harry Lakenham. "He cannot be planning to go with them."

"I fear he does. Fanny, please." Miranda gripped her sister's arm. "You must not go to him."

"I will! I will! He is sure to be killed…I know

it…" Fanny's voice had risen to a shriek and several people turned to look at her.

"Don't worry, they will not take him if he is inexperienced. Is he a friend of yours?" It was a casual question, but something in Richard's tone caused Miranda to throw him a sharp glance. His eyes were on Fanny's face, and in that moment he betrayed himself.

Miranda groaned inwardly. This was yet another complication and one which she could well do without. She could not doubt that Richard was in love with Fanny, and he could not fail to be hurt. Suddenly she felt fiercely protective towards him.

"Pull yourself together, Fanny!" she urged. "See, they have turned Harry away…"

It was true. As she watched, the two intrepid flyers climbed in the basket and signalled to their assistants. Harry had been motioned to one side with a couple of stalwarts between himself and the balloon. They jumped out of the way as the ballast was thrown out and the wind filled the silken dome. As it began to rise, Harry saw his chance. He dodged the men and leapt for the basket, catching at a trailing rope, already high in the air.

As the crowds watched in horror, Fanny crumpled at Miranda's feet. She fell to her knees beside her sister, but Richard was there before her. He lifted Fanny tenderly in his arms.

"We must get her home at once," he said.

Miranda nodded dumbly, but she could not take her eyes from the struggle taking place above her head. As she watched, Harry gained the rim of the basket, causing it to sway alarmingly. Then he was pulled to safety inside. Next moment he was on his feet again, waving cheerfully to the onlookers below.

Miranda heard a murmur of disgust from those beside her.

"Doubtless he did it for a wager," one man said. "But he might have killed them all. I have no patience with such folly."

Miranda was in complete agreement with his sentiments, but Fanny was her more immediate concern. She followed Richard through the press of people with Charlotte by her side.

"You will come home with us?" she asked Charlotte. "We shall never find your brother in these crowds, and we cannot leave you here alone."

Charlotte herself was pale and trembling. "I feel quite faint myself," she admitted. "If Lord Lakenham had fallen… It does not bear thinking about."

"Then don't think about it. It was the most stupid thing I have ever seen, and I don't propose to give myself a fit of the dismals over Harry Lakenham's idiocy. It would have served him right if he had fallen and broken a leg."

"He was more likely to have broken his neck." Charlotte shuddered and was still trembling as their carriage reached its destination.

"You are back early," Mrs Shere began as Miranda stepped into the hall. Then she saw Richard with Fanny in his arms. "What is it? What has happened?"

"My sister fainted, and Charlotte is not well. There was an accident during the Ascent, but no one has been hurt…"

"Bring her in here and put her on the sofa, poor child. Miss Fairfax, do sit down! You shall take a glass of brandy."

Charlotte took a glass from Richard's hand, sipping at the spirit with a small moue of distaste. It soon restored her, and she cast an anxious look at Fanny, who lay inert upon the couch.

"Here, my love!" Mrs Shere forced a little of the brandy between her niece's pallid lips. "This will make you feel better."

Fanny had recovered consciousness in the carriage, but she had not uttered a word since her collapse. Now her eyes met Miranda's in a heart-rending plea for reassurance.

"Tell me the worst," she murmured at last. I must know…even if he is dead."

"Lakenham is not dead, though he deserves to be," Miranda told her sharply. "I know that his stupid action was a shock for you, as it was for all of us. Charlotte almost fainted too." She looked a warning at her sister as she spoke. In her present state of near-hysteria, Fanny was only too likely to betray herself. "Let me take you to your room… you should have rest and quiet."

"That will be best," Mrs Shere agreed. "If Mr Young will be good enough to see Charlotte home? My dears, I can't believe such folly! Apart from all else, it has quite ruined your outing."

Miranda caught Richard's eyes. With his usual courtesy he had agreed at once to escort Charlotte home, but his normally cheerful expression had disappeared and she knew the reason why. Fanny's outburst had convinced him that she was in love with Harry Lakenham.

Miranda was quick to caution Fanny when they were alone.

"I know that you could not help fainting. It was a terrifying experience, but, Fanny, do take care what you say. Aunt Emma must have wondered…"

"I could not help it. I was sure that Harry must have been killed. You would not lie to me? He is really safe?"

"The last time I saw him he was waving to the crowd with all the effrontery in the world, and it did not make him popular. Everyone realised that he might have killed others beside himself."

"It was just a high-spirited prank," Fanny pouted.

"You did not think so at the time, and I doubt if it would have seem so to the widows of the men he might have destroyed."

"You never make allowances for him. He is young…"

"He is, indeed, and, in my opinion, far too light-minded to think of getting wed. I'm not surprised that his grandfather is against it. Had you been a duchess, with the largest dowry in the world, Lord Rudyard must have been of the same opinion."

Slow tears rolled down Fanny's cheeks. "I love him…" she said brokenly.

"Well, I don't admire your choice. If you married him, you would not have a moment's peace of mind. A handsome face is no substitute for common sense."

"I don't expect you to understand. You have never fallen in love…"

"When I do, it won't be with a man like Harry Lakenham."

"Then I'm surprised you didn't take that fat old creature who offered for you when we first came here. Surely he was staid enough for you?"

"Mr Norton?" Miranda smiled. "He was a little too staid, even for me. Oh, Fanny, I don't mean to criticise. No one can tell where their heart will lead them…"

She grew silent. For some reason the memory of a harsh, dark face swam into her mind. Heston would be a rock, a man upon whom any sensible woman might rely. It was strange how that penetrating gaze could soften into a smile which had the oddest way of making her heart turn over. She brushed the treacherous thought aside. How could she reproach Fanny further when her own fancies were just as wayward?

"Won't you rest?" she begged. "Richard had promised to return this evening to see how you go on."

"I won't come down. If he wishes, he may call again tomorrow." Fanny turned her face away. "I wish that life were not so dull at present. You have forbidden me to see Harry, and Count Toumanov is away at Oxford."

"Haven't you had enough excitement for one day?" Miranda teased gently. "Would you like me to sit with you this evening? I could read to you, or we might play cribbage?"

"You need not! I don't care to listen to any more lectures."

"As you wish." Miranda was losing patience. She changed quickly and left the room before she was tempted to utter words which she might regret. It was useless to argue further. She would abandon Fanny to her sulks.

During supper she was obliged to relate the day's events again for the benefit of her uncle.

The Alderman's face grew dark with anger. "That young man needs taking in hand," he announced. "Such folly! When Lord Rudyard gets to hear of this escapade the lad will be sent to the country on a repairing lease, and high time too."

"It was very bad," Mrs Shere agreed. "But I fear that young Lakenham has been indulged too much by his grandfather. His mother and father are both dead—"

"That is no excuse! How true is the old adage 'to spare the rod and spoil the child'."

"He is a charming boy," Aunt Emma ventured.

"Too charming!" came the gruff reply. "That has

been his undoing… Now let us speak no more of it. It will ruin my digestion."

This dire prediction did not affect his appetite and he made an excellent meal. As usual, Mrs Shere left him to his port and led Miranda through into the salon.

She was playing a favourite song upon the spinet when Richard was announced. Miranda closed the instrument at once, and walked towards him.

"Your patient is better, I trust?" He bowed to both ladies as his eyes searched their faces.

"My sister is much recovered from her fright, though she is tired. She will not come down this evening, but she will be glad to see you in the morning."

Richard hid his disappointment with a good grace. He did not refer to the incident again, confining himself to an exchange of pleasantries, and a remark about the mock battle on the Serpentine which was to take place during the following week.

It was not until Mrs Shere was called out of the room that he spoke of the subject closest to his heart.

"I have no right to ask," he told Miranda. "Do not answer me if you think it indiscreet, but has Fanny formed an attachment for Lord Lakenham?"

"Mere calf-love," Miranda said briskly. "I suspect that it is a youthful infatuation on both sides. If I am not mistaken, it will come to nothing."

"I must hope that you are right." His eager look dismayed Miranda. "I do not ask from a mere vulgar curiosity. The thing is…well…I have always been fond of her, even when we were children. I felt that she needed protecting, you see."

"You are right," Miranda told him drily. "And more from herself than from any outside influence."

He smiled at that. "You were always the strong one, Miranda. It's hard to believe that you are twins."

"Fanny has many qualities that I lack."

"I doubt if that is so." He coloured to the roots of his hair. "Seeing her again after so long…well…I won't deny my feelings. I had hoped to ask her to become my wife."

"Dear Richard, how good you are! Fanny is a lucky girl, if she did but know it."

"But she must not know of my wishes, at least for the moment. I would not have her feel awkward with me, or obliged to say…to say…"

"To refuse you? No, you are quite right. Let her get over this youthful passion. If I know her, it will not take long."

"You think your mama would not object to my

offering for Fanny? She seems to believe that both of you should marry well."

"How could she object, my dear Richard? You are the son of one of her oldest friends. As to marrying well…in my opinion, Fanny could not do better than to wed a man with such a loving heart as yours. Mama will be satisfied with the thought of my own match." Miranda looked a little conscious as she spoke, but Richard did not notice.

"Indeed, I wish you happy, Miranda. I cannot doubt it. Lord Heston is such a splendid fellow, isn't he?"

Miranda gave him a mechanical smile. She nodded, thinking as she did so that Richard might be the answer to her prayers. If he and Fanny were to make a match of it, she would be free to cry off from her own supposed betrothal. The prospect should have cheered her, but she found it unaccountably depressing.

Chapter Eight

Richard was an early visitor on the following morning and Fanny greeted him with unaffected pleasure. She had recovered from her fright and was disposed to regard with a kindly eye any visitor who promised an opportunity to chatter and make plans for the coming week.

Now she dimpled as she welcomed him, drawing him aside to sit with her by the window.

Miranda regarded them with some anxiety. To flirt with any personable young man, even a childhood friend, was as natural to Fanny as breathing. Thank heavens Richard understood her. It would be cruel to raise his hopes by leading him on in that careless way she had.

Richard caught Miranda's eye, and a faint smile curved his lips. Inwardly, Miranda blessed him.

His face betrayed nothing of his inner turmoil. To all appearances he was his usual amiable self. He knew very well that Fanny's lively manner did not indicate a change in her feelings for him.

"More visitors!" Fanny jumped to her feet and looked out of the window. "Why, it is Charlotte and her brother! Now we shall be gay!"

She abandoned Richard and hurried to greet her friends.

"Are you recovered, Charlotte? What a fright we had! I thought that I should die of terror!"

"So did I!" Charlotte's manner was still subdued. "I cannot forget the sight. Last night I could not sleep. Mama is furious. She had intended to write to Lakenham's grandfather, but now she says that she will speak to Lord Heston instead, rather than worry the old man."

"Lord Heston?" Miranda was surprised. "What can he do?"

"He acts in some way as Harry's guardian. He is not, of course, but there is a connection. Heston is Lord Rudyard's godson. You did not know of it?"

Miranda shook her head.

"Heston keeps an eye on Harry to oblige his grandfather. Lord Rudyard is said to be a martyr to gout. He can no longer get about as he was used to do."

"I see." Miranda grew thoughtful. Much that she had not understood before was now becoming clear to her. She had wondered why Heston should take so keen an interest in Harry's affairs. His concern had seemed to her to go far beyond the claims of friendship.

She sighed. Even had Heston been in London on the previous day, she doubted if he would have been drawn to attend a Balloon Ascent. In any case, Harry was no longer a child. Heston could not be expected to watch over him as if he were still in leading-strings.

Her irritation grew. Harry Lakenham, like her sister, sailed through life with little regard for the peace of mind of those about them. When she next saw him, she would give him a piece of her mind.

The opportunity came at once. They had not been sitting for more than a few moments when the door was opened cautiously and Harry's laughing face appeared.

"Must I throw my hat in, Mrs Shere?" he cried.

"Come in, you wicked creature!" Mrs Shere strove to preserve a stern expression, but Harry was a favourite of hers. She was not proof against his charm. "I should send you about your business. It is certainly what you deserve…frightening us as you did!"

Miranda was furious. Harry must be mad to come here. She could not look at him. Instead, her eyes flew to Fanny's face, and was dismayed by what she saw there. Fanny's heart was in her eyes. In another moment she must betray herself.

Miranda stepped in front of her twin and greeted Harry with cold civility.

"Are you very angry with me?" he said penitently. "You look so severe, Miss Gaysford. I confess I am quaking in my boots…"

"That I must doubt, my lord!" Miranda stepped aside and allowed him to make his bow to Charlotte and her brother.

Then he moved to Fanny's side. "Helmsley tells me that you are the person who suffered most from my ill-judged behaviour," he said softly. "Indeed, I am sorry for it. Will this make amends?" He handed her a small parcel.

Fanny could not answer him. Her hands were shaking as she busied herself with the wrappings.

"Let me!" He took the packet from her and opened it to reveal a book of poems. "They are by George Byron," he explained. "I remembered that you liked his work."

"Thank you." Fanny's reply was almost inaudible.

"You feel more yourself, I hope?" Harry continued eagerly. "I should have called last evening to see how you did, but we landed far out in the country and I did not see Helmsley until midnight."

"Then you were not injured?" Fanny murmured. "Oh, if you only knew how much I have suffered!"

"It was the sudden shock which overcame your nerves," Miranda broke in quickly. "Charlotte was in much the same case and so were many others…" She picked up the book of poems. "I had not imagined that you were a lover of poetry, Lord Lakenham." It was a desperate effort to change the subject.

Harry grinned at her. "I'm not," he said frankly. "Can't understand what the women see in the fellow. All these romantic vapourings… He's naught but a poseur…sleeps with his hair in curling papers."

"That can't be true," Mrs Shere protested. She, too, was an admirer of the noble lord. "It is simply malicious gossip."

"Upon my word, it is the truth. M'friend called on him one morning and saw it. Byron admitted that he was as vain of his ringlets as a girl. Begged Scrope Davies not to speak of it, of course, but the joke was too good to keep it to himself."

"You will ruin my niece's pleasure in her book,"

Mrs Shere reproached. "No matter what is said of Lord Byron, there is still his poetry, which I find most uplifting."

"Are you an admirer of his work?" Richard addressed Miranda in an effort to keep the conversation away from dangerous subjects. He had supported his introduction to Harry Lakenham with perfect civility, but there was an indefinable air of tension in the room.

"He is not quite in my style, though the fault must lie with me, I fear." Miranda smiled at him. Byron had spoken to her on one occasion, drawn by her beauty and clearly expecting to be met with the same adulation which he regarded as his due from the female sex. She had been unimpressed, finding this lion of London society so self-centred as to be a bore. He had soon moved away in search of a more appreciative audience.

"Have you missed Heston? He is at Oxford with the Prince, I hear…" Harry's eyes danced with mischief as he teased her.

Miranda resolved to pay him back in his own coin.

"Lord Heston returns to town today, so I understand. Doubtless he will wish to seek you out without delay."

"I expect so, if only to give me a roasting…" Harry

pulled a comical face. Then, undeterred by this warning of Heston's displeasure, he grinned. "He'll be full of stories. The Prince is a wit, you know."

"We heard that the Regent has a humorous turn of phrase," Mrs Shere agreed.

"It's clever, but not always kind." Harry began to laugh. "He described the Marquess of Wellesley as a Spanish grandee grafted on to an Irish potato. The Wellesleys are of Irish stock, as you know. It was so apt. Richard Wellesley is a stiff old stick."

"Yet the Duke of Wellington thinks highly of his brother, I believe. It is said that the Marquess is the cleverer of the two." Richard spoke quietly, but Harry Lakenham looked up.

"My dear sir, you sound like Adam Heston..." He was smiling, but there was a challenge in his eyes. His careless gossip had not met with universal approval and it did not please him.

Miranda turned to Charlotte. "Shall you watch the procession to the Guildhall?" she asked quickly. "Heston has promised that we are to go..." The rest of her words died upon her lips when the door opened and the subject of her conversation walked into the room.

At the sight of his tall figure, Miranda's heart

began to pound. She could not decide if this disturbing sensation had arisen from joy or fright.

As always, Heston's face was impassive, but by now she knew him well enough to realise that he was very angry. She rose and went towards him.

"I am glad to see you, my lord," she said with perfect truth. It was strange, but there was something so dependable about him.

"Are you, my dear? I am glad to hear it." He kissed her hand and then her cheek.

"We did not expect you this morning," she continued brightly. "Here you find us talking about the procession to the Guildhall…" She prayed to heaven that he would not give full vent to his displeasure in the presence of her aunt.

"I see." His indifferent gaze roved from one face to another as he greeted the assembled company with his usual civility, albeit with some reserve.

It was enough to persuade Charlotte and her brother to take their leave. Richard was about to follow them when Heston stopped him.

"Mr Young, you have not forgot that you are to join our party?"

"Your lordship is very kind. I had not forgot—indeed, I am looking forward to it." Richard bowed and walked towards the door.

"Wait, I will go with you…" Harry made as if to join him.

"Must you rush away so soon?" Heston's gentle words stopped Harry in his tracks.

"I have just remembered an appointment." Harry's face was the picture of guilt.

"An urgent appointment, I am sure… Will you wait upon me, say, at six o'clock? I shall be expecting you." Heston's tone made it impossible for Harry to refuse. He gulped, nodded, and hurried away.

"My lord, you will not be too hard on him?" Mrs Shere pleaded. "It was just a boy's trick. Lord Lakenham did not think that it might have serious consequences."

"You are too generous, ma'am." Heston gave her a faint smile. Then his frown returned. "That is Harry's problem…he never considers the consequences of his actions until it is too late. I have been at fault. I should not have agreed to his coming to London, but that is easily remedied."

"What do you mean?" Fanny spoke so sharply that Mrs Shere shot her a quick look of reproof.

Heston bent his penetrating gaze on Fanny. "Harry must return to his grandfather," he announced. "I had thought him grown to manhood, but he is still a thoughtless child. In the country he may fall out of trees and into the river without harming others."

Fanny gasped and burst into tears. Then she fled from the room.

"Oh, dear! My lord, you must forgive my niece. Her nerves are on edge since yesterday. Poor child…such a shock. I must go to her…"

Heston waited until the door had closed behind her.

"And how are your nerves, my dear?" he said smoothly. "I heard that you had fainted in the Park."

"No, I did not!" Miranda snapped. "It was my sister who was overcome…"

"Curious! But then I expect that you are made of stronger stuff…I won't say I'm surprised."

Miranda did not answer him.

"What does surprise me, however, is to find Lakenham here this morning… No doubt you will tell me the reason?"

"He…he came to apologise," Miranda stammered. "My sister and Charlotte Fairfax and many other ladies felt ill when they saw Lord Lakenham in danger of his life."

"Touching! But then, you have such tender hearts, have you not? It has always been a source of some amazement to me that you ladies form such attachments for gentlemen with rakish tendencies."

"Harry is not a rake," Miranda cried hotly.

"He is well on the way to being so. Harry is a lightweight, and well you know it."

"Do I?"

"I think so. I have never imagined you to be a fool. You think me hard, perhaps? Let me assure you that if Harry stays in London, not satisfied with forming an unfortunate attachment, he will also fall into the hands of ivory-turners and will lose his patrimony as soon as he comes of age."

"That must be a source of anxiety to you," Miranda said with a touch of irony.

"It is." Heston ignored the sarcasm. "I have known men die before the age of thirty, ruined by drink and gaming." There was no trace of mockery in his voice and Miranda felt ashamed of her outburst.

"I know that it can happen," she agreed.

"Well then, my love, we are in charity with each other once again, I hope? I have some news for you. My mother longs to meet you. Next week she will come here from Warwickshire…"

"Your…your mother?" Miranda eyed him with dread.

"Of course. Why should you be surprised? I have a mother, you know. I did not spring to life fully formed, like some character of old."

"You have not mentioned meeting her before," Miranda said faintly.

"I was not sure that she would come to London. She is an artist, and painting is her life. I thought perhaps a quiet dinner in Brook Street, to include your aunt and uncle and your sister, if that would please you?"

Stunned by this news, Miranda could only acquiesce.

"It will give you an opportunity to see your new home. You may like to make some changes to the furnishings, but I will leave that in your hands…"

Miranda looked at him in desperation. "My lord…"

"No, don't talk! We have been parted for too long." He drew her to him and sought her lips.

"Please, you must not!" she protested.

"But I must! Kiss me, dearest! I have thought of you each waking moment since I saw you last."

"Humbug!" she cried fiercely.

A quiver of emotion disturbed the calm of Heston's expression, and his shoulders began to shake.

"How unkind!" he reproached in a bland tone. "At our first meeting you struck me. Now you throw my words of love back in my face… I am beginning to believe that I am betrothed to a termagant."

Miranda was strongly tempted to inform him that

he was not betrothed to anyone, but she bit back the angry words.

"I am aware that you find our situation amusing," she retorted.

"Oh, I do, my dear, I do! I haven't been so entertained in years. You are a constant joy to me. I had begun to believe that there wasn't a woman in London possessed of any spirit...and you have always some surprise in store for me."

"I shall try not to disappoint you in that respect." Miranda spoke with feeling. She had a number of surprises in store for this self-assured creature. Her eyes began to sparkle. Then she recalled how quick he was to sense her every mood. She stole a glance at him, but he was regarding her with that false expression of tenderness which she disliked so much.

"I doubt if you could ever disappoint me, even if you would," he murmured in sentimental tones as he slid an arm about her waist. He drew her to him, and then his hand stole up her spine. As he began to stroke her neck, little shivers of delight swept over her. He bent his head and kissed her beneath her ear.

"Must you always stiffen when I touch you?" he whispered. "Relax, my love. You will enjoy it more." He took the small pink lobe between his teeth and nibbled at it gently.

Miranda did not pull away from him. Insensibly she was losing the power to resist his caresses, but she made a last determined effort. There was something she had to say.

"My lord, may I ask you something?"

"Anything, my dearest!"

"I have been thinking. Would it be wise to send Lord Lakenham out of London in disgrace? He is high-spirited. It may persuade him to do something foolish."

Heston released her and rose to his feet. There was a curious glitter in his eyes.

"You think that he might yet elope? How could that be, my dear, when you are promised to me? Or do you still have a *tendre* for him?"

"Of course not! I was never in love with Harry—" Miranda's hand flew to her mouth. She had betrayed herself at last. Now she waited for the explosion of wrath and demands for explanations which must be sure to follow her outburst.

"I did not think you were…not for a moment. On your part it was a business arrangement, was it not? My hope that you will not cry off from our engagement must lie in the fact that my fortune is greater than his."

The cruel words struck Miranda like a blow to

the heart. Tears stung her eyes, and her mouth was trembling.

"You may believe what you will," she whispered.

"What else can I believe? You made your position very clear. You shrink from my caresses and you answer my attempts at tenderness with insults."

"Tenderness? From you? Sir, you shall not think me a fool. I know very well what you are about."

"I wish that I could say the same, my love."

His words were casual enough, but they filled Miranda with dread. How much did he suspect? She hardly dared to look at him, but when she did so he appeared to be absorbed in studying the intricate pattern carved into the lid of his snuff-box.

"You speak in riddles, my lord. I do not understand you…"

"You will come to do so, I suspect, though it may take a lifetime. You do not find it a lowering thought to consider the trials ahead of you?"

Miranda had recovered her composure. She gave him her most enchanting smile. "I shall do my best to bear them," she said sweetly.

"You do not lack courage, as I have observed before. Will it carry you through an evening at Almack's?" He produced two of the coveted vouchers and laid them upon a table.

"You wish me to make an appearance there? Well, I suppose that I must do so. You will not wish me to be exposed to further insults from your friends."

Heston looked mystified and then he laughed. "You are referring to Lady Eddington? She is no friend of mine. I thought merely that you might like to satisfy your curiosity about the place, and Alexei finds it amusing."

"You will invite Count Toumanov?"

"Only if you do not object. I believe you find him entertaining…" His voice was bland.

"I find him charming." Miranda gave her tormentor a hostile look. "He is so kind."

"A worthy trait of character! Would that I could lay claim to it…sadly, I am irredeemable."

"In that, at least, we are in agreement, sir. When is this visit to Almack's to take place?"

"If Alexei is to join us, it must be tonight. Those hallowed portals are open only on Wednesdays, and by next week he will be gone."

"He returns to Russia?"

"Unless his master gives him leave to stay. It is unlikely." Heston looked at his watch. "Much as it distresses me, my love, I must tear myself away from your side for the moment."

"I will try to bear it, sir."

Heston grinned at her. "Always the hard word, my dearest? Until this evening, then…shall we say at nine?"

Miranda walked to the door and opened it a trifle. He would not attempt to kiss her again in full view of the servants. When she looked up at him she saw his mocking smile.

"Minx!" he chided. "That would not stop me, but you may have your way. Don't worry about Harry Lakenham, by the way. I could not send him out of London, even had I wished to do so. I am not his guardian, but I'll give him a dressing-down he won't forget. What his grandfather may decide is something else."

Miranda was thoughtful as she made her way upstairs to Fanny. Heston was the most extraordinary creature she had ever met. She needed time to think…to understand her own emotions…

In the course of the last hour her feelings had fluctuated wildly. At the sight of his tall figure she had experienced an unguarded moment of joy. It had been followed almost at once by dread of his reaction to the sight of Harry in her company.

Then she recalled the words which had hurt her so. She closed her eyes in agony. Heston had made his opinion of her only too clear. He considered her a fortune-hunter, no better than the expensive Incognitas who swarmed about the capital.

He had not made the best of bargains, either. At least those harpies gave value for money, and it was not unreasonable of him to expect the same from her.

Her face burned. If he only knew how she had longed to melt into his arms, to return his kisses, to trace the curve of that mobile mouth... She dared not. It was much too dangerous. Only by keeping him at arm's length could she hope to carry out her plan.

But what was that plan? With every day that passed her motives grew more hazy. Her own honesty compelled her to admit that Heston was right in his judgment of Harry's character. She herself had given him no reason to think well of her; in fact, she had been at pains to do the opposite. Why should she object when he accused her of being what she had claimed to be?

She entered the bedchamber to find Fanny staring at the ceiling.

"Has Heston gone?" her twin demanded.

Miranda nodded.

"Of all the rude, arrogant, overbearing men in the world, he must be the worst," Fanny cried. "How dare he speak of Harry so?"

"He had some justification," Miranda pointed out.

"I don't know how you can defend him. Harry was right…he needs a setdown. To threaten to send my darling away as if he were a naughty child? I tell you—Harry will not go."

"Lord Heston is not his guardian. He has no power to banish him from London, so he tells me."

"He did not give me that impression," Fanny sulked. "Did you get round him, then?"

"There was no need. The decision rests with Harry's grandfather. Heston will speak to Harry, of course, as someone must do."

"Pompous creature! One might suppose that he had never been young. Lord Rudyard, I suppose, will get a full report from him?"

"I doubt it, Fanny. Heston, whatever his faults, does strike me as a tattle-tale. Others will be ready enough to put Lord Rudyard in possession of the story."

"It must come to the same thing," Fanny mourned. "Harry will be sent away and we shall never see each other more."

"You still feel the same about him?"

"Of course I do. I know you think me fickle, but yesterday, when I thought Harry dead, I knew I could not live without him."

"Luckily he is still alive and so are you. Now do

cheer up. Heston has obtained two vouchers for Almack's for us."

"You are not serious?" Fanny brightened up at once.

"Indeed I am. We are to go this evening. Heston has asked Count Toumanov to make up our party. That is, if you feel well enough…?"

"I would not miss it for the world!" Fanny jumped out of bed, a beaming smile upon her face. "We must tell Aunt Emma. She will be so pleased."

"You feel you can bear Lord Heston's company, then?" Miranda asked wickedly.

"I shall ignore him. The Count is so charming. I shall leave you to put up with Heston's rudeness and sarcastic comments."

"Thank you so much! It promises to be a very pleasant evening…"

Fanny regarded her twin. "You seem to deal together," she said. "He never takes his eyes off you."

"I hope you are mistaken. He worries me, I will admit. I am beginning to wonder if he suspects."

"Nonsense! How could he?" Fanny waved the suggestion aside. "What are we to wear tonight?"

Her final decision required more than an hour of serious consideration, but at last she settled upon a gown of spider-gauze, with ribbon braces.

"Our zephyr cloaks will go well with this toilette," she announced. "Do you think them suitable?"

Miranda nodded absent-mindedly. She had taken little interest in the selection of gowns which Fanny had paraded for her approval. Heston filled her mind to the exclusion of all else.

Was he playing some deep game? It was becoming more and more impossible to doubt it. He had taken her so far along the road to matrimony that she could see no escape.

Yet he could not mean to go ahead with it. A fortune hunter, tainted by the smell of trade, and penniless into the bargain? No, it was impossible. He was planning some hideous retribution. Perhaps he intended to leave her at the altar, the butt of the Polite World. Or at best he might jilt her even earlier, and go abroad.

In her own heart she did not believe him capable of either of those actions, but the alternative might be worse. Surely he could not intend to marry her and punish her for the rest of her life? She pushed the thought aside. She was allowing her overwrought imagination to overcome her common sense.

She went to find her aunt.

To her surprise, that lady found herself unable

to give the proposed visit to Almack's her un-qualified approval.

"Your sister should rest," she announced. "She is not yet recovered from the shock of her experience yesterday."

"The invitation has raised her spirits, ma'am."

"Well, of course, we must all be delighted by the vouchers, but…" Mrs Shere hesitated "…my dear, I cannot think it right that you should appear there in the company of two young men, and without a chaperon. Lady Medlicott does not have the entrée. She could not go with you."

"Heston did not mention the matter, and, Aunt, as you well know, he is a law unto himself…"

"Not at Almack's, dearest. Why, Willis turned away Wellington himself because he was wearing pantaloons instead of knee breeches…the rules are very strict."

"It is not quite the same thing. Heston is my… er…betrothed. That must make all perfectly respectable." Miranda looked a little self-conscious as she spoke, but her embarrassment went unnoticed.

"I don't know, I'm sure. Still, dear Lord Heston will always behave with propriety. You and your sister may go, my dear, though I believe that I should mention it to him."

In the event, there was no need for Mrs Shere to undertake this duty. When Heston appeared, resplendent in black coat, satin knee-breeches, silk stockings and buckled shoes, he was quick to assure her that Alexei's sister, the Princess Chaliapine, would be happy to undertake the role of chaperon.

"Her husband will be with her, ma'am," Alexei told her with a smile. "Between us, we shall take good care of the young ladies."

Mrs Shere beamed at him. She had a soft spot for a handsome young man, and Alexei was a dazzling figure in his dress regimentals.

Even so, there was no comparison between the two men, Miranda thought to herself. Heston lacked Alexei's classical features, and he was so large that he might have appeared clumsy. Yet he did not. There was some quality about him…an air of physical grace, perhaps?

Above all, a certain air of authority in his bearing drew all eyes, making the man beside him seem insignificant.

Chapter Nine

When they reached King Street, the guardian of Almack's, the great Willis himself came forward to greet them.

"Welcome, my lord!" He made a low obeisance. "This is an unexpected pleasure…"

Heston nodded an acknowledgement, chatting amiably as the ladies removed their cloaks.

"Is my sister arrived yet?" Alexei enquired. "She is the Princess Chaliapine."

Willis bowed again. "I believe that you will find the Princess in the ballroom, sir. May I take you through?"

"Great heavens! We'll never find her in this crush." Alexei gazed about the crowded ballroom.

Yet their arrival had not gone unnoticed, and a laughing girl soon appeared at his side. She was accompanied by a burly man much older than herself. He was dressed in Russian military uniform, and Miranda guessed from his insignia that he must be a high-ranking officer.

"Xenia, may I present the Misses Gaysford to you and the General?" Alexei took his sister's hand and kissed it. "You have heard me speak of them, I know."

"Very often!" the Princess teased. Then she turned to his companions and held out both her hands.

"How delightful! And I am to be your chaperon? I could not wish for prettier charges, and I shall not be too strict, I promise."

Even the General smiled at that. It was clear that he was devoted to his lovely wife. So slender as to seem ethereal, the Princess yet bore a strong resemblance to her brother with the same clear ivory complexion, a full mouth which revealed perfect teeth when she laughed, and large almond-shaped hazel eyes. Her gown of creamy silk was cut with the simplicity which showed the hand of a master couturier, and it formed an ideal background for a necklace of the largest diamonds Miranda had ever seen. The overall effect was that of some exotic creature from another world.

In the face of such splendour Miranda felt ill at ease, but the Princess was quick to banish her shyness. She was perfectly unaffected and natural in her manner, and her charm was such that Miranda warmed to her at once.

"Adam, you are the luckiest man in London," the Princess announced. "I might have guessed that you would steal away one of these two beauties for yourself. There is no need to wish you happy, my dear friend. You cannot fail to be so." She took Miranda's hand.

"I am so glad to meet you," she went on. "Alexei has spoken often of the lovely Gaysford twins. I see now that he did not exaggerate."

"Princess, you are too kind," Miranda murmured.

"Not at all! It is quite true. Have you met the Patronesses yet? They are quite formidable. Such *grandes dames!* But you must not be afraid of them."

"I do feel nervous at the thought of meeting them," Miranda admitted.

"But you have brought Adam here. That must most certainly be a mark in your favour. In the ordinary way he shuns the place, and they do not care to be ignored, you know. Now here comes Lady Castlereagh. See if she does not make a fuss of him."

Miranda looked up as the wife of the Foreign Secretary bore down upon them. This high-ranking lady was not only married to the leader of the

House of Commons, she was the second daughter of the Earl of Buckingham, and centuries of authority showed in her bearing.

"So, Heston, you have deigned to visit us at last?" Her mock severity left his lordship undisturbed.

"As you see, Emily. May I present to you my bride-to-be and her sister?"

Both girls made their curtsies, and were rewarded by a bow from her ladyship.

"Charming!" she murmured. "Heston, you never cease to astonish me!"

A quiver of emotion disturbed the calm of his lordship's expression. "You flatter me, ma'am. I had not thought it possible."

"Wicked creature! Do you think to put me out of countenance?"

"I should not dare to attempt such a thing. It would be useless."

Lady Castlereagh smiled. Then she turned to Prince Chaliapine and his wife, keeping them in conversation for some minutes.

Alexei had moved aside with Fanny, and Miranda found herself alone with Adam Heston.

"Well, is this temple of fashion all that you expected?" He looked down at her with a question in his eyes.

Miranda gazed about her. The room was crowded and both men and women were ablaze with jewels which caught the light and dazzled the onlookers. Toilettes of great magnificence adorned the persons of the ladies, showing to advantage against the regulation costumes of such gentlemen as were present.

"Everyone looks very fine," she admitted cautiously. "But I had not expected such a crush."

His lip curled. "My dear, this place is considered the seventh heaven of the beau monde. To receive an invitation is to achieve the peak of happiness, whilst to be excluded can only mean despair."

"I wonder why?" Miranda murmured, half to herself.

"I have wondered too. There is a desire to mix in "select" company, as some would have it. One must dance and gossip in the best company, after all, and it is a recognised marriage mart."

She looked up sharply. Was this yet another gibe? She would never know, for Heston's attention was fixed upon the doorway. Following his gaze, she saw Harry Lakenham in the middle of a group of friends.

Her companion uttered a low exclamation beneath his breath. "Damn the boy!" he said savagely. "He did not say a word to me. Did you tell him of our visit here?"

"No, I did not!" Miranda snapped. "We have not seen him since we knew that we were to come to Almack's. What is more, my lord, you will please not to use that tone with me!"

He was about to reply when Princess Chaliapine rejoined them.

"Do you like to dance?" she asked Miranda. "It is my passion, but they have strange notions here. The quadrille is not yet allowed, although I hear that Lady Jersey is considering it. We must be satisfied with the old English country-dances, and those energetic Scottish reels. It is a pity, as I so love to waltz."

"Would you cause a scandal, Xenia?" The harsh, dark face softened as Heston smiled down at her.

"I shall not have the opportunity, my dear. I doubt if the musicians have ever heard of it." She allowed herself to be led away by the gallant who had come to claim her hand.

"Shall you care to join them?" Heston asked.

"I think we are too late, my lord. The sets are made up."

"Good evening, Miss Gaysford."

Miranda turned to find Harry Lakenham at her elbow. She recognised the man beside him as Heston's cousin, Thomas Frant.

"Ma'am, I'm happy to see you again," said Thomas. "I shall hope for a dance this evening—that is, if Adam will allow it."

"Mr Frant, I shall be happy to partner you," Miranda replied.

Thomas looked startled by this evidence of independence, but he took her card and marked it for a Scottish reel.

Miranda did not glance at Heston. He did not own her, she thought fiercely, and she would dance with whom she chose. She half-expected some caustic remark, but his lordship was addressing Harry.

"Is not Almack's a little tame for you?" he said. "I had not thought to see you here tonight."

"We came for the gaming." Unconcerned, Harry grinned at him.

"You may have done so," Thomas announced, "but I intend to dance. Some fine-looking women here tonight, saving your presence, ma'am. Who is that gorgeous creature over there…the one with the diamonds worth a ransom?"

"That is the Princess Chaliapine," Heston informed him in repressive tones. "The General standing by the wall is her husband."

Thomas sighed. "Ain't it always the way? The beauties are snapped up before you can say 'knife'.

Will you introduce me, Adam? The General won't object if I ask her for a dance…"

"Ain't she a little above your touch, old boy? Dancing ain't your thing, you know. You caper like a farmer's boy," Harry told him frankly.

"Good of you to say so!" Thomas had stiffened. "You ain't much of a hand at it yourself."

Heston sighed. "Come, my dear, let us leave these two young cockerels to their quarrelling."

He led her through the throng and into the supper-room. There he found her a seat in a secluded corner.

"May I bring you something to drink?" he asked. "Sadly, I fear it is a choice between orgeat and lemonade."

"I should like some lemonade, my lord."

"Very wise! Are you hungry?" There was mischief in his eyes as he asked the question.

Miranda shook her head, but when he returned he carried a plate which he set before her with an air of triumph.

"Positively Lucullan!" he announced as he inspected the food through his quizzing-glass. "Do pray note the interesting way in which this bread and butter has curled at the edges. It must be concern for the health of the patrons here. Fresh bread is thought to be so bad for the digestion."

Miranda's sense of humour got the better of her. She looked up at him with laughter in her eyes.

"You did warn me," she admitted.

"I could not be sure that you believed me. Now, my dear, you must not be shy. I shall not blame you if you fall upon this feast with ravenous appetite."

"My lord, you are a most complete hand. Suppose one of the Patronesses should hear you?"

"I should be banished at once, and thereby cast into obscurity."

Miranda giggled in spite of herself as she pushed the plate away. Then she remembered. She must not allow herself to be charmed into being in charity with this formidable creature, even though his wit amused her.

"We should rejoin the others," she murmured. "My sister will be wondering what has become of me."

"Will she? I had supposed that perhaps Alexei might divert her thoughts from more pressing problems."

Miranda shot a suspicious glance at him, but his expression was bland.

"Well, I should like to dance," she said hastily. She was on dangerous ground and she was anxious to change the subject. Heston would be unable to speak to her throughout the country dance.

"And so you shall, my love." He held out his arm and she had perforce to take it.

They took their places in the next set, and once again her companion succeeded in surprising her. He moved through the figures with a grace peculiarly his own.

"You told me that you did not care to dance," she accused as they joined hands.

"That depends upon my partner." He looked down smiling at her upturned face, and something in his eyes made her heart turn over. In her confusion she missed a step.

"Careful!" he whispered. "We are the cynosure of all eyes."

"I beg your pardon, sir. I was not attending…" Her eye fell upon the couples in the adjoining set. Surely that was Fanny with Alexei, and this must be her second dance with the same young man.

As the music stopped, she moved to her sister's side. "Pray don't dance with the Count again," she whispered in a low tone. "It must give rise to comment."

"Don't be such a prude, Miranda! You are become as stuffy as Heston himself. I may not speak to Harry, and now I may not dance again with Alexei. Do you intend to make my life a misery?"

"Of course not, but you will not wish to lose your voucher. The Contess Lieven has been watching you…"

Fanny looked dismayed. "I meant no harm," she sulked.

"I know it, but you must choose from another of your beaux. There are enough of them, if I am not mistaken…"

Fanny brightened. "I did dance with Mr Frant, but he trod upon my toes, and Alexei is such a perfect dancer."

"He is not the only one. Why not give your hand to Mr Rushton? He has been hovering about you for this age."

Fanny smiled prettily upon the gallant who had pursued her from their entry into the ballroom, and crowned his happiness by giving him her card.

Satisfied that a crisis of ill humour had been averted, Miranda turned her attention to the dancers.

The Princess Chaliapine was so graceful, she thought in admiration. Light on her feet, she executed entrechats with consummate grace as Thomas Frant endeavoured to keep up with her.

Inspired by her example, Thomas sprang into the air, determined to be a credit to his partner, and to emulate her performance. It was then that disaster struck. Thomas landed in a heap upon the ballroom floor. He made a quick recover, but his face was scarlet as the music ended.

Beside her Miranda was aware of Harry Lakenham, convulsed with laughter.

"Shouldn't have tried it, dear old boy," he choked out as Thomas came towards him. "You ain't the build. Getting fat as a flawn."

A picture of injured dignity, Thomas did not take this chaffing in good part.

"Lakenham, you will apologise for that remark," he said stiffly. "Otherwise you may name your friends."

"For laughing because you landed on your rump? Come off it, Thomas…"

"I don't like your tone, and you may not speak such words to me. I take it you ain't afraid to meet me?"

Harry's face changed. "Do you accuse me of cowardice?" he said quietly.

Miranda gasped. She could not believe what she was hearing. What had started as a simple joke had turned into a quarrel and now into something much more serious. Desperate to avoid what promised to turn into a duel, she threw a glance of appeal at Heston.

Her plea was just too late. He had already stepped between the combatants.

"Stop this, you idiots!" he said in icy tones. "Will you make yourselves the laughing-stock of London? Harry, you would do well to keep a still tongue in your head. And Thomas, as for you, if you cannot take a joke against yourself, it is a poor business. You had best shake hands and forget this nonsense. For one thing, you embarrass the ladies."

For a full minute Harry continued to glare at his challenger. Then he laughed and stuck out his hand.

"My fault entirely, Thomas. Shouldn't have liked it if you'd said the same to me. I need to have my head examined... Will you forgive me and accept my apology?"

Thomas took the proffered hand. "My fault too, old thing. I must have looked like a grounded whale. Can't blame you for laughing...thing is, I felt a fool."

"I expect you turned your ankle, sir," Miranda broke in swiftly. "It is easily done, and very painful. I did the same myself on one occasion..."

"Did you, Miss Gaysford?" Thomas brightened. He had felt the humiliation keenly, but now Miranda's words in some way restored his dignity. "That must have been it. I'll take care not to slip again."

"Then you may beg pardon of these ladies, both

of you. Take yourselves off to the gaming rooms, for heaven's sake. We've seen enough of you for one evening."

This command was enough to quell any argument, and with Heston's severe gaze fixed upon them both young men made their apologies and disappeared.

Behind her Miranda heard a tired sigh. Fanny's face was drained of all colour, and she was clutching at Alexei's arm.

"Will you excuse us?" she asked. "I find I have torn a flounce. My sister will help me pin it up."

Heston gave her an ironic look, but he made no comment as she seized Fanny's hand and led her through the crowd to the nearest retiring-room.

Once there, she swung round upon her twin.

"Do pull yourself together," she urged. "If you are to faint whenever Harry takes one of his odd starts, your secret will soon be common knowledge."

"I didn't faint," her twin protested in a low voice.

"You were on the verge of doing so. Take care, or you will betray us both. As for Harry, I am out of all patience with him. I could box his ears. How you can bear…?"

"I can't." Fanny turned her face away.

"Oh, love, I'm sorry, but his behaviour is too bad."

"I know it. It is so lowering, to be always on pins, wondering what he will do next."

Miranda was surprised. She had expected the usual fierce defence from Fanny, coupled with excuses for Harry's folly. A tiny flicker of hope stirred in her heart. Perhaps Fanny was beginning to grow out of her infatuation. She picked up her sister's card and studied it.

"We should go back to the others," she said quietly. "Your next partner will be searching for you, and I'm sure you don't want the suicide of a disappointed beau upon your conscience."

Unresisting, Fanny allowed herself to be led back to the ballroom.

As Miranda had predicted, her next partner was waiting to claim her twin, but Heston was quick to intervene.

"My dear sir, will you excuse Miss Gaysford?" he said mildly. "She has the headache...I expect it is the heat."

Overcome by being noticed by the famous Corinthian, the young man murmured a wish that Fanny might soon recover, and bowed himself away.

Miranda looked at Fanny, but her sister was too dispirited to take exception to the summary dismissal of her partner.

"Do you wish to go home?" his lordship asked. His tone was gentle, and Miranda threw him a look of gratitude.

Fanny shook her head. "I am quite well, my lord, but if we might sit down…"

"Of course." Heston led them to a vacant sofa by the wall. "You will perhaps like to watch the dancing for a time."

The Count was dancing with his sister, his skill clearly matching her own.

"They make a handsome couple, don't they?" Miranda was anxious to draw Heston's attention from her sister's woebegone expression.

"Indeed they do. Looking at Alexei now, one could not guess less than two years ago he was with Platoff's Cossacks, driving the French from Russia."

Fanny's ears pricked up.

"He never speaks of it, my lord."

"No, he would not. No one who took part in that terrible campaign cares to recall the horrors witnessed by both sides, but Alexei was decorated more than once."

Miranda shuddered. Even in Yorkshire they had learned of that fearful winter of 1812, when the French armies, which had conquered most of Europe, had been defeated by the Russian snows and the bravery of the men who were determined to defend their homeland.

The Cossacks, she knew, had appeared as avenging hordes from the wide and icy wastes, falling upon the starving and retreating French to wreak appalling havoc. Then, ghostlike, they had disappeared, only to return when least expected.

"The Count looks too young to have seen such sights," she murmured half to herself.

"It changed him, as such experiences must do…" Heston rose to greet two of his acquaintances who came to offer their congratulations on his betrothal. They were among the many to whom Miranda had been introduced that evening.

"I shall never remember half their names," she whispered to Fanny.

Her sister was not attending. Alexei had returned to her side, and there was hero-worship in her eyes.

"Tell me about Russia," she begged. "Oh, I do not mean to remind you of the war, but the cities must be very fine."

"You would like St Petersburg, Miss Gaysford." He began to speak of the wonders of that city, and Fanny hung upon his every word.

"Do you care to dance again, my dear?" Heston's

eyes rested upon Fanny and the Count, and then returned to Miranda.

She consulted her card. "The next dance is to be a Scottish reel, I believe. I am promised to Mr Frant."

Heston laughed. "Do you think he will venture upon the floor again after his mishap? If he does, I must commend his courage, and your own."

"His courage is not in question," Miranda replied. "Here he comes…"

Thomas looked a little self-conscious as he stood before her. "Perhaps you will not care to partner me?" he ventured shyly. "I shall understand—"

"Nonsense, I am looking forward to our dance." Miranda allowed him to lead her out. "You will not trip again, you know. It happens very rarely."

Thus encouraged, Thomas began the reel with great enthusiasm, bounding high in the air, but without attempting the more intricate flourishes. He acquitted himself well and, when the dance was over, he was flushed with pride.

"There, you see! Did I not tell you? I knew you would enjoy it."

"I had a splendid partner, Miss Gaysford. I say, you really are a brick! Adam is a lucky dog, and I shall tell him so."

When he took her back to Heston, it was to find that the Princess Chaliapine had rejoined their little group.

"Adam, can you spare Alexei?" the Princess asked. "Chaliapine is called away, and I need an escort home."

"We, too, should be going." Heston looked a question at Miranda and she nodded her assent. "Don't worry, I will see the ladies home."

"But I fear I have broken up your party." The Princess looked so penitent that Miranda smiled and shook her head. "You are quite sure? I promise to make it up to you when we meet again." With that, she took her brother's arm and went in search of her carriage.

"She does not care to see me in Alexei's company," Fanny murmured in an undertone.

"Hush!" Miranda felt uncomfortable. She looked at Heston, but he was engaged in conversation with a friend. "Is that so wonderful? You should not have danced with him so much. It cannot have gone unnoticed."

Miranda was quite sure that it had not, but the Princess had been too well bred to comment upon this social gaffe.

Such criticism was enough to send Fanny into the sulks and she was silent on the journey home. Once indoors, she excused herself with a plea of exhaustion, leaving Miranda to explain away this uncivil behaviour. She was about to speak when Heston forestalled her.

"Your sister is not herself tonight?"

"Lord Lakenham has given her another shock, I fear. She was frightened, as I was myself, when he quarrelled with Mr Frant. I could not believe that they would call each other out over such a trivial matter."

"Men have fought for less," Heston said indifferently. "Once the actual challenge has been made, it is almost impossible to draw back."

"But that is ridiculous!" Miranda began to pace the room. "There can be no need to accept a challenge…a man of good sense would let it go unheeded."

"And be accused of cowardice? I see you have not heard of General Thornton, who was excessively fond of the dance. Theodore Hook gave him the title of "The Waltzing General", to which Thornton took exception. When they quarrelled Hook insulted him further, but Thornton did not call him out. He was accused of cowardice and asked to resign from his regiment."

"What nonsense! At least you, my lord, put a stop to the quarrel tonight before it could go further…I was so thankful."

"Were you, my dear?" Heston took her hands and drew her to sit beside him. "I am delighted to hear that I have won your approval at last."

Miranda was silent.

"It may surprise you to hear that I am entirely of your own opinion in this matter. Too many men have lost their lives over incidents of little consequence."

She looked up at him then. "It does surprise me," she told him frankly. "I doubt if I shall ever understand you."

"Did I not tell you it would take a lifetime?" He dropped a kiss upon her nose. "Now what is it in particular that you do not understand?"

"I don't know. It's hard to explain. You mix in the highest circles, and yet you do not seem to share the opinions of Polite Society."

"Because I do not care for Almack's, and I disapprove of duelling? It's true... I may yet become a social outcast...it is a lowering thought."

Miranda could not repress a smile. "You are impossible!"

"So I'm told. Now I must go, my love. It is late and you are looking tired."

"Thank you so much, my lord. There is nothing more heartening than to be told that one is looking hagged."

"I did not say that." He wound a finger around a copper curl and tugged it gently. "You could not look other than beautiful, but must you always be as prickly as a porcupine?" He began to stroke her cheek.

Miranda jumped to her feet. "Sir, will you take a glass of wine?" she asked hastily.

"That would be delightful." His face was bland. "I confess to feeling parched. Those fearsome liquids which were served tonight are sufficient to decimate the population. You will join me, I hope?"

Obediently she filled two glasses and took a seat as far away from him as possible.

"Tell me about your sister," he said suddenly. "Her nerves are sadly on edge, I fear."

Miranda eyed him nervously. What was the reason for this sudden interest in Fanny? Was he too afraid that she would become involved with Alexei Toumanov?

"She…she is sometimes a little high-strung, my lord. She was delicate as a child. Mama was always afraid that she would lose her."

"I see. Yet nowadays she looks the picture of health."

"Oh, yes, she is quite recovered. She grew out of her childish ailments…"

"But old habits die hard, and you continue to indulge her?" Heston gave her a quizzical look.

"Of course not!" she replied hotly. Then she blushed at the lie. "Well, perhaps we do, a little… but, sir, you must not think ill of her. She has a loving heart."

"And you?" He drew her to her feet. "What of your own heart?"

Miranda could not answer him. He was so close, and suddenly she felt breathless. Beneath the fine cambric of his shirt she could feel the beating of his heart, and his nearness made her tremble. She hung her head, not daring to look at him. Then a long finger slid beneath her chin and he raised her face to his. His mouth came down on hers and the world was lost.

When he released her she clung to him, afraid that her limbs would no longer hold her upright. He kissed her again, and this time so tenderly that the tears sprang unbidden to her eyes.

"I wish you felt that you could trust me," he murmured gently.

Miranda stiffened in his arms. "I don't know what you mean," she cried in confusion.

"Oh, yes, my dear, I think you do." With those words he left her.

Chapter Ten

Miranda walked upstairs unsteadily. Coming as they had done at the close of a passionate embrace, Heston's final words had robbed her of all hope of sleep.

She allowed a drowsy Ellen to undress her and dismissed the girl. Then she slipped into a dressing-robe and sat by the window, gazing at the gaily illuminated streets with unseeing eyes.

Heston suspected something. He had made that clear when he had invited her to take him into her confidence. She longed to do so, but it was impossible. How could she trust him? To divulge her secret would mean that she would lose him for ever.

And that she could not bear…not now, when all her happiness lay in his hands. Her own honesty compelled her to admit the truth. She loved him dearly, and would do so for the rest of her life.

She could not think how it had happened. She had hated him so at first. Now the very sight of his tall figure heightened all her senses. In his company the world became a different place, so wonderful that until now she felt she had been blind to all its glories.

Yet it was all so hopeless. A tear rolled down her cheek. Her deception could not be hidden for ever, and when it came to light he would believe the worst of her.

It was too much to bear, especially as he too seemed to have changed in his attitude towards her. On one or two occasions his gentleness had surprised her, and more than once his manner had been almost tender. Perhaps she had imagined it.

Either way, it did not matter. She had no hope of winning his love. It was true, she did not understand him. Why did he persist in continuing with this mock betrothal? They had gone so far along the road to marriage, but he could not mean to go through with it at the end.

She buried her flushed face in her hands. She knew it now. She longed to be his wife, but a future with a man who held her in contempt could only be a living hell.

* * *

A disturbed night left her heavy-eyed and listless and brought a comment from her uncle on the following day.

"You must not overdo it, my dear child," he reproached. "Burning the candle at both ends, I fear. I must speak to his lordship."

"We shall not see him today. His mama arrives from Warwickshire, so he will be engaged. He has asked if we will dine with them in Brook Street as she will wish to meet my family. That is, if you agree."

"Naturally, my dear. We must not be lacking in observance to her ladyship, but to be correct they should dine here first."

Miranda summoned up a spurious show of enthusiasm. She would not have her uncle think that she was ashamed of her relations.

"I'll send a note to Brook Street," the Alderman assured her. "In the ordinary way I would not suggest it, but Lord Heston ain't in the least top-lofty, in spite of all that's said of him. He makes himself at home here, though I doubt if he's ever set foot in Bloomsbury before."

"You are mistaken, sir. He knows the Museum well."

"Is that so? Well, the gentry have their own ideas

of entertainment. At least her ladyship need not fear our food. She won't get a better dinner in London. I'll speak to the cook at once."

"Shall I do that?" Mrs Shere asked anxiously.

"No, Emma, not on this occasion. No expense must be spared." He went off happily, humming with pleasure as he considered the feast which he intended to lay before his honoured guests.

"My dear, you should have a quiet day." Mrs Shere patted Miranda's hand. "Why not read your book? It always takes you out of yourself, as I well know. How many times have I asked you something, and you have not heard me? We shall deny all visitors for this morning."

"Pray do not do so, ma'am. If Richard calls, I think we shall be glad to see him. He is a restful person."

"As you wish, my love. Is Fanny still asleep?"

"I believe so. She was very tired when we came home…"

"We must take better care of you. Alas, it is always the same at the start of an engagement…so many invitations and congratulations, and so much to be done. You have not fixed a wedding-date?"

"Not yet."

"Well, I must suppose that Heston wishes to

consult with his mama. And then, you know, we must make arrangements for your own mother to bring the family up to London for the ceremony…"

Suddenly Miranda could bear no more. She excused herself on the thin pretext of searching for her book.

Fanny was still asleep, so she picked up the thick volume and returned to the salon, intending to curl up on the window-seat for the next few hours.

Mrs Shere gave her an anxious look. "My dear, I have been thinking. If you were to take up tatting, it would help to pass the time…"

Miranda chuckled. "Aunt Emma, you have seen examples of my tatting. You can't believe that I have a gift for it?"

"Well, then, perhaps some tapestry work? You might cover the dining-chairs in your new home."

"No, no, you cannot wish that upon Lord Heston. Ma'am, we should have no guests. Who would sit on them?"

Her aunt was forced to smile. "They are suitable occupations for a lady," she said half-heartedly. "But there, my love, you had always a lively sense of fun. Perhaps you are right." She went away to oversee the running of her household, and Miranda was left in peace.

As her aunt had predicted, she was soon lost in her book, and though roused at times by the sound of the front door-knocker, no visitors were allowed to disturb her.

It was time for luncheon before Fanny came to find her. A night's rest had done much to restore the spirits of her twin, and now she sparkled with vivacity.

"I vow I have never laid so long abed," she cried. "I have missed all our morning callers. Tell me, who has been to see us?"

"Aunt is guarding us today." Miranda smiled. "No one has been admitted."

"Oh, how dull! I had wished to see Alexei, that is, if he called, but perhaps I have not missed him. There is still the rest of the day…" She stood by the window, gazing along the street.

"I half-expected Richard," Miranda admitted. "I asked that aunt Emma should not send him away."

"Did you?" Fanny's tone was indifferent. "Well, better his company than none at all, I suppose."

"How can you say such things? I know quite well that you are as fond of him as I am."

"Richard is well enough in his way but, when I compare him with Alexei, I confess that he seems dull. Miranda, did you ever hear anything so exciting as the story of the Cossacks when the

Russians fought the French? And to be decorated twice? Alexei is a hero."

"I agree, although there are degrees of heroism, you know. I have felt often that it must be difficult to be a non-combatant, held by other ties of duty."

"You can't mean that! I don't agree at all!" Fanny's eyes grew dreamy. "How I should love to visit Russia…to see St Petersburg…to skate on the frozen lakes…and to drive in a troika through the snow, wrapped in wonderful furs."

"And outrunning the wolves if possible?"

"There you go again! Sometimes I think you have no soul. You are always so prosaic."

"I have a keen imagination, Fanny. Shall we go down to luncheon?"

It was clear that Alexei's heroism had raised him even higher in her sister's estimation. Miranda suspected that Harry Lakenham now appeared to be no more than a foolish boy in Fanny's eyes.

She hoped that it was so. With Fanny cured of her infatuation, all might yet be well. A rueful smile curved her lips. It was a vain hope and she knew it in her heart.

Fanny now showed every sign of transferring her affections to the handsome Count Toumanov, but Miranda doubted if he had thoughts of anything more than a light flirtation. Such protestations of devotion were common currency in Polite Society and were not taken seriously by girls with more experience than her sister.

Fanny, as she knew of old, would build them up in her imagination until she had convinced herself that she and Alexei were in the throes of a *grande passion.*

Miranda could only comfort herself with the thought that the Tsar and his entourage would soon return to Russia. Little harm could come to Fanny in the next two weeks.

She looked across at her twin, and then she thought of Richard. Dear Richard! He was far from being the shining knight on a white charger who appeared in Fanny's dreams. How could he compete with a handsome warrior, resplendent in a military uniform, who had taken part in so many dashing adventures?

If only he could rescue Fanny from a burning building, or snatch her from the path of runaway horses. Miranda's sense of humour bubbled to the surface, and she laughed aloud. There seemed little likelihood that any such desirable events would occur in the near future.

"There, my love, you are much better for the rest, as I knew you would be. I am glad to see you more yourself again. Will you not share the joke with us?" Mrs Shere said fondly.

"It was nothing, Aunt Emma…just a silly fancy… Do you go out this afternoon?"

"I think not. I have just been saying that I have obtained a copy of Ackermann's *Repository of Fashion.* I thought that we might look at it this afternoon. It will take some time as there are a full four hundred and fifty plates to study if we are to decide upon your brideclothes."

Fanny clapped her hands. "Famous!" she cried. "We shall like that above anything…"

"It can do no harm to look at it." Miranda threw her twin a warning glance. "But, Aunt, we have so many gowns. We shall never wear them in a twelvemonth. It would be extravagant to order more."

"Do not let your uncle hear you say so. Your brideclothes are to be his present to you."

Miranda murmured her thanks, but she was determined that the Alderman should not be put to any more expense on her behalf.

This resolution was sorely tried as the ladies examined the coloured plates. Tempting visions of the latest fashions appeared before her eyes. Charming light dresses in both white and coloured sarsnets, chamerry gauzes, muslins and tiffany were all suggestions for the summer. Many of them were trimmed with gold or silver fringe. Most had short puffed sleeves, but all were caught high beneath the bosom with matching or contrasting ribbons.

"Pray look at these dear little hats!" Fanny exclaimed in delight. "They are so unlike my own poke bonnets. They just sit on the back or the side of the head, and this one, with the plumes of feathers, is the most ravishing of all."

"I declare! We shall be spoilt for choice. My dears, do examine the shoes. They are charming."

Obediently Miranda looked at a selection of demi-boots in satin with gilt buttons, black kid shoes with a yellow underlay, and similar versions in a blue and black print.

Fanny was exclaiming over white silk slippers with self-ruching and binding.

"These would be my choice," she said with longing.

"Of course! They would be just the thing for heavy snow…" Miranda teased.

"But, my dear, we shall have no snow before November at the earliest." Mrs Shere was mystified. "And it is not yet the end of June."

"I am just funning, Aunt, but you will agree that white silk is not very practical?"

"It would quickly soil, but that cannot be a consideration when you become Lady Heston. Perhaps this grey silk, with the lower part of black leather, is a better choice? You may not have much time, you know, once your wedding date is set, and nothing is more trying than to be rushing about at the last moment. It quite ruins all ones pleasure."

Thus pressed, Miranda had an inspiration.

"You will not take it amiss, ma'am, when I tell you that Heston has decided views upon a suitable toilette? Perhaps I should consult him before making a decision?"

"Has he, my dear? I confess you have surprised me. I had not thought that gentlemen took much interest in such matters, preferring only to see the results. Still, his lordship is so elegant himself. I expect that you are right. He will advise you on what is suitable for the life you are to lead."

Miranda gave an inward sigh of relief. It would be wrong to involve her uncle in spending money upon a wedding which would not take place. Such conduct would be inexcusable.

But so much of her conduct had been inexcusable, she thought sadly. Even if Fanny was in the way of falling out of love with Harry Lakenham, it would not help her own disastrous situation. How could she confess the truth to Heston?

She was roused from such dispiriting thoughts when Richard was announced. He had forsworn his former dress in favour of a blue coat with brass buttons, leather breeches, and immaculately polished top-boots. His shirt-points no longer reached half-way up his cheeks, and he looked much more comfortable.

After the usual civilities had been exchanged he looked at Mrs Shere.

"Ma'am, I was wondering... If you do not object to travel in a hackney carriage, you might like to drive out to the Park this afternoon with Fanny and Miranda."

"My dear boy! What a happy thought! We should enjoy a breath of air, but there is no need for a hackney." She pulled at the bell-rope and ordered her own coach.

"Off you go, my dears, but put on your pelisses. I think it is not warm enough for just a spencer."

As Fanny hurried away, Miranda begged to be excused.

"I should like to sit quietly for a time," she said. "Will you forgive me if I do not join you?"

Mrs Shere gave her an arch look. "I understand perfectly, my love. You will not wish to be abroad in the town if Lord Heston should chance to call."

Miranda coloured. "I doubt if he will do so," she replied. "He did not speak of it last evening."

"Well, well, one never knows! In any event, you will not be lonely. You may keep your uncle company. He will soon be home…"

They had not been gone above half an hour when the Alderman returned from the city.

"Aha! You have caught me playing truant from my business, my dear." Mr Shere looked so like the picture of an errant schoolboy that Miranda smiled.

"Let me guess," she teased. "You were worried about the plants in your glasshouse."

"I admit it. In the summer months, you know, they need more care, and some must be watered twice a day. I leave instructions, but John is inclined either to drown them, or to miss one or two."

Miranda laid aside her book. "Will you let me help you? I can't tell exactly when the time is right to water them, but if you were to tell me…"

"It is just a matter of experience." He looked doubtfully at her figured muslin gown. "You will not wish to soil your dress…"

"I shall be careful," she promised.

"Very well, then." The Alderman removed his coat and followed her into the garden. Once there, his progress to the glasshouse was delayed incessantly as he paused to examine one or other of his extensive collection of exotic plants and shrubs.

"It is a pity the garden is so small," he sighed. "I have been thinking…perhaps I should buy a villa on the outskirts of the city, with more ground."

"I suspect that in your heart you are a countryman, sir." Miranda gave him an affectionate look.

"Your aunt would agree with you. She claims to be a gardening widow as it is…but I cannot resist a new plant. They are mighty expensive, though. I heard that the Marquess of Blandford gave five hundred pounds for a rarity."

"So much?"

The Alderman winked at her. "I haven't yet fallen so far from grace. Now let us see how we go on in here…" He opened the door to his glasshouse. "Hmm, it is as I thought. Take up this small pot, my dear. Do you feel how light it is? That tells you that it is in need of water. With more experience one may know by simply tapping the pot…"

Miranda picked up a watering-can.

"No…no…not that way. Set it in this bowl of water until the soil darkens. That way you will not get moisture upon the crown."

He moved about among his treasures, murmuring an occasional instruction to her until he was satisfied that all was well. Then, as they were leaving the glasshouse, his eye fell upon a tangled jasmine by the door.

"Dear me, this will not do! It has fallen away from the support and will come down if we have high winds." He took a small knife from his pocket and cut some small lengths of twine. Then, with infinite care, he began to tease out the winding tendrils of the plant.

Miranda sat upon a rustic bench and watched him. It had always been a source of amazement to her to find that his chubby hands could be so gentle. Totally absorbed in his task, he had forgotten her for the moment.

She found it soothing just to sit there, not speaking, yet grateful for his presence. There was something about his solid figure which was comforting, and she could forget her troubles for a time.

Suddenly she was aware of being watched. Looking up, she found to her surprise that Heston was standing not three yards away, his eyes intent upon her.

"My lord, we did not expect you today," she cried in confusion. She rose to her feet, scattering the knife, the lengths of string, and the ball of twine. Her heart was pounding in the most alarming way.

Heston bent to retrieve the fallen objects, apologising as he did so for telling the servant that there was no need to announce him.

"Quite right, Lord Heston! You need stand on no ceremony with us…indeed, I hope that you will not. But now, as you see, you have caught me in all my dirt, so I won't offer to shake hands." The Alderman looked delighted to see his unexpected visitor.

"I see that you are busy, sir. That is a fine jasmine, and the scent is so powerful, is it not?" Heston put out a long lean hand to examine one of the leaves.

"It is a good variety, my lord. Repton recommends it…"

"You know his work? I wonder if you believe, as I do, that he will change the nature of gardening in this country?"

"He has some very fine ideas. I make use of some of them here."

"So do I, Mr Shere. Perhaps you may care to visit me in Warwickshire, where he did some work for me?"

The Alderman's eyes were bright with interest. Heston had hit upon the subject closest to his heart.

"You are most kind." He bowed. "You received my note, Lord Heston?"

"Indeed I did. We shall be honoured to dine with

you tomorrow, though I should warn you that my mother is not much accustomed to company. By her own choice she leads a somewhat solitary life…"

"She will not object to coming into Bloomsbury?"

"My dear sir, it is quite her favourite part of London. When she visits the capital, which is not often, she spends her days in the Museum. Sometimes I have suggested that she might take up residence there…"

The Alderman laughed heartily. "It would be uncomfortable to live among the antiquities, I should imagine, although I have not seen them. My lord, will you excuse me? I shall get a roasting from my wife if she discovers that I have received you in my present state." He hurried into the house.

"Your mother is well?" Miranda ventured when she and Heston were alone. "I trust she did not find the journey trying?"

"I doubt if she noticed it." Heston grew thoughtful. "She is not quite in the common way, you know, and she is very shy. To be in company is a torture to her. I think I need not ask, but, my dear, may I beg you to be kind to her?"

"You are quite right. You need not ask that of me," Miranda answered gently. "Shyness is an affliction which those who do not suffer from it find hard to understand."

"Yet you do and I think that you have never been shy in all your life."

Her enchanting smile peeped out. "You may have noticed, sir, that I find it difficult to keep a still tongue in my head when I have strong opinions upon a subject."

"Yes, I had noticed," he agreed drily. "On occasion there can be a certain…er…paralysing frankness about your conversation."

Miranda flushed to the roots of her hair. Was he referring to that dreadful interview when she had announced herself ready to become his bride? She felt ready to sink with embarrassment, and she would not meet his eyes.

He looked at her bent head and his lips twitched with amusement. "No answer for me? I can't believe it! I was congratulating myself upon winning for my bride the only girl in London who does not look at me as a terrified rabbit might gaze upon a stoat."

"Now you are gammoning me," she murmured. "That can't be true, my lord."

"Indeed it is! I have pondered upon the matter. It is so disheartening that on occasion I have been tempted to put a period to my existence…"

Miranda repressed a giggle. "How astonishing!" she replied in a demure tone. "There can be no reason for this strange effect you have upon the ladies. After all, sir, your manner is so engaging on first acquaintance."

"Minx! That's milled me down." He took a seat beside her and smiled down at her upturned face. Miranda's heart turned over.

"You…I mean…it was good of you to invite my uncle to see Repton's work on your estate," she said hastily. "Gardening is his passion."

"I guessed as much. He and my mother will deal together famously. In her painting she has recorded every flower in the grounds."

"I wish I had her gift, but I believe it to be inborn."

"You are right. One can acquire a certain facility, but there can be no comparison with the work of a true artist." He looked about him. "All this is very pleasant and comfortable." He drew her head down to rest upon his shoulder. "I have a confession to make," he said.

"Yes, my lord?" Miranda was startled, and she stiffened. Was he about to tell her that he knew of her deception? A moment's reflection convinced her otherwise. Heston would not be sitting here at his ease if that were the case.

"I met your aunt and your sister in the Park. I came here in the hope of finding you alone."

"I see," she answered faintly. "Was there some reason, sir?" She prayed that he would not start to question her or ask her again to trust him.

"Need you ask?" His fingers tickled the back of her neck, and a shiver of pleasure ran down her spine. She ought to pull away from him, to make some excuse to go indoors, but she could not. His caresses were beginning to produce such sensations of delight that she was losing all power to resist him.

"My uncle is pleased that you and your mother have agreed to dine with us tomorrow," she whispered. It was a last desperate effort to divert his mind from this seductive love-making. "You seem to have changed your mind about his ill intentions…"

Heston held her away from him and looked deep into her eyes. "In these past few days I have changed my mind about so many things," he told her. Then his lips found hers and once again she was swept away into a world where only they existed.

When he released her her head was spinning, but his next words brought her back to reality with a jolt.

"May I hope that you too have changed your mind?" he asked. "Or do you still intend to punish me, my love?"

Miranda stared at him in horror. He must have seen through all her plans. Racked with despair, she could think of nothing to say to him.

Then providence came to her aid in the shape of Fanny, who came tripping down the path.

She stopped short at the sight of Heston.

"Why, my lord, I did not expect to see you here," she said. "I thought you had a pressing engagement…"

"I had," he told her smoothly.

Fanny looked at her sister's face and then at his. What she saw there brought a look of astonishment to her face. It was quickly hidden.

"Then I must beg your pardon for disturbing you," she faltered.

"Lord Heston was just leaving," Miranda told her. "Did you enjoy your drive?"

"Oh, yes. After you left, Count Toumanov stayed on with us, sir. We set him down at the Imperial Hotel in Piccadilly. Is it not strange that the Tsar should choose to stay there, rather than at Carlton House?"

Heston laughed. "After the cold of the Russian steppes, the Tsar may have found the heat at Carlton House somewhat stifling. The Prince is afraid of draughts, even in the height of summer, and the windows are never opened."

"But does not the King of Prussia stay there, and General Blücher, too?"

"On their own terms, Miss Gaysford. I hear that they sleep on army cots, rather than in the luxury of canopied beds."

"How very odd of them!" Fanny was about to question him further when Miranda gave him her hand.

"We shall not detain you further, sir. It was good of you to call in answer to my uncle's note."

She saw the laughter in his eyes, but he accepted his dismissal with good grace.

"Miranda, you do not fool me for a moment," Fanny began as soon as he had left. "I have suspected for some time that you don't dislike Heston as you once did."

Miranda was silent.

"Why don't you answer me? Surely you cannot have a *tendre* for him?"

"Would it be so strange?" her twin said slowly. "I believe I have misjudged him…"

"Oh, pray don't say so! He means you harm, I know it! To make you fall in love with him…what better way to injure you?"

"I don't think that of him."

"Then you are a fool! You will not tell me that

he holds you in regard? Think of the things he said to you."

"I can't forget them."

"Then how can you care for him?"

"I don't know, except that he has changed, and so have I."

"Then you had best go on with this remarkable betrothal, and I wish you joy of him." Fanny's face grew bitter.

"You need not do so. He will never marry me. How could he when the truth is out?" Her anguish was too deep for tears and she turned away.

Chapter Eleven

Fanny did not broach the subject again. She was tempted to do so, but the closed look on Miranda's face warned her against it.

Instead, she set herself the task of diverting her sister's thoughts into lighter channels, and Fanny could be charming when she chose.

"Will you not read aloud to me?" she coaxed. "I have finished *The Mysteries of Udolpho,* whilst you are still reading *Ivanhoe!*"

"But I am halfway through the book. You will not understand the story."

"You could tell me the beginning. Perhaps we might go to the library tomorrow…"

"Do you mean to meet Harry Lakenham again?" Miranda asked.

"Of course not. I have not seen him, so you need not be suspicious." Fanny gave her a bright smile.

Miranda was satisfied. Her sister was incapable of dissembling. It was clear that Harry's star was fading, or Fanny would not look so cheerful.

"Very well then. In any case, the library will be closed tomorrow. Have you forgot the Procession to the Guildhall?"

"But that is not until the following day."

"So it is. I must be dreaming...tomorrow is the day when Lady Heston is to dine with us."

Fanny looked uncomfortable. "I'm sorry for what I've done, believe me, especially as..."

"As you no longer think of marrying Harry Lakenham?" Miranda said steadily.

"Well, you see, I am not sure...he has behaved so badly, as you said yourself."

"Is it not rather late to be convinced of that? I wish you had discovered it before we found ourselves in such a tangle."

"It's easy to make a mistake," Fanny pouted. "You have done the same with Heston."

"So I have. There is no point in recriminations, is there?"

"At least you are free to cry off from your supposed betrothal, if that is what you wish."

Miranda lost her temper. "You think it will be easy? When he is coming here tomorrow with his mother?"

"She may take you in dislike and forbid the match." Fanny's brow cleared. "That would be the obvious solution."

"I intend to make sure that she does not take me in dislike. Heston has asked particularly that we make her welcome, and we shall do so."

"You are very anxious to oblige him."

"In this particular case I am, and I expect the same from you. None of your tricks, remember! You will be civil to her, if only for Uncle's sake."

"I shan't forget my manners," Fanny sulked.

"Make sure that you don't. I warn you, Fanny, I won't put up with any of your nonsense!"

Fanny grew more conciliatory. When Miranda spoke in that particular tone it was time to retreat.

"Is Lady Heston very *grande dame?*" she asked. "Did Heston tell you anything about her?"

"Only that she is shy and does not go much into company…"

"How odd! I mean, with her position in society and all her wealth, one might suppose…"

"She is an artist…a gifted painter."

"Well, that is something. Better a Bohemian than a fearsome dragon like the Countess Lieven. Did you see the high-nosed way she looked at us at Almack's?"

Miranda gave up. "Do you wish to hear the story of *Ivanhoe* or not?" she snapped.

Fanny subsided. "More than anything," she said meekly.

The candles were guttering in their sockets before Miranda laid aside the book. Then Mrs Shere appeared.

"Not abed yet?" she reproached them. "I saw your light and wondered if aught was amiss."

"We were reading, Aunt. I beg your pardon…we have been wasting the candles."

"As if that mattered, my dear child. Still, it is late, and we shall have a busy day tomorrow. You will need your rest."

She kissed the twins and left them to their slumbers, but it was a long time before Miranda fell asleep. The thought of meeting Lady Heston filled her with dismay, and it was long after midnight when she closed her eyes.

On the following day the household was astir at an early hour. Amid the bustle Miranda sought out her aunt.

"Is there anything we can do to help?" she asked.

"Perhaps the flowers, dearest girl? The cook tells me that we have no milk…I might have expected it. Milk has been so difficult to come by with all these people in the city. As for the linen…it has not yet been returned. Those washerwomen leave our orders to put those of the foreigners first. I will look out some more just in case…" She hurried away.

Miranda decided to leave the flower arrangements until later in the day. They would wilt in the sultry heat.

The day before her stretched out endlessly, and she was glad to accompany Fanny to the library. It would help to pass an hour or two.

Luncheon that day consisted of cold meats and salads and she was glad of it. Her appetite seemed to have deserted her. When it was over, she took Fanny with her and went into a chilly pantry which normally did duty as a flower-room. John had plunged the cut blooms up to their necks in water to keep them fresh.

She and Fanny began upon their task, but even that did not take long. Afterwards the hours seemed to crawl. It was the oddest thing. In Heston's company the time flew by, but without him the hands of the clock refused to move.

"What are we to wear tonight?" Fanny asked. "I suppose we must be very fine."

"Your white gowns with the French bead edges

would be suitable," Mrs Shere suggested. "And perhaps a small wreath of flowers in your hair?"

"I think I'd prefer a ribbon," Miranda answered hastily. The flowers would make her look too much like a bride.

"As you wish, my love. The ribbons should match the blue tiffany sashes, and you will wear your pearls tonight, I hope? You would not have his lordship think that you despised his gift, and yet you have not worn it."

Miranda nodded her assent. There was no way she could refuse. Mild panic seized her as she thought of the woman she was to meet that evening. How many others would be drawn into this deception before it ended? And how she disliked herself for going on with it.

When the twins came down that evening Mrs Shere inspected them with approval. Miranda was wearing her pearls, much against her own inclination. Beautiful though they were, she felt that they must burn her skin and brand her for the trickster which she felt herself to be.

"I have not seen you in better looks, my dears," Mrs Shere said kindly. "Now, tell me what you think of the dining-table…"

They accompanied her into the panelled room. In the soft candlelight, the huge silver epergne which formed the centrepiece glistened with reflections. Beside it stood small pillars holding wreaths of trailing plants.

Miranda caught her breath. "How lovely!" she exclaimed. Then something about the table settings caught her eye. "Aunt, the servants are mistaken. They have laid for eight, and we are only six."

"Did I not tell you? I vow that today my head has been in such a spin that I forgot. I have invited Count Toumanov and also Mr Young. Eight is such a comfortable number for a dinner, and we could not have four ladies and two gentlemen."

Fanny's eyes began to sparkle. "How clever of you, Aunt!"

"Well, you know, my dears, I thought it might take away any little awkwardness which might occur. Lady Heston is well acquainted with the Count, and she will like to have a friend here. As for Mr Young, he is always welcome, and Lord Heston seems to think well of him."

"So he should!" Miranda cried warmly. "Richard need not fear to be in any company."

"Of course not, dearest!" Mrs Shere patted her hand. "You must be calm. To meet one's future mother-in-law is always an ordeal, but she cannot fail to love you as Heston does himself."

There was no time to say more, for at that moment Richard was announced. As he came towards them, Miranda blessed him. Dear Richard, always so calm and pleasant, and so dependable. She gave him her hand.

"How do you go on?" he murmured in an aside. "This cannot be very pleasant for you."

"It is hateful," she replied. "But I have no choice."

"There is always a choice, Miranda, though you may not care to make it…"

"Oh, don't," she cried in desperation. "Please don't! If you only knew…"

She looked up as the rest of the party was announced, allowing Heston to take her nerveless hand in his. Then he led her forward.

"This is my bride, my dear Mama. I hope you will love her as I do."

Miranda sank into a deep curtsy, hardly daring to look up at the woman who stood before her.

When she did so, she was reassured. Lady Heston was very tall, but so thin as to make her son seem larger than ever. There was little resemblance between them, except for the raven darkness of their hair and brows. In place of hard grey eyes, her ladyship's were of a blue so dark as to appear violet. What struck Miranda most was the peculiar sweetness of her expression, combined with a certain reserve.

"I am glad to meet you," Lady Heston murmured in a musical voice. "Adam is so happy, and I must thank you for it."

Miranda shot a fleeting glance at Heston, but he was regarding them with an air of benevolence. She could hope for no help from that quarter. She felt a surge of indignation. How dare he claim to love her when both he and she knew that it was untrue? When it came to deception, she was not the only one who had cause for self-reproach.

She felt even worse when Lady Heston took her hands and kissed her, knowing what it had cost this shy and sensitive woman to make such a gesture of affection.

"Ma'am, you are very kind," she said in a low voice. "Adam tells me that you are an artist, with an interest in flowers and plants. My uncle shares that interest. You might care to see his collection…?"

"Will you show it to me later?"

"It would by my pleasure, Lady Heston, but my uncle is the expert. I have little knowledge, and could not give you the Latin names."

The Alderman had been listening to their conversation. Now he stepped forward with an offer to take her ladyship into the garden.

Miranda sighed with relief. She had no wish to enter into a private conversation with Lady Heston. Her ladyship might appear to be reserved and even diffident, but loving her son as she did her perception would be keen. She must soon discover that all was not as well as it might appear to the less interested observer.

Fanny was deep in conversation with Count Toumanov and Richard was chatting to her aunt. Miranda stood by the long windows watching Lady Heston as the Alderman trotted beside her down the garden path.

"Did I not say that they would deal famously together?"

She turned to find Heston by her side, and frowned at him.

"Now do not look black at me," he reproached. "What have I done to deserve it?"

"You need not have claimed to love me," she replied with strong feeling. "We both know that it is not true."

"You must forgive me," he told her smoothly. "It was but a natural desire to set my mother's heart at rest. She disapproves of arranged marriages, with no serious attachment on either side. I fear she regards them as a certain path to disaster."

"She is quite right," Miranda said hotly.

"Do you think so, my dear? You have surprised me yet again…" He gave her a dangerous smile. "I had not supposed that your affections were engaged. Am I to hope that you are learning to think of me with kindness?"

The colour rose to Miranda's cheeks, and for the moment she was robbed of speech. She turned away from him, throwing a pleading glance at Richard as she did so.

He came to her rescue at once, leading Mrs Shere to join them, with the expressed desire to pay his respects to Lord Heston.

His lordship was all civility, but his lips twitched.

"What should we do without our childhood friends?" he murmured to Miranda. Then, in his usual easy manner, he began to speak of the Prince's recent visit to Oxford.

"The Regent was well received there?" Mrs Shere enquired. "I fear that he is not always treated well in London, and I cannot think it right that the people should behave so ill as to hiss and boo him, when perhaps they do not understand…"

Heston bowed. "The visit was a great success, ma'am. His Royal Highness is popular in that city. In his speech he said all that was gracious."

"It was a great occasion." Alexei brought Fanny over to join them. "Two hundred persons dined at the Radcliffe Camera." His eyes twinkled. "There were lighter moments, Mrs Shere, in spite of all the gold plate. General Blücher enjoyed the wine to such an extent that later he got lost in search of his lodgings."

They all smiled at that.

"And my master insisted upon strolling down the High Street afterwards to see the candles shining a welcome in every window. He may be Tsar of All the Russias, but the spectacle pleased him immensely."

"He is thought to be extremely handsome, is he not?" Fanny's eyes shone. "How I look forward to seeing him tomorrow."

"Where will you be?" Alexei asked eagerly. "I shan't forget to wave to you as we pass."

Heston was explaining the exact position of their vantage point when his mother came up to him. Her arms were filled with flowers, and she was smiling.

"See how spoiled I am," she murmured, "I feel so guilty… Mr Shere has stripped his garden for me."

"Let me take them, your ladyship." Richard

stepped forward and relieved her of her burden. "Should they go into water?"

Mrs Shere signalled to a footman, who bore the blooms away. Then the Alderman returned, and Lady Heston went to him at once.

"I have done more damage than a plague of locusts, my dear sir. I must hope that your garden will recover…"

The Alderman waved her apologies aside. He was glowing with pride. "Happy to have pleased you, ma'am. As I say, some of the roses are cuttings from the Empress Josephine's collection at Malmaison. A friend was good enough to bring them over."

"I have seen them only in paintings by Pierre-Joseph Redouté until today."

"By next year they will be well established. I shall hope that you will come to see them. The Gallicas, in particular, should be very fine…" He was about to launch into a discourse upon his favourite topic when Mrs Shere caught his eye.

"Well, well, I must not be a bore upon this subject," he said cheerfully.

At that moment the gong sounded and they went in to dine.

In spite of her aunt's efforts, Miranda had feared

that the atmosphere at the dining-table must be strained. As she glanced about her, she sensed with some surprise that it was not so.

Seated at the Alderman's right hand, Lady Heston had clearly found a friend. She was chatting to him without the least trace of reserve.

Seated at the other end of the table his wife had Lord Heston by her side, and he at once engaged her in a conversation which touched upon the Prince Regent's courtesy in translating General Blücher's speech in German for the benefit of the General's English audience.

Miranda turned to Richard, who was seated on her right.

His eyes were fixed upon Fanny, who faced him across the table, and was absorbed in listening to the Count.

"Take heart!" she murmured inaudibly. "She is quite recovered from her previous infatuation."

"And in the way to falling into another one?" His face was sad. "How can I compete? I can't appear in a splendid uniform, or tell of my adventures. There isn't much adventure to be found in Yorkshire."

"The Tsar and his entourage will leave next week," Miranda told him. "You have heard of the old saying that out of sight is out of mind?"

Richard brightened visibly. Then his face fell.

"There will be someone else, with more to offer than I."

"Stuff! You shall not think so poorly of yourself."

She might have gone on, but the conversation became more general. Peace with France was to be proclaimed on the twentieth of June, and later that week the Fleet was to be reviewed at Portsmouth.

"Shall you go there, my lord?" The Alderman addressed himself to Heston. "It will be a fine sight."

"I believe so, sir. I'm not yet sure if I shall accompany the Prince, but Alexei will go, of course." He glanced across at his friend with a slight smile in his eyes. "It won't be a favourite occasion for him. He is the worst of sailors."

"You are right!" the Count shuddered. "Give me a horse beneath me rather than a rolling deck. The motion of the sea is the worst sensation in the world. Shall you go to Portsmouth, sir?"

The Alderman shook his head and laughed. "We shall content ourselves with the mock battle on the Serpentine in August."

"Very wise, if I may say so. Is it not to be a recreation of the Battle of Trafalgar?"

Fanny clapped her hands. "Oh yes, and it is to be exact, down to the cannon and the rammings, and the smoke. Someone told me that the crews are to be dwarfs, to make the ships seem larger."

"The Regent does nothing by halves, ma'am." Heston turned to Mrs Shere. "He intends that the celebration of the first centenary of the House of Hanover shall be an unforgettable spectacle."

"I cannot blame him," Mrs Shere replied. "It will be a grand occasion, and the more so because we shall have our feet on dry land. I share your dislike of the motion of the sea, Count Toumanov. I cannot be easy even in harbour."

"Dry land is much to be preferred," Alexei agreed. "Alas, I shall not see the battle. We return to Russia after the Fleet Review."

Fanny's face fell. "Oh, no!" she began. Then a sharp look from Miranda silenced her. Her sister's obvious disappointment went beyond the bounds of propriety.

"You do not stay on?" she asked. "We shall all be sorry to lose you."

"It is not for another two weeks or so. Meantime, there is much to see and do. I have not yet visited the Temple of Concord, or the Chinese Pagoda…"

A general discussion of these wonders relieved Miranda of the need to speak overmuch herself. She had eaten little of the splendid meal, although the Alderman's cook had lived up to his reputation.

White almond soup with asparagus had been followed by a fine turbot with a side dish of fish quenelles in bouillon, and another of tiny vols-au-vent filled with shrimps, as well as a salver of whiting.

There was something for every taste, from salmis of duckling in wine and epigrammes of chicken to ham braised in Madeira and a baron of beef.

Miranda looked about her. Her own lack of appetite had gone unnoticed due to the Alderman's concern that Lady Heston should eat more. Smiling, that lady shook her head.

"I seldom dine on more than a single course," she protested. "But I must compliment you upon your chef. Everything is so delicious. It will put our own man upon his mettle, I assure you."

Heston was quick to agree with her. He, at least, had done full justice to the meal, as had Alexei and the Alderman himself.

Heston looked at Miranda's plate. "Have you been influenced by George Byron?" he teased in a low voice.

"I don't understand you, sir."

"It is one of his little foibles. He dislikes to see women eat, preferring to think of them as ethereal creatures."

"What nonsense!" she cried warmly. It was enough to persuade her into accepting a serving of summer fruits in jelly.

"You are not an admirer of the noble lord," he asked carelessly. "I thought I saw a book of his upon your table the other day."

"That belongs to Fa—to my sister. Lord Lakenham gave it to her." Miranda could not look at her companion. Once again she had come so close to giving herself away.

Apparently he had not noticed the slip. "Lakenham gave her a book?" He looked incredulous.

"It was a peace-offering," she explained hastily. "He was sorry to have caused her to faint at the Balloon Ascent."

"Very civil of him," Heston said smoothly. "If he continues in his present ways, he will be forced to buy up half the books on sale in London. Don't you agree?"

"I have no idea. We have not seen him, sir." It was a curt reply and she flushed. She had warned Fanny to be civil to their guests, and now she herself was guilty of rudeness.

Heston waved aside the cheeseboard and changed the subject. "We shall not stay late this evening. Tomorrow we must make an early start if we are to get through the crowds before the procession begins."

She nodded as Mrs Shere broke in with a question about the arrangements for the following day.

Miranda turned to Richard.

"I believe I shall go back to Yorkshire after the Parade," he said. He looked so disconsolate that her heart was wrung with pity.

"Pray don't leave just yet," she begged. "Your father will spare you for another week or two…"

"But will it do any good?" he sighed. "Fanny does not look at me."

Miranda frowned a warning at him. Heston had sharp ears. If he heard Fanny's name on Richard's lips, all would be lost.

"Give her time!" she insisted. "You heard the Count. In two weeks' time he will be gone, and that will be your opportunity."

"I hope you may be right." His face cleared a little. "I'll stay if you feel that I have the slightest chance of winning her."

"Of course you have," she encouraged. "Would that I could discover a monster for you to slay…"

She smiled at that, though he looked rueful. "I know you think her foolish, but I love her so. I would care for her, you know, and she would have all she could desire. Once away from London, she will be different."

"I agree," she told him quietly. "Perhaps it was not the best idea for us to come here. Mama was delighted and Uncle believed that it would be an opportunity for us but things have gone so sadly wrong."

Richard pressed her hand. "Are you quite sure of that?" he asked.

"I'm afraid so. I can see no way out of our difficulties that will not hurt the people I love best."

His face was grave, but he pressed her hand again. "I believe you to be mistaken, and that all will yet be well for you."

She was about to deny his words when Mrs Shere rose from the table and the ladies withdrew to the salon.

"Do you like music, your ladyship? Both our girls play so well upon the spinet..."

Miranda threw her aunt a glance of gratitude. She had been wondering what on earth she was to say to Lady Heston if they should find themselves tête-à-tête.

A pleasant smile of encouragement sent her to

the instrument, with a gloomy-looking Fanny beside her.

On the pretext of searching through the music, she managed to have a private word with Fanny.

"For heaven's sake, smile!" she urged. "Would you have everyone notice that you dislike the thought of Count Toumanov going away? They may imagine that you have a *tendre* for him."

"London will be so dull without him," Fanny sighed.

"Then we had best go back to Yorkshire."

This dire prospect startled Fanny. "You cannot mean it! How can you say such a thing? You cannot leave Heston, can you?"

"No, I can't, and well you know it. Now turn the music, and try to look as if you are enjoying it."

Subdued, Fanny did as she was bidden and Miranda began to play a favourite piece. As always, she found the music soothing, and it as not until she reached the final bars that she was aware of being watched. She looked up quickly to find Lady Heston's eyes upon her. In their depths she saw a question, or was it her imagination?

Their aunt beckoned to the twins. "Come and sit down with us," she said. "My dear, we have been discussing a date for your marriage."

Miranda froze. Why had she supposed that matters could not possibly grow any worse? She stared from one face to the other, but it was Fanny who broke the silence.

"Must it be just yet?" she asked in a hollow voice. "There is so much to be done, and Mama will wish to make arrangements to come to London…"

"Naughty girl! You must not put difficulties in your sister's way, my dear child." Mrs Shere turned to her ladyship. "You must forgive my niece, ma'am. The twins are so close that they dislike the thought of separation, one from the other."

"That is perfectly natural," her ladyship agreed quietly. Her thoughtful gaze rested upon Miranda's face. "There is a special bond between twins, so I understand, and you are identical, are you not?"

"Yes, your ladyship." Miranda sat down suddenly, clenching her hands as she waited for the next blow to fall. It came soon enough.

"We have decided upon the first week in September, if Lord Heston agrees. That will give us more than two full months to make our preparations, and allow plenty of time for your mama to come down for the ceremony."

Fanny dared not argue further, and Miranda could think of nothing to say. To protest would be unthinkable. How could she disgrace her aunt and uncle by announcing her decision to end her betrothal at this moment?

She prayed that something would happen… anything to extricate her from her present predicament.

Her prayers were answered briefly when the door opened and the gentlemen came to join them.

Mrs Shere rang for the tea-tray.

"Your ladyship, if you will be kind enough to ask Lord Heston for his views?"

"Upon what, ma'am?"

"We have been speaking of your marriage," his mother told him. "We thought perhaps the first week in September? Is that agreeable to you?"

"Much too far away!" He grinned at her. "But if it suits my bride, then her wish is my command."

He sat down beside Miranda and took her hand. "What do you say, my dear?"

She knew then that she must end this hoax without delay, but this was neither the time nor the place. She kept her eyes fixed firmly upon the carpet.

"It shall be as you wish," she said.

Chapter Twelve

As Heston had promised, the company did not stay late, but Miranda was only half-aware of their leaving.

She felt that she was drowning in deep water, and reality no longer had a meaning for her. She was drifting as though through a dream from which she must awaken. Even her own voice sounded strange to her.

Fanny and Richard watched her with concern. They alone knew how she was suffering. They stood together in one corner of the room, and Fanny's lips were trembling.

When they were alone that night, she flung herself upon the bed and wept as if her heart must break.

"Don't cry!" Miranda told her quietly. "It can serve no purpose."

"But what will you do?" her sister wailed. "I did not think it would come to this…"

"What did you expect? When one is betrothed, marriage must follow."

"But you are not betrothed!"

"Sadly, I am, and everyone knows it." Miranda felt like an automaton. She was moving about the room, taking off her gown and her undergarments and even the ribbon in her hair, but she was not aware of it.

"But you can't marry Heston…you can't."

"No, I can't. I won't cheat him to that extent." Something in her voice made Fanny look at her, and then she began to weep afresh.

"You love him, don't you?"

"Yes I do. I had not intended it, but there it is."

"Then, dearest, you must wish to marry him. If you love him, would it not be possible…to go ahead with it, I mean?"

Miranda's smile was a ghastly travesty. "You think I should deceive him further? Sometimes I wonder what you must *think* of me. I won't do it, Fanny. Tomorrow I shall tell him everything."

Fanny paled to her lips. "Oh, please, you can't! He will blame me, I know it. If you must cry off, why not start a quarrel? That would give you the excuse…and then no one would need to know—"

"Your part in this hoax, or mine? I might take your advice if I thought that it would serve, but it won't."

"Why not?"

"You don't know Heston as I do. He would see through it in a moment. Sometimes I think that he suspects already."

"How could he?"

"I don't know. It is the things he says and the way he looks…"

"If he loves you, he will not care, and he must do so or he would have taxed you with it."

"If he loves me?" There was no amusement in Miranda's laugh. "Fanny, you know what Heston thinks of me. He has made his opinion only too clear."

"Then I think it wrong of him to pretend to love you, especially to his mama. He is guilty of deceit, as much as any of us."

"It really doesn't matter as to who is most to blame. The point is that I must put an end to it. We can't go on like this and I shall tell him so in the morning."

"Oh, please, you can't! Not tomorrow, I beg of you…everyone will be there to see the Procession and I could not face them all. We shall be disgraced and sent back home at once."

"It can't be helped."

"Yes, it can! I think you are being very selfish, Miranda. I do not care to be sent away from London. Alexei has only a few more days with us, and you might think of me instead of yourself."

This remark caused Miranda to gaze at her sister in stupefaction. Words failed her for the moment.

"Besides, you will think of something…some other way to free yourself," her sister announced. "You spoke of telling Heston that you had mistaken your heart. Would that not be better than to shame us? You must consider Aunt and Uncle."

Miranda was silent.

"Won't you wait a little while?" Fanny coaxed. "It is not as if you were to be wed next week. September is a full two months away… In the meantime, anything might happen."

She looked a little conscious as she spoke and Miranda's heart sank. Surely Fanny did not expect an offer from Count Toumanov? It stiffened her resolve to put an end to the hoax without delay, but there was much to consider in her sister's pleas.

She grew thoughtful. A scandal must be avoided if possible. She had been badly shaken to hear that a date was to be set for her wedding, but as her composure returned she knew that it was panic which had overwhelmed her. Her plan to confess everything to Heston had been born of desperation and a feeling of being trapped.

"There may be another way," she admitted with reluctance. "I can but try…a quarrel might serve."

On the following day she was given no opportunity to carry out her scheme. The household was astir at an early hour, but the Strand was already crowded as the Alderman's coach bore them towards the building which was their destination. Their progress was slow, but they arrived at the appointed hour.

Heston had used his influence to reserve a series of rooms with long windows which would give them a splendid view of the Procession. Nothing had been neglected for their comfort, from easy chairs to tables laid for a late breakfast.

His mother was already seated by a window, sketching the scene before her and Heston was chatting to Richard Young.

He turned as they entered and came towards them with a smile.

"We shall have some hours to wait," he said. "Will you take some refreshment?"

He was the perfect host, apparently casual, but

Miranda noticed that his eyes missed nothing which might add to their pleasure in the occasion.

How could she possibly quarrel with him? Miranda thought in despair. He neither did nor said anything which she could take amiss. In any case, this was not the occasion upon which to carry out her plan. She gave up all thought of it for the time being and began to enjoy herself.

Whatever the future held, she would forget her troubles for this one day. It might be the last occasion upon which this man whom she loved so much would look at her, if not with love, certainly with admiration in his eyes.

That she could not mistake. When their meal was over, he came to her and took her hand.

"Unfair, my love!" he murmured softly. "How can you tease me so?"

"My lord, you speak in riddles. I do not understand."

"Don't you, my dearest? Can it be possible that you do not know how delicious you look today? It is a severe test of my self-control. I want to take you in my arms and kiss you here and now."

"Please, my lord…someone will hear you." The colour rose to Miranda's cheeks, but she was glad that she had chosen to wear her new walking-dress of French cambric, with a charming Oldenburg hat. She was not immune to flattery, although it was mortifying to be forced to admit it.

"Now I have made you blush," he teased. "Will you always do so?"

Miranda's face grew warm. She did not pretend to misunderstand his meaning.

"Sir, I beg that you will not continue with this conversation. Do you wish to provoke me into quarreling with you?"

He laughed and patted her hand. "No, I won't do that. Did you think to escape me with a quarrel?"

With these thought-provoking words, he moved away to speak to Mrs Shere.

Miranda stayed where she was, frozen into immobility. It was as she had feared. Heston seemed always to be able to read her mind.

"You are very quiet." Richard slipped into the seat beside her. "I can't say that I blame you."

"No, it is all getting out of hand, and I don't know how to put and end—"

"Do you wish to?"

Miranda looked up in surprise. "You know that I must. I am so ashamed of all the lies and the deceit."

"That's understandable, but Fanny tells me—"

"Fanny should not gossip," she cried in anger.

"She did not tell me anything that I did not already know," he told her gently.

"Oh, Richard, is it so obvious that I love him?"

"It is to me, but then I've known you since you were a child. What of Lord Heston?"

"He wishes only to punish me. I tricked him into this betrothal, in a way."

"I doubt if there is a soul alive who could trick him into anything." Richard looked at her with smiling eyes. "You misjudge him, my dear."

"I don't think so. What other reason could he have?"

Richard laughed aloud. "Neither you nor your sister could claim the prize as the ugliest women in London," he chaffed.

"There are others with more beauty."

"But none with the same spirit as your own. Oh, I'll admit that you might have angered him at first, but has it not occurred to you that he might have changed his mind?"

"I wish it might be so," she faltered. "But I cannot believe it."

"Then you must be blind. Do you think him a man of honour?"

She looked at him dumbly. Then she nodded.

"So do I. It would be beneath him to seek to

harm you." Richard spoke with conviction. "Don't do anything foolish, I beg of you. In time all will be well."

"What are you trying to say?"

"If you will have it straight, I believe Lord Heston loves you."

For the first time a little flame of hope burned in Miranda's heart. Then she shook her head.

"That isn't possible, but even if it were true it cannot help me. How could I accept that love knowing all that I do? No marriage can be built upon a lie."

"It might be built upon love, as I hope my own will be... Do you hear the cheering? The Procession must be close."

He led her over to the window and settled her in a chair as the clatter of horses sounded in the distance.

The Procession was a tribute to the Prince Regent's love of splendour. First came a company of the Eleventh Light Dragoons in their uniforms of blue and buff, and they were followed by a number of carriages bearing the officers of the Prince's household. Then came those of the foreign generals, and the state carriages of the Regent's brothers, all of them Royal Dukes.

It was all a feast for the eye, and the number of

dignitaries seemed endless. All the members of the Cabinet were there, together with the Speaker, in splendid isolation in his own coach. Then came a troop of Horse Guards, their accoutrements glittering in the sunlight as they preceded the Royal officers of state and certain of the foreign suites.

The Regent himself looked sullen, and even the presence of his popular allies did not prevent the crowd from booing and making cat-calls as his eight cream horses drew the State Coach past.

"Shame on them!" Mrs Shere cried indignantly. "Today, at least, they might have honoured him."

"He does not look as if he is enjoying himself," Fanny murmured. "It must be galling to hear the cheering for the others. But, Aunt, he is enormous, positively gross, in fact. What a disappointment!"

"Fanny, remember where you are!" Miranda hissed. "I hope that Lord Heston did not hear you."

Fanny was not attending, for at that moment the Tsar's procession came into view.

"At last!" she cried in high excitement. "Here come the Russians and the Tsar himself." She clasped her hands in rapture. "He is everything I had expected...tall and slim...and so handsome. Some may think him dandified, but I do not agree..."

A murmur of amusement went around the room, but Fanny did not notice.

"Where is Count Toumanov? I do not see him, and he promised to ride upon this side." She leaned out of the window, peering anxiously at the cavaliers below.

"Dearest, do take care," Mrs Shere pleaded. "You must not risk a fall."

Fanny was oblivious of the danger. She leaned out even further. "There he is!" She began to wave her handkerchief and was rewarded when Alexei looked up briefly and grinned at her. "Does he not look splendid, and see how well he controls his horse?"

"Yes, yes, my love. Now do pray close the window, or her ladyship may take a chill."

It was unlikely on that pleasant summer day, but Fanny obeyed her, unconscious of the fact that her conduct had gone beyond the bounds of propriety.

"How I should like to have attended the banquet!" she cried. "I wonder that Uncle could not have obtained an invitation for us."

"He will tell us all about it later!" Miranda was aware of her aunt's dismayed expression. Fanny's present behaviour was the outside of enough. She shuddered to imagine what Lady Heston must think of such a lack of restraint.

Apparently her ladyship had not noticed. She was preoccupied with her sketching and seemed lost to all else.

Heston touched her lightly on the shoulder. "Do you care to stay here for a while?" he asked. "I shall not be long, but I must see the ladies home."

Richard offered at once to perform that office for him, but Heston shook his head.

"Then I shall bear her ladyship company, if she will permit," Richard said shyly.

"How very kind of you!" Lady Heston had taken a liking to this quiet young man who seemed so diffident. "Then I shall not mind how long Adam is away. Now tell me, Mr Young, do you feel that I have captured something of the atmosphere today?" She held out her sketchpad to him, and came over to Mrs Shere.

"Will you come to Brook Street with your nieces whilst Adam is in Portsmouth?" she asked. "We must learn to know each other better, but first I hope that you will bring the Alderman to dine. Shall we say three days from now?"

Mrs Shere thanked her, and the ladies took their leave. Fanny continued to chatter brightly on the journey back to Bloomsbury, but when Heston had left them her aunt took her to task.

"It grieves me to say so, but I was ashamed of you today, my dear. How could you behave so ill? That hoydenish way you leaned out of the window, and called to Count Toumanov? I could not believe my ears."

Fanny looked startled and dismayed. "I did not think—"

"Then it is high time that you began to do so. How could you disgrace your sister in that way? What your mama would have said I can't imagine."

"Pray don't be cross with me." Fanny's eyes filled. "I was so excited…"

"Well, it will not do. I cannot help but notice that you are either in high alt, or down in the cellars, my dear girl. Such nervous excitement is not good for you. I wonder if I should write to your mama?"

"Please don't!" Fanny began to cry in earnest. "I didn't mean to be so bad, and I will try to be better."

As always, the sight of tears had their usual effect upon Mrs Shere's tender heart. She laid a comforting hand on Fanny's arm.

"It is the thought of your sister's marriage which has disturbed you so, I think. But you will grow used to the idea, believe me. Now dry your eyes, my dear one. Lady Heston did not seem to notice your behaviour and for that we must be thankful.

Dear me, I must confess that I find her somewhat odd. To be drawing at such a time is most unusual."

"She has been so kind," Miranda ventured.

"To be sure she has. You are fortunate in your mother-in-law, my love. I doubt if she will take the trouble to interfere in anything you may wish to do."

Miranda forced a smile. "She is devoted to her son, my dear ma'am. His wishes will come first with her."

"But of course. With his father dead, he is the head of the household, and so capable. Dear Lord Heston! How very lucky you are, my dear."

Miranda had reservations upon that point. Luck was the last word she would have used to describe her present situation, but she murmured a feeble assent.

When their aunt had left them, Fanny rounded upon her.

"You might have supported me," she complained in an injured tone. "Aunt Emma was so cross and you did not say a word in my defence."

"If she had not done so, I was about to speak to you myself," Miranda told her grimly. "Aunt was right…you embarrassed both of us."

"Oh, you are grown as high in the instep as Heston himself… I do not know you any more. Are we to sit like statues, unsmiling, and without a word to say? That may be your idea of fun, but it is not mine."

"No one asks that of you, but can't you see how you expose yourself to gossip?"

"As if I cared!" Fanny tossed her head. "Since you have known Heston you are changed. You were used to be light-hearted. Now all you care about is the proprieties—"

"That isn't true! But we aren't children any more. What passed for high spirits long ago in Yorkshire is not acceptable in Polite Society, and you know how tongues can wag." Miranda sighed. "Sometimes I think that members of the *ton* have nothing else to do."

"I have done no harm," Fanny sulked. "Lady Heston did not notice, and his lordship does not know that I exist."

"Don't be too sure of that!" Miranda warned. She knew that it was not so. Nothing that her sister did or said escaped Heston's notice. That penetrating gaze rested frequently upon her twin and she had seen speculation in his eyes. His apparently casual manner hid a mind that was razor-sharp, and it never ceased to worry her.

Fanny bridled. "What has he been saying to you?" she demanded. "He need not think to criticise me, for I will not have it. It seems I can do nothing right. You are all against me, except for

Richard. He is the only one who does not say a word except in kindness."

"Richard is very fond of you." It was an incautious statement in view of the fact that Miranda had promised not to reveal his true feelings for her sister, but Fanny was unmoved.

"I know that. He is fond of both of us. When we were small I was used to wish that he were my brother, instead of Jonathan and William. He did not torment us as they liked to do."

"He is the best of creatures," Miranda said warmly. "It is a pity…" She stopped in confusion. She had been on the verge of saying too much, but Fanny was not attending.

"I think I have behaved quite well," she announced. "I did not make the least fuss because Alexei cannot visit us this evening."

"How could he possibly do so? The celebrations will go on until the early hours, and he is in attendance upon the Tsar. He did not come to London just for pleasure, as you know."

"Well, I think it most unreasonable of his master to keep him at his duties for so long."

"How fortunate that we are not in Russia! You would probably be beaten with a knout for that remark."

"You may make a joke of it, but he did promise…at least, he suggested a party after the Procession on the night we met, if you recall."

"It was only a suggestion. There was nothing definite settled, and his duties must come first."

"I suppose so. Oh dear, how dull we are this evening!"

"Well, I, for one, have had enough excitement for one day. We made such an early start this morning, then all the crowds, and the Procession. After supper I shall seek my bed."

This suggestion met with approval from her aunt. Mrs Shere's eyes searched Miranda's face, then she nodded to herself with a strange little smile of satisfaction.

"What is it, Aunt Emma? You are looking positively conspiratorial. Have you some secret plans for us?" Fanny could not hide her curiosity.

"I have a surprise, but you are not to know of it until tomorrow."

Not all Fanny's wheedling could persuade her to reveal her secret before the twins retired.

Fanny returned to the subject at breakfast on the following morning.

"Now do pray tell us, Aunt," she coaxed prettily.

"I vow I have not closed my eyes all night for wondering."

"What a story! When I looked in upon you, you were sound asleep!" Mrs Shere glanced from one twin to the other. "Very well, then. We are to go for a drive, but I shall not tell you our destination."

"How exciting! I love a mystery!" Fanny clapped her hands. "What are we to wear? Must we be very fine?"

"We may be out for quite some time, so perhaps your Sardinian blue pelisses with the matching bonnets, and an extra shawl for warmth. And your parasols against the sun?"

Miranda chuckled. "I see that this is to be a serious expedition, ma'am, if we are to go from one extreme of temperature to another."

"There is no harm in being prepared against the weather," her aunt reproved. "It may be high summer, but in this climate one can never tell… The morning is fine, but before the day is out we may have rain, or even blazing sunshine."

"Are we to be out all day?" Fanny's face clouded, and Miranda threw her a warning look.

Fanny must not raise objections to the outing, however much she hoped that the Count would call. Aunt Emma may have believed that Fanny's behaviour on the previous day was just high spirits, but she would not be deceived for long.

And only Fanny could believe that Alexei would offer for her. To be seen to throw herself at the young man's head would bring down Mrs Shere's severest disapproval upon her. It would be the last straw as far as their aunt was concerned. She would write at once to their mama.

And much good that would do her, Miranda thought ruefully. However unlikely the chance of such a thing occurring, her mother would be in raptures as the thought of having a Countess in the family.

Her frown quelled Fanny's objections for the moment, although she heard a few mutterings of rebellion as they tied the ribbons of their bonnets.

"I can't think why we must be out all day," Fanny complained. "I believe it will be too tiring, but I suppose we may come home if I am not feeling well."

"To make an instant recovery if Count Toumanov should happen to call? You will do no such thing! Aunt has arranged this outing for our pleasure, and you will do nothing to spoil it."

"You always think the worst of me," Fanny complained in an injured tone. "You are becoming such a crosspatch."

Miranda was tempted to inform Fanny that her behaviour would try the patience of a saint. Instead she turned the conversation to their new bonnets.

"I like these curled plumes, don't you?" she said. "I wonder how they managed to dye these feathers to the exact shade of blue?"

Fanny looked at her reflection in the glass and gave a nod of satisfaction.

"They are pretty," she agreed. "Though I wonder if we should not wear the new small hats instead?"

"Aunt Emma suggested bonnets." Miranda began to laugh. "They are more likely to protect our faces from either snow or blazing sunshine."

Fanny picked up her shawl. "I wonder where we are to go? I thought we had visited almost everywhere of interest. Pray heaven it is not to be another outing to the Museum!"

"I doubt it. I did not see any parasols unfurled in there, nor gentlemen in fur hats."

They went downstairs together to find Richard waiting for them in the salon.

"Oh, is it you?" Fanny murmured. "We are to go out today, you know."

"And I am to accompany you. Mrs Shere arranged it with me yesterday…"

That was not the full extent of Mrs Shere's arrangements. The next arrival was Lord Heston, attired in a riding coat, buckskin breeches, and gleaming Hessians. He took Miranda's hand.

"Beautiful as always!" he murmured. "You are ready, my dear?"

"Why, yes! I did not know that you were to come with us, sir."

"With *you*," he corrected. "Shall we go? I do not care to keep my horses standing."

"But my aunt intends to travel in the family coach…" Miranda looked across at Mrs Shere for confirmation, and was surprised to see a conspiratorial smile again.

Still chuckling, her aunt proceeded towards her own coach and stepped inside. She was followed by Fanny and then by Richard, and the carriage set off along the cobbled street.

"I hope you know our destination, my lord, for I do not." Miranda allowed herself to be handed up into Heston's racing curricle. She was somewhat mystified by these curious travelling arrangements. There was room and to spare for both herself and her companion in the coach. Perhaps Heston preferred to drive himself upon this strange expedition.

"I know my own, and yours." Heston's expression was enigmatic and suddenly she felt sudden panic. Her aunt's coach had turned to the left at the far end of the street, but his lordship guided his team to the right.

"What are you about?" she cried. "Surely we should follow them?"

"Why should we do that? They are not going in our direction."

"You will please to stop at once. How dare you trick me in this way? I did not agree to spend the day with you…my aunt will be distraught."

"I doubt it, dearest one. She knows of my intention."

"And what is that, my lord?"

"Why, I have kidnapped you! Sadly, only for the day, but I believe that we should make the most of it."

"And you arranged this with my aunt? How could she agree to such a plan? I can't believe it!"

"But you must. She thinks you too much in your sister's company, and so do I. It is a strain on both of you."

Miranda's fury knew no bounds. "My relations with my family are none of your concern," she cried. "You dislike Fa—my twin. You have made that clear, but you do not understand, and nor does my aunt."

"I think we do," he told her calmly. "I have no wish to come between you and your sister—"

"You could not!" she burst out.

"That may be so, but confess it. Shall you not enjoy a drive to Richmond? It is peaceful there, away from the noise of the city. Both your aunt and my mother thought you in need of rest."

Miranda was about to fly at him. Then she recalled her ladyship's sweet smile. That gentle person must have seen her inner torment. She had been about to inform Heston of her strong dislike of being discussed in her absence, but she checked the angry words.

"That was kind of her. I had not thought—"

"That you were looking 'hagged'? That is your own expression, I believe? No, my love, you could not look other than ravishing, but there is an expression in your eyes. Sometimes, I have thought…" He left it there, and Miranda did not answer him.

No purpose could be served by either admitting or denying his words. She leaned back against the cushions as he took the road to the west.

Chapter Thirteen

For a time he drove in silence, a fact for which Miranda was profoundly thankful. She had no wish to return to the topic of Fanny and herself, and to comment upon the weather or the charm of the countryside through which they passed held no appeal for her. It was the type of trivial conversation which Heston would find trying, though why she should care for that was puzzling.

She smiled to herself. On occasion she had noticed how his eyes would glaze with boredom when faced with a gabblemonger. At least he could not accuse her of that.

She was intensely aware of his strong hands on the reins as he sprang his team of matching chestnuts. He seemed at one with the splendid animals, never pushing them too hard, or dragging at their tender mouths, yet allowing them to cover the miles to Richmond at a spanking pace.

It was always a pleasure to watch an expert, she admitted to herself, and he was right. To escape from the city with its crowds and its fearful stench was exactly what she most needed on a day like this.

"My compliments, ma'am! You are no chatter-box!" He drew the curricle to a halt at a small inn. A groom materialised as if from nowhere, and Heston threw him the reins.

"Glad to see your lordship! It's been some time!"

"Too long, Ben! How do you like my cattle?"

The groom ran an appraising eye over the team.

"You ain't lost your eye for bloodstock, sir, and that's a fact," he grinned. "Shall I stable them?"

"Just for a few hours, if you please." Heston took Miranda's arm and led her into the inn.

There he was greeted with evident pleasure by the landlord.

"Ah, Flodden, there you are. You kept your private parlour for us?"

"As if you need to ask, my lord!" The man bowed low, but there was no trace of servility in his manner. As he straightened Miranda was aware that she was the object of scrutiny from a pair of sharp blue eyes.

"My dear, this is Flodden. He is an old friend of

mine." Heston clapped their host upon the shoulder. "Now, you old rascal, where is Annie? I must make her known to Miss Gaysford, who is to be my bride."

Flodden was clearly startled by this news, but he made a quick recover, leading them through into an inner room where the table was already laid for two.

"You will take a glass of wine, my lord, to clear the dust?"

"Champagne, I think. The occasion calls for it…"

As Flodden limped away Miranda saw that he was badly crippled. One leg was bent at an awkward angle, and his left arm was almost useless. His short stature and slight build, as well as something in his walk, made her suspect that he had been a jockey.

When he returned he was accompanied by a buxom woman who was twice his size. The contrast between them was incongruous, but there was a certain dignity in Mrs Flodden's bearing that commanded respect rather than amusement.

She flushed with pleasure as Heston rose to greet her.

"Well, Annie, how do you go on? Still ruling the roost with an iron hand?"

Mrs Flodden smiled at this sally, but she shook her head in reproach. Then she made her curtsy to Miranda.

"Now, tell me, how is Mary? No further setbacks, I hope?"

"Not since your lordship sent the physician down from London. She hopes to see you, sir, to thank you herself."

Although Miranda had never succeeded in putting Heston out of countenance, the older woman's words clearly embarrassed him.

"I'll come at once," he said quickly. "Perhaps Miss Gaysford will like to remove her coat and bonnet."

Miranda's curiosity was aroused. She followed the landlord's wife to an upper room where she found all in readiness for her to wash away the dust of travel.

"Have you known Lord Heston long?" she asked.

"For many years, ma'am, and what we should have done without him I don't know."

Miranda looked up, a question in her eyes, but Mrs Flodden would not go on.

"Ma'am, we are forbidden to speak of it. You saw how Lord Heston looked when I tried to thank him for his goodness. I fear that I disobeyed his wishes…" She handed a towel to Miranda. "Will you excuse me?"

She hurried back to her kitchen, clearly preoccupied with thoughts of the meal already in preparation.

Miranda made her way downstairs. Her untouched glass of champagne stood upon a side table, the bubbles still rising to the surface. She took a sip or two, realising suddenly that she was both thirsty and hungry.

Now that she was alone she had leisure to look about her. The place was spotless in the brilliant sunshine which flooded through the windows. Horse brasses on the walls gave back reflections, as did the lovingly polished oak of a fine dresser.

She was examining a drawing of a horse race, flanked by a number of rosettes, when Heston returned.

"Was Flodden a jockey?" she asked. The connection of the oddly assorted couple with Heston had intrigued her.

"Yes." This short reply was not an invitation for further questioning, but Miranda persisted.

"What happened? Why is he…?"

"A cripple? There was an accident. He was riding a young horse in its first race. Something startled the creature…perhaps the shouting of the crowd…and it ran into the rails."

"And he was crushed?"

"No, he was thrown over the rail and into a heavy post on the other side. It was not thought that he would live."

"My lord, I know that you do not care to speak of it, but why you? Why did you help them? I could not help but notice their gratitude."

"Inquisitive!" He tugged at a straying curl. "It was my horse, you see. Flodden had ridden for me for years."

"And you set them up here?"

"What else could I do? His livelihood was gone, and the child was sick."

Miranda was silent. Many owners would not have spared another thought for the injured man since he could be of no further use to them. Compassion was not a virtue which she had noticed much among the *ton*.

"And Mary?" she ventured.

"Their daughter is much improved since she came to live in Richmond. I have promised that she shall meet you later, if you do not object?"

"Of course not. I should like to meet her." She eyed Heston with new respect. Perhaps it was not so strange that she should be in love with him. Behind that hard exterior lay a warm heart. If only some of that warmth might flow in her direction.

She had emptied her glass without thinking, and he refilled it for her.

"Hungry?" he asked.

"I'm starving!" Miranda smiled up at him. "It must be the drive and the country air."

"I'm glad to hear it. Annie is a fine cook. She will be disappointed if we don't do justice to her efforts."

He spoke no more than the truth, and for the first time in weeks Miranda ate with a hearty appetite. She had expected the usual country fare of ham and beef and heavy meat puddings, and was surprised to be served with a feather-light omelette, followed by small strips of chicken breast in a tangy sauce. The salads were so fresh that they could only have come from the Floddens' garden that very morning.

She was lavish with her praise when Mrs Flodden appeared.

"I did not wish to overface you, miss. The day is so warm, but if his lordship is still hungry there is a saddle of mutton…"

Heston shook his head and laughed. "Annie, you would have me as fat as a flawn. I doubt if I could eat another mouthful." There was a wicked twinkle in his eyes.

"Not my fruit pie? Oh, sir, I made it specially, knowing how you like it, and the apples are our own, stored from last year."

"Well, if I must…" he said with mock reluctance. Miranda was undeceived.

"Lord Heston is joking, Mrs Flodden," she announced. "He tells me that your pies are famous. You should punish him by refusing to let him taste them."

"Oh, ma'am. I couldn't do that!" Mrs Flodden was shocked. "I'll fetch the pitcher of cream."

She stood over him anxiously, waiting for his verdict.

"Delicious! Annie, you haven't lost your touch. I believe I might manage another morsel." In the end he consumed a full half of the pie, much to the satisfaction of his hostess.

"You have led me astray once more," he told her with a grin. "Now I must walk for at least three hours or I shall fall asleep."

"Oh, sir, you can't be meaning to keep the young lady out for all that time in the heat?"

"If she falls by the wayside, I shall sweep her into my arms and bring her back to you, I promise." He saw her worried frown. "Don't worry, Annie. We shall keep to the shade of the trees down by the river. I think Miss Gaysford will enjoy a stroll."

Miranda was quick to assent. There was something about this quiet place which had done much to restore her peace of mind, and she felt at ease with these good people.

Heston took her arm and led her through the

inn and down through the kitchen garden to a wicket gate. Beyond it a narrow path ran down towards the river.

He drew her arm through his and they strolled along in a companionable silence.

"Still cross with me because I brought you here?" he asked suddenly.

"No, I have enjoyed it very much. You were right. It is good to get away from the city."

"And your worries?"

Miranda did not answer him. How could she explain that the main cause of her apprehension was standing by her side.

She pointed to the swans. "May we not take a closer look at them? They have some cygnets."

"Feed them if you wish. Annie sent me out prepared." He produced a bag of broken bread from his coat pocket, and handed it to her. "Not too close though. They can be dangerous at this time of year."

Obediently she stood well back from the river bank and threw the bread into the water. It attracted the swans at once and they came towards her, their long, snake-like heads striking out towards the floating food. When it was gone they lost interest and swam away.

She turned to find that Heston was seated on the

trunk of a fallen tree, regarding her intently. He patted the seat beside him.

"Come here," he said gently. "I want to talk to you."

She wanted to refuse, but somehow she could not. She hesitated, knowing that it was folly to be alone with him like this.

"I shall not eat you, my dear love, but if you will not come to me then I must come to you." He rose and walked towards her. Then he took her in his arms.

"Please don't!" she murmured.

"Why not, my darling? Don't you know how much I love you?"

His words brought her to her senses. She broke away abruptly.

"Haven't you punished me enough?" she cried in a broken voice. "On top of all else, must you pretend that you care for me?"

"You are sure that it is pretence?" He was so still that he might have been carved from stone.

"What else can it be? I admit that I was wrong, if that is what you want from me. I knew that you had no intention of offering for me, and I should not have pretended that I did."

"It was not a very serious pretence, my dear." His face was calm. "On the contrary, you gave me the impression that you wished to put me out of countenance."

"But you…but you…"

"I decided to call your bluff."

"Well, you certainly did so." Miranda's voice was bitter. "May we not end this farce here and now? I release you from your promise."

"But I have no desire to be released. Did I not make that plain?"

"Oh, no, you cannot mean it? How can you behave so ill? You know that I have not the least desire—"

"That I must beg leave to doubt." He bent his head and found her lips, and again the world was lost.

"Will you still tell me that you don't care for me?" he murmured. "Your body gives you the lie."

"You are mistaken!" Miranda struggled to free herself.

"Am I? I think not! I asked you once before to trust me. Is it so hard to do? Is there always to be this barrier between us?"

"I don't know what you mean."

"I think you do. This secret that you guard so closely? Must it never be revealed?"

"It is not mine alone to tell," she cried, goaded into flinging caution to the winds.

"Your sister again? Well, I had suspected it. I

won't press you to reveal her confidence, but one day you will come to me in your own good time."

"You speak in riddles, sir. Now, if you please, I should like to return to London."

"I wonder why that should not surprise me?" His expression was imperturbable as he took her arm once more and led her towards the inn.

Miranda was desperate to get away, but she was not to be released so soon.

"I have promised to take you to see Mary," he announced. "I hope you will be kind to her."

Accompanied by Mrs Flodden, he led her through to a small private parlour at the far end of the inn.

At first she did not see the child who lay among a pile of cushions on a sofa by the window. Then she was aware of being inspected by a pair of bright blue eyes. The thin little face was a perfect replica of Flodden's own.

"Here is Miss Gaysford come to see you, Mary. She is very shy. Promise that you will not frighten her as you do me?" Heston sounded solemn.

"Sir, you are teasing me," a small voice cried merrily. "I don't frighten you."

"Indeed you do! Sometimes, when we have been playing spillikins, you looked so fierce that I was positively shaking in my boots."

A peal of laughter greeted this sally. Heston was clearly a favourite with the frail little girl.

Miranda guessed that she could not have been more than eight or nine, although the traces of pain upon the child's face made her look older. She was desperately thin, with stick-like arms and legs, but her face was alive with intelligence.

Heston went across to sit beside her on the sofa.

"Well, what do you think of the lady who is to be my wife?" he said gravely.

Blue eyes and grey regarded Miranda so seriously that she began to smile.

"Mama told me that she was beautiful, and she is," the little girl announced. "She looks like the picture in my book."

"You mean the wicked witch?" Heston asked mildly.

"No, sir…I mean the fairy princess."

"I am relieved to hear it. I should not care to be married to a witch. She might put a spell on me."

"And turn you into a frog?"

"I shouldn't put it past her. It would be most inconvenient to be a frog, you know. I should have to hop about the garden and eat flies."

"Instead of Mrs Flodden's apple pies? You would not care for that, my lord," put in Miranda.

Miranda could not hide her amusement, especially when Mary nodded her agreement.

"He would not," she confirmed. "Mama says that Lord Heston is a splendid trencherman. I think it means that he eats a lot…"

"What a reputation!" Heston rose to his feet. "All these agreeable compliments will turn my head. Mary, we shall come to see you soon. If you do as the doctor says and eat up all your food, you may be well enough to come for a drive."

The child's eyes shone. "I will!" she cried. "Do you promise?"

"I give you my word on it. Now say your goodbyes to Miss Gaysford, for I must take her home."

A small, claw-like hand appeared from among the cushions and Miranda took it in her own.

"I hope we shall be friends," she said with a twinkle in her eyes. "Then you may teach me how to frighten his lordship."

"Both of you?" Heston threw his eyes to heaven in mock dismay. "I shall be a quivering jelly."

Mary was still laughing when they left her.

They had covered several miles of the journey back to London before she questioned him about the child.

"Is Mary very sick?" she asked.

"She was always delicate, but she is improving. There have been setbacks, naturally, but the spirit is there. It has pulled her through on many an occasion."

"She seems devoted to you."

"Purely due to my expertise at spillikins." Heston smiled down at her and her heart turned over. She turned her head, so that he should not see how her love for him betrayed her.

He drew the team to a halt in the shelter of some trees. Then a large hand reached out to cover her own.

"Can I have been mistaken? My love, we deal so well together, and in these last few days I have felt that you have changed. I think you do not dislike me as you did. In fact, I have begun to hope that you could learn to care for me."

Miranda did not answer him.

"You do not deny it?" he said eagerly.

She cast about wildly for some reply which would put an end to this dangerous conversation. Perhaps a half-truth would serve.

"I have misjudged you from the first," she replied in a low tone. "Perhaps we might be friends—"

"And that is to be all?"

Before she could protest he took her in his arms and kissed her soundly. Her mouth opened like a flower beneath his own, and he began to tease her with little flickering movements of his tongue. Her arms crept about his neck and she strained towards him, faint with longing for a fulfilment which she did not understand.

When he held her away his face was serious.

"Will you tell me now that you do not wish to marry me?" he asked.

"I can't!" Miranda did not recognise her own voice. The words had seemed to come from a stranger.

"You have not answered my question."

When she did not reply he sat in silence for a time. Then he turned to her again.

"Promise me this at least? Do nothing hasty for the moment. Next week I shall be in Portsmouth for some days. It will give you time to consider. On my return you may give me your answer."

When she began to speak, he stopped her.

"Don't worry, my dear. If you are still of the same mind I shall not press you further. You may put an end to our betrothal in any way you wish."

These were the words which she had once longed to hear, but the triumph felt like ashes in her mouth. There was nothing left to say, and indeed if she had tried to speak she must have burst into tears.

Heston picked up the reins and guided his team

back on to the road. For the rest of the journey back to London both of them were silent, but in place of the easy camaraderie on the drive down to Richmond there was now an atmosphere of tension.

It was not until they reached their destination that Heston broke the awkward silence. He threw his reins to the groom, jumped down from the driving seat, and held out his arms to help Miranda from her perch.

"Cheer up!" he murmured as his lips brushed her ear. "Even friends are allowed to enjoy each other's company."

She responded with the faintest of smiles, and was in no mood to listen to Fanny's strictures after he had gone.

"What a trick to play on us! I am surprised that Aunt allowed you to go jauntering off with Heston on your own, and for so long…"

"Haven't you enjoyed your day?"

"No, I have not. We saw no one that we knew, and if there is one thing I detest it is a picnic. There were so many creepy-crawlies, and stinging insects too. I could not eat a bite."

"Then you must be very hungry…"

"Much you care when we might all have gone to Richmond."

"Lord Heston wished to speak to me alone."

"Are there not rooms enough in this house where you might be private with him without trailing out to Richmond on your own?"

Miranda did not reply.

"What had he to say?" her twin asked with a nervous laugh.

"He has offered to release me from my promise to him." Something in her face warned Fanny to proceed with caution.

"And did you agree?"

"I agreed to do as he requested."

"And that was?"

"To wait and to consider. I am to give him an answer when he returns from Portsmouth."

"Oh, you are a darling!" Fanny threw her arms about her sister's unresponsive form. "You did it for me, just as you promised."

"It must come to the same thing in the end. I cannot marry him..."

"Well, in my opinion he would make a most disagreeable husband, always looking down his nose, and making those strange remarks which no one can understand." She saw the pain in Miranda's eyes and stopped.

"Of course I do not know him as you do," she continued when her sister did not speak. "You seem to have seen something else in him, though what I can't imagine—"

"Leave it, Fanny!" Miranda begged in desperation.

"Very well," Her sister brightened. "You need not make a decision yet, you know. Anything may happen in the next two weeks..." Her face grew dreamy.

Miranda knew that she was thinking of Alexei Toumanov. Had he joined them on the infamous picnic, the stinging insects would have gone unnoticed. She could only be thankful that the handsome Russian was due to leave the capital so soon.

"I wonder that Harry Lakenham has not called upon us recently," she said. "You have not seen him?"

"We met him in the Park the other day," Fanny told her in casual tones. "He was with his friends, so we did not stop to speak."

"He seems to have taken his dismissal very well."

"It was you who told him that he must not try to see me."

"Not alone and in secret, but I did not say that he should avoid your company altogether."

"It cannot signify! I expect he feels as I do, that we were both mistaken in our hearts."

This cool dismissal of what was to have been the love affair of the century took Miranda's breath away. Angry words rose to her lips, but she suppressed them. The same thing had happened many times before, but on previous occasions no harm had been done. She struggled for composure.

"What a pity that you did not discover it before," she said quietly. "Much trouble might have been avoided."

"I can't help that, and I don't know why you should look so black at me. I thought you disapproved of Harry."

"I think him too young and foolish to be considering marriage."

"Well, then, you must be satisfied, and your precious Adam Heston will be delighted."

"Not if he thinks that you have formed an attachment for the Count…"

The colour rose to Fanny's cheeks. "What an idea! Pray why should he think that? Alexei has not spoken."

"Nor will he do so, Fanny."

"Are you so sure? He has been most particular in his attentions."

"He likes to flirt, as do most young men, but you can't believe that he is serious?"

"You think I am beneath his notice?" Anger sparkled in Fanny's eyes.

"Of course not, but I don't want you to be hurt. You should not refine too much upon his gallantries. They may be nothing more than the usual outrageous flattery which passes for conversation in the Polite World."

Fanny tossed her head. "Why should you be the only one to marry well? I have a fancy to be a Countess."

Miranda said no more. Further warnings would be useless. Her only hope that her twin would be saved from further folly lay in the fact that the Count would return to Russia within the next two weeks.

She was dismayed to find that he, together with his sister and her husband, were to be their fellow dinner-guests at Brook Street on the following evening. At Lady Heston's invitation Richard had also joined them.

He looked overawed at the prospect of visiting Lord Heston's home.

"How do I look?" he asked Miranda in an undertone. "I expect it will be all magnificence…"

"You are the epitome of elegance," she told him with a smile. She felt somewhat nervous herself, but her blonde silk gown, ornamented with cobweb-like blonde lace, was so becoming that it gave her confidence.

In the event, the evening was not the ordeal she had expected. Heston's major-domo, whilst perfectly correct in his manner, showed no trace of stiffness, and she guessed that he was an old retainer.

He announced their party to the group already gathered in the salon, and Heston came to greet them with all the easy address which was natural to him.

Miranda could not meet his eyes, but he took her hand and kissed it, and then saluted her upon the cheek.

"Friends?" he murmured.

She gave him a look of gratitude. She had dreaded a certain awkwardness after their last meeting.

His lordship appeared to have forgotten it. To her surprise it was the Count whose manner had changed. It was imperceptible to most of the party, and throughout the meal he joined in the conversation so merrily that he kept them laughing with his stories of life at the Russian court. Yet he made no effort later to monopolise Fanny for himself.

Miranda looked across at the Princess Chaliapine. She, too, was speaking with her usual vivacity, but it was impossible not to wonder if she had spoken to her brother, warning him not to raise hopes which could not be fulfilled.

She prayed that Fanny would not give herself away. Her twin was incapable of dissembling, and she was already looking dissatisfied to see the Count in conversation with the Alderman and Mrs Shere.

Miranda threw a speaking look at Richard, and he moved at once to Fanny's side.

Accompanied by Lady Heston, Miranda went to join them.

"This has been a delightful evening, your ladyship," Richard told his hostess warmly. "It was kind of you to include me."

"It was a pleasure, Mr Young. Now you three young people may advise me. I have a small gift for the Alderman. Do you think that he will like it?" She took up a small parcel from the table and unwrapped it to reveal a painting.

"How beautiful! It is one of my uncle's roses… He will be delighted!"

Miranda bent to examine the work more closely.

"Why, you have caught every detail," she murmured in wonder. "I had not realised that the petals were shaded so, and that the leaves are not all a solid green…"

Even Fanny was intrigued. "Ma'am, it is hard to

believe that you have made the painting so quickly. Why, it is not more than a day or two since you took the flowers."

"That is experience, my dear, and a sad habit of ignoring all else in order to paint."

"How better could you spend your time, my dearest?" Heston had joined their little group. "We are all waiting for your *magnum opus.*"

"Now, Adam, I beg of you…" Lady Heston shook her head in reproach.

"Please tell us what it is, ma'am, if you do not object."

Richard was so clearly interested that her ladyship did not refuse.

"I am trying to record the flora and fauna in our part of Warwickshire," she admitted shyly. "It is a lengthy task."

"But well worth doing, Lady Heston. It will be a wonderful record for the future." Richard quite forgot his own diffidence as he began to tell her about the countryside in Yorkshire.

Heston took Miranda's arm. "We are *de trop,*" he told her with a smile. "If you ladies do not rescue me, I shall be forced to display my ignorance. Do you care for cards, or a game of billiards?"

"Billiards, my lord? I have never played, but I

should like to try." Fanny's expression brightened in an instant.

"Then you shall do so." He led them through the hall and into a massive billiard-room, complete with baize-covered table and cues in racks upon the walls.

Fanny showed a surprising aptitude for the game.

"What fun it is!" she cried. "I had thought it only a game for gentlemen." She grew excited as her score increased, and her face was vivid with enjoyment. For the moment she had forgotten the Count's defection.

Miranda sighed with relief. "When do you go to Portsmouth?" she asked Heston.

"In a day or two. Alexei is to go ahead of the main party, to make sure that all is in readiness for the Tsar's suite." The penetrating eyes held amusement in their depths. "You have no need to worry, I assure you."

"No…no, of course not. It is just that…"

"You need say no more. I am not blind. Now will you not try your hand at this absorbing game? If you allow your sister to outshine you, she will be insufferable."

A smile took the sting out of his words and Fanny laughed at him as she relinquished her cue.

"You shall both try to beat me," she announced.

"Not I!" his lordship shuddered. "I have too much regard for the surface of this table."

"Lord Heston, you are joking!" Fanny reproached. "I suspect that you are an expert at this game."

"This…and others…" he murmured in Miranda's ear. "Now let me show you how to hold the cue."

He stood behind her, long arms stretched out, and his hands covering her own. "Don't rush at it," he advised. "Take it gently, and keep your eye upon the ball."

His nearness made Miranda feel faint with longing. She tried to pot the ball, and missed completely.

Fanny's laughter echoed round the room. "That is not the way," she cried. "Here, let me show you."

Miranda dropped the cue and turned, only to find herself still enclosed within his lordship's arms. Beneath the fine cambric of his shirt, she sensed the beating of his heart, and the pounding in her own breast threatened to overcome her.

Then Heston moved away. "We shall be missed," he said lightly. "Shall we join the others?"

They returned to the salon to find the Alderman lost in admiration of his painting. "I have just the place for it," he said with pride. "I'll have it framed to match the gilding in the drawing-room. Then I shall see it every day."

He was still gloating as they returned to Bloomsbury.

Chapter Fourteen

Fanny was unusually quiet on the following day. The reason was not far to seek, but Miranda did not question her.

"I thought Alexei seemed a little strange last night, did not you?" Fanny asked at last.

"He was pleasant, as he always is."

"Yes, but…well…he is used to be more loverly."

"You could not expect him to flirt openly in company."

"You mean in the company of his sister, I suppose?"

"Among others."

"No, it is she who does not like me. I knew it from the first. A Princess, indeed! Why, her husband is old enough to be her father."

"That is not our concern."

"Not yours, perhaps, but it is mine. She is so puffed up with family pride—"

"Oh, Fanny, that isn't true! I find her charming."

"That is because she doesn't try to interfere in your affairs." Fanny's laugh was angry. "It is to be hoped that she does not intend to join us for our visit to the Pantheon. Without her, Alexei is so different."

Her hopes were realised on the following evening, and Fanny was so delighted by the absence of the Princess that she failed to notice Alexei's continued reserve.

As always, his manners were delightful, but there was certainly a change in him.

It was obvious to Miranda. Alexei was his usual charming self, solicitous for their comfort and as entertaining as always, but he did not seek to engage Fanny in private conversation.

Surely her sister must realise that his interest in her went no further than the lightest of flirtations. A look at Fanny's expression convinced her otherwise. Her twin was gazing up at the Count with adoration in her eyes. She could not have made her feelings clearer if she had spoken them aloud.

"Out of the frying pan and into the fire?" Heston murmured wickedly. His words were for Miranda's ear alone, and she threw him a look of reproach.

"My sister is too susceptible," she admitted with an uneasy laugh.

"Unlike yourself?" There was something in his eyes which challenged her to deny it.

"We…we are very different, she and I," she said hastily.

"Indeed you are! It would be difficult to find two women less alike in temperament. I confess that your previous attachment to Harry Lakenham and his to you has often puzzled me."

His remark was so unexpected that it caught Miranda unawares. Her head went up and she looked at him in panic. Then she made a valiant effort to cover her confusion.

"Why should you find it strange, my lord? I explained my reasons well enough…"

"So you did! It was a splendid explanation, but I was thinking more of Harry…"

"I don't know why you should feel his wish to marry me outrageous."

"Not outrageous…just astonishing! Did he not quail at times?"

"That remark is unworthy of a gentleman, sir. You make me out to be some kind of dragon."

"Not a dragon, my love, although I have seen you breathing fire upon occasion." He looked down at her and she heard the laughter in his voice. "Now how shall I find the words to describe you when you are upon your high ropes...perhaps a pretty little hissing kitten, out to defy the world?"

"That is nonsense!" she said coldly. "Now, if you please, I should like to listen to the play."

"Of course. I, too, shall enjoy it. It is such a comfort to know that both your own undying passion and that of Lakenham is unlikely to survive into old age."

Miranda did not reply, although she herself had wondered why Harry no longer called upon them. After all, in the first hot throes of love he had been prepared to defy his grandfather. Yet that devotion had not survived an enforced separation. She realised that it was for the best, but it said much for the fickleness of a man's affection. Most probably they were all the same with their honeyed words at one moment, and indifference in the next. It was a lowering thought.

"Cheer up!" Heston teased. "I shall not change."

"No, I don't suppose you will," she snapped. "And that, my lord, is not a source of comfort to me!"

"Milling me down again?" His shoulders began to shake. "I shall advise my friends that they need not visit the great Jackson for lessons in the art of self-defence. They should come to you instead."

Miranda gave him an unwilling smile. Such a notion was so ridiculous that it appealed to her sense of humour.

"That's better!" he approved, and relapsed into silence until the interval. The one-act play which opened the evening's entertainment had not been received with much acclaim, but before the main performance could begin a buzz of excitement ran around the theatre.

Then the audience rose and began to clap and cheer. A woman had entered the opposite box, and now she came forward, bowing to the crowd.

Miranda knew at once that it was the Prince Regent's estranged wife, Caroline of Brunswick. Rumour had not lied, she decided. The Princess was heavily built, with rather coarse features. Her colouring was difficult to distinguish beneath the garish layers of paint and powder. Against the thick white coating blotches of scarlet rouge stood out in such startling contrast that they gave her the appearance of a clown.

The plunging neckline of her gown revealed a magnificent bosom, but it was cut even lower than those of the demi-reps who plied their trade on such occasions.

As Miranda watched the Princess threw back her

head and laughed, displaying broken and dis-coloured teeth.

The vulgarity of her manner did not dismay the crowd. They cheered her to the echo.

"I did not know that the Princess was so popular," Mrs Shere announced.

"We are about to find out just how popular," Heston said with a significant glance at the ad-joining box.

It was unfortunate that the Regent himself had chosen that particular moment to arrive at the theatre. He went unnoticed for a moment or two, and was forced to content himself with a back view of those of his fellow countrymen who had chosen to welcome the Princess Caroline. Then a murmur ran through the crowd. They turned and stood in silence as the heir to the throne took his seat.

The audience could not have made their opposi-tion clearer, but the Prince's manner remained un-changed. He did not betray by the flicker of an eyelid that he was acquainted with the woman in the opposite box.

"Why, this is more exciting than the play," Fanny whispered to Miranda. "The Prince and his wife are looking through each other."

"I think it sad," Mrs Shere said quietly. "Sometimes

men and women are ill suited to each other. They cannot be blamed for that."

"The blame is laid at the Prince's door," Heston told her. "He is considered to have treated both his wife and his daughter in a shabby way. The people will not stand for it. They have a love of justice, as you know."

"Perhaps they do not know the whole," Mrs Shere said kindly.

"You are generous, ma'am, and you are right. The Prince believes his wife to have an unfortunate influence on his daughter."

Mrs Shere was silent. She, like everyone else in the capital, had heard rumours that the Princess Charlotte had been actively encouraged by her mother into conduct which lacked propriety. On one occasion, Caroline of Brunswick had locked her into a bedroom with a handsome aide-de-camp, telling the couple to enjoy themselves.

"That will be ended when the Princess Charlotte is wed," Mrs Shere assured him.

"Let us hope so, ma'am, but she has just cried off from her engagement to the Prince of Orange, believing it to be a trick to get her out of the country."

"Oh, no, I don't believe it! Whatever his faults, the Regent has always loved his daughter." Mrs Shere spoke with conviction. From his early days, when the Prince was known and loved by all as the handsome Prince Florizel and the hope of the country, Mrs Shere had been his staunch supporter.

Heston smiled down at her. "Ma'am, the Prince stands in need of more friends like you," he said. "It is too easy to think the worst of him."

Miranda threw him a warm glance of approval. She was unsurprised to find him ready to defend his friend. Extravagant the Prince might be, changeable in his politics, easily swayed by the termagants who took his fancy, and emotional to a fault, but beneath the surface Heston had found a warm-hearted, cultivated man who believed in a civilised way of life, and would settle for nothing but the best in any field of the arts.

During the next interval she was able to study the Royal Party more closely. The Prince's appearance was as artificial as that of his wife. The paint and powder failed to disguise the fact that he had paled at the sight of her, and now looked morose.

Against the brilliant splendour of the satin coat and breeches which clothed his massive form, the dress of his Allies appeared simple and unostenta-tious. But it was for them that the cheering had begun again as they entered his box. The Regent had joined them in bowing to acknowledge the plaudits of the crowd, but there was a bitterness about his expression which Miranda could not fail to mark. He had suffered a public humiliation and she pitied him.

"Will the Princess Caroline be invited to attend the Proclamation of Peace with France tomorrow?" Mrs Shere enquired.

"No, ma'am. She does not attend official occasions." Heston frowned. "It is to be hoped that she won't invite herself and cause a disturbance."

"Shall you go with the Prince, my lord?" Miranda asked.

"No, I think not. You know my views upon this so-called peace, my dear. In my opinion it is but a temporary cessation of hostilities. We haven't crushed Napoleon yet."

He spoke in a low tone, for which Miranda was profoundly grateful. Mrs Shere had suffered enough as her eldest son had fought his way through the Peninsula with Wellington.

Miranda looked at the Prince again. "If you are right, will the Regent lead his troops in battle? I heard that he had always longed to do so."

"The King would never permit it."

"But why? His royal brothers hold the highest ranks in the army."

"That was one cause of the estrangement between Prince George and his father. He does not lack personal courage, but he was made to appear a coward through no fault of his own. It was in part a desire not to risk the life of the heir to the throne, but the main reason was the old king's dislike of his eldest son. Any request was met with a refusal as a matter of course."

"They are an unfortunate family," Miranda sighed.

"Indeed they are, but let us drop this depressing subject. Tomorrow I intend to leave for Portsmouth."

"So soon? The Review of the Fleet is a full five days away…"

"Would you keep me by your side?" he teased.

Miranda looked up to see a twinkle in his eyes.

"Your private arrangements are none of my concern, my lord…" She turned away, but not before the tell-tale colour had risen to her cheeks.

"Crushed again, and just as I was beginning to hope." He took her hand and raised it to his lips. "I intend to call upon Lord Rudyard," he told her. "He is not in the best of health, and as he lives near Midhurst, it seemed an excellent opportunity…"

"To report upon myself and Harry?" Miranda's tone was sharp.

"Why, no!" He looked at her in mock surprise. "I see no need for that."

"He is sure to ask." She felt uncomfortable.

"I don't intend to worry him with details of a matter which is now in the past. And Harry is behaving better than we might have hoped. I haven't seen him at the gaming tables, and to my knowledge he hasn't attempted any more balloon ascents."

Miranda could not take so sanguine a view of Harry as a reformed character. In the past few months she had come to know him well, and his absence from his usual haunts had worried her.

For a time she had suspected that he and Fanny might be meeting in secret, but since her sister had transferred her affections to Alexei Toumanov she had dismissed the idea. Fanny was transparent and, apart from the fact that she had had no opportunity to make furtive assignations, it was clear that she no longer had any wish to revive her former love affair.

"Will Count Toumanov go with you?" she asked.

Heston shook his head. "Tomorrow he is on duty. He will follow later."

Fanny looked across at her twin with a radiant smile. Without Heston by his side this would be an opportunity for Alexei to declare his love. She was in the highest of spirits for the rest of the evening.

* * *

Throughout the following day her air of suppressed excitement did not go unnoticed by the Alderman and his wife.

"What a child you are!" her aunt said fondly. "Such enthusiasm for our trip into the city! I hope it will be all that you expect, my dear."

They were not to be disappointed. As the family coach turned into the Strand, the crowd slowed them to a halt. The city was in gala mood and there was dancing in the streets. Every building was decked with flags and banners, and the fountains ran with wine.

"What a sight!" Tears sparkled in Mrs Shere's eyes as she turned to her husband. "May we not go into St Paul's Cathedral, my love? I should like to give thanks that our boy will now be safe…"

"Perhaps another day, my dear Emma. I think we should not leave the coach, or there is every likelihood of our being either separated or trampled underfoot."

The press of people was so great, and the shouting so loud, that the horses grew uneasy. The Alderman was quick to see the danger, and he ordered his coachman to turn for home. It was not easily accomplished, and it was late afternoon before they reached Bloomsbury again.

Mrs Shere sank into a chair. "What an exhausting day! I am glad to have seen the celebrations, but what a blessing it will be when all these foreigners leave the city…"

Miranda smiled at her. "You will like to have a quiet evening, ma'am, with perhaps a little music?"

"More than anything, my dear, if you are not too tired to play."

After their evening meal Miranda took her place at the spinet, signing to Fanny to turn the music for her. It soon became apparent that her sister's attention was elsewhere.

"Do pay attention, Fanny. You have missed the place three times."

Fanny's eyes were upon the clock, and her face grew longer as the hours ticked by.

"It is so late," she whispered. "He won't come now."

"Of course not!" Miranda did not pretend to misunderstand. "Tonight there is a dinner at Carlton House."

"A dinner at Carlton House, do you say?" The Alderman settled himself more comfortably in his chair. "The Prince will be hard put to beat the dinner we gave him at the Guildhall. Did I tell you that we had the first turtle soup of the season?"

"Many times," his wife assured him with a smile. "My dear, would you not be more comfortable in your bed instead of dozing in your chair? These girls must be tired to death."

It was a disconsolate Fanny who sought her bed-chamber that evening.

"I quite thought that Alexei would have come tonight," she told Miranda.

"But I explained. The dinner will go on until the early hours."

"Yes, that must be it, but pray do not suggest that we go out tomorrow. He is sure to call…"

Her hopes were to be dashed. They had a number of visitors on the following day, but the Count was not among them.

"Do you think that he is ill?" she asked Miranda anxiously. "There must be a reason why he does not come to see us."

"We have no way of finding out." Miranda did not have the heart to voice her own interpretation of the reasons for the Count's absence. Fanny had been unable to hide her feelings for him, and he was too much of a gentleman to encourage her in a hopeless passion.

As the days passed Fanny grew more and more distraught. When Richard arrived she could not wait to question him.

"We have been worried about Count Toumanov," she said. "Have you heard that he is ill?"

"He was looking well when I saw him yesterday. He was on his way to Portsmouth."

This apparently innocuous remark brought a gasp from Fanny. She fled the room with her handkerchief to her eyes, and Miranda could only be thankful that she and Richard were the only witnesses of her distress.

His face fell. "Miranda, I know that you told me not to give up hope, but I can't believe that Fanny does not love the Count."

"Another infatuation!" Miranda told him calmly. "By next week he will be gone. Richard, if you are still of a mind to wed my foolish sister, I suggest that you seize the opportunity to offer for her. The love of a dear friend cannot but help to mend a broken heart."

"She won't look at me." His face was sad. "She thinks of me as a brother."

"Then you must change her mind." She gave him

a rueful look. "But who am I to advise you? I cannot manage my own affairs."

"How do you go on with Heston? Don't tell me if you don't wish it. I have no right to ask, but I should like to see you happy."

Miranda hesitated for a moment. "He says he loves me," she replied. "But I can't believe it."

"I believe it. I have thought so for some time, as I once told you."

"Even supposing it were true, I cannot marry him. In the first place, I should be forced to tell him of the way I have deceived him. What man could hear of it without disgust?"

"You are convinced that he has no suspicion of what has happened?"

"I am. I know well enough what his reaction would be." She shuddered. "I could not bear to hear what he would say…"

"Miranda, you misjudge him. He is one of the wisest men I know. His pride might be hurt, but he would soon forgive you."

"You sound like Aunt Emma. I know you mean to comfort me, but it is to late for that. He offered to release me from my promise to him…did Fanny tell you?"

"No, but I must hope that you didn't accept."

"I can do nothing else. When he returns from Portsmouth, I shall give him my decision."

"If he accepts it, he is not the man I think him." With those enigmatic words he prepared to take his leave.

"Will Fanny care to see the battle on the Serpentine?" he asked. "It is not until next week, but…"

"By then the Count will be gone. No doubt she will welcome the diversion." Miranda gave him her hand.

"What a staunch friend you are!" He bowed and left her.

Miranda went in search of Fanny, only to find her sister weeping in their room.

"How could Alexei do this to me?" her sister moaned. "He must have known how much I longed to see him."

"You certainly made it obvious. Fanny, I wish you will listen to me…"

"I won't! I won't! You don't understand! You have never cared for anyone as I care for him."

"Perhaps not!" Miranda lied. "But must you advertise it to the world? Richard was distressed to see you so upset."

"Richard understands. He is the only person in the world who does not criticise me."

"Then I am surprised that you are not kinder to him."

Fanny ignored this last remark. "When does the Court return from Porstmouth?" she asked. "There is so little time left to us. Perhaps Alexei does not know of my feelings for him."

"Then he must be blind. Fanny, I beg of you… please try for a little conduct. You lay yourself open to gossip."

Fanny was not attending. "That must be the reason. He thinks that I don't care for him. What a fool I have been! When he returns, I shall make my feelings clear."

"Oh, love, please don't! Think how mortifying it would be to discover that he does not feel the same."

Fanny glared at her. "Why should he not? The most mortifying thing to me is to discover that you are eaten up with jealousy. Do you want him for yourself?"

The gibe was unworthy of a reply and Miranda changed the subject.

"Richard has asked if you would like to see the mock battle on the Serpentine next week. Shall you care to go? It is to be a re-creation of the battle of Trafalgar."

"I suppose so. Anything would be preferable to this dreadful boredom. How dull we are without Alexei!"

Miranda held her tongue. She, too, was finding that life had lost much of its savour. It came as a surprise to realise just how much she had grown to enjoy her daily battle of wits with Adam Heston.

She missed the stimulation of his company, the laughter, the teasing, and above all the excitement when he held her in his arms.

She could not deny that she loved him with all her heart and she longed for the sight of his tall figure, the warmth of his smile, and his passionate caresses.

Without him the future would be bleak indeed. More than anything in the world she wanted to become his wife. It was cruel to think that she had found her love at last, only to be forced to give him up.

Yet their next meeting must be their last. The Review of the Fleet was to take place on the following day and then he would return from Portsmouth to seek her answer.

The thought of refusing him was agony, but she must be strong. To see him just once more was all she could hope for now. She looked so sad that Fanny was moved to question her.

"Are you ill?" she asked. "You don't look at all the thing."

"I have the headache, that is all."

"So have I," Fanny sighed. "This waiting is enough to give anyone the megrims. I believe we should go shopping. That will cheer us up, and Aunt Emma will enjoy it."

She hurried away to find their aunt and returned with the news that the carriage would be at the door in half an hour.

Miranda as too preoccupied to take much interest in their expedition, though she did her best to hide her worries. Perhaps the Tsar and his retinue would sail back to Russia direct from Portsmouth after the Review. There had been some talk of it. That would prevent Fanny from carrying out her plan to tell Alexei of her love.

Three days later her hopes were dashed when the Count was shown into their drawing-room.

Chapter Fifteen

Fanny jumped up at once, oversetting her embroidery frame and scattering the brightly coloured silks across the carpet.

"At last!" she cried. "Oh, how I have missed you!"

Miranda was ready to sink with embarrassment at this open declaration and a glance at Mrs Shere told her that her feelings were shared. She tried to retrieve the situation.

"We have all missed your company, Count Toumanov. Is that not so, Aunt Emma?"

"Indeed it is! The Review went well, I hope?" Mrs Shere tried to hide her anger at Fanny's shocking lack of decorum.

"It was a great success, ma'am, but now, alas, I am come to take my leave of you." He did not look at Fanny as he spoke.

An audible gasp drew all eyes to her. Her colour rose and then receded, leaving her very pale.

"No, not yet!" she pleaded. "Oh, I cannot breathe! Sir, will you help me into the garden?"

"I will take you to your room." Mrs Shere rose to her feet. "Count Toumanov, will you excuse us? My niece has not been well."

"I am sorry to hear it, and I must hope that Miss Gaysford will make a quick recovery…" He opened the door and stood aside as Mrs Shere thrust Fanny from the room.

An awkward silence followed their departure.

Then the Count walked over to the window. For some moments he was lost in thought.

"Have I been at fault?" he said at last. "I would not willingly give pain."

"The fault is not yours, sir." Miranda felt unable to discuss her sister further. It had been an appalling scene, and she wished to spare the young man further embarrassment.

"Adam did not return to London with you?" she asked.

"Forgive me, Miss Gaysford, I had quite forgot. I am charged with messages for you. Adam sends his duty to Alderman and Mrs Shere, and rather more than that to you, I fancy." He managed a faint smile. "He is gone to see his godfather."

"I thought he had intended to call upon Lord Rudyard on his way down to Portsmouth."

"He did so, and found the old man sadly pulled down. Adam was so worried that he decided to return."

"I see. Then we must expect him when we see him."

"That won't be too long, I imagine. He is anxious to return to you, as I'm sure you know." The Count pulled on his gloves. "This has not been the happiest of leave-takings, Miss Gaysford, and for that I must blame myself. I should not have come today."

"After all our happy times together? We should have taken it amiss if you had not called to say farewell."

Miranda hoped that her words would reassure him, but his face was troubled as he took his leave of her.

She was given no time to worry about it, for at that moment the door burst open and Ellen rushed into the room.

"Miss, will you come at once? Your sister is in strong hysterics, and Mrs Shere can do no good with her…"

Miranda hurried up the stairs. She could hear Fanny's screams from the first landing. Fanny was lying on her bed, laughing and crying by turns.

"Shall I send for the doctor?" Mrs Shere turned an anxious face towards her.

"Leave her with me." Miranda walked over to the bed and slapped her twin across the face. The laughing and screaming stopped as Fanny subsided into hiccuping sobs.

"My dear child, I had not the least idea that your sister had formed an attachment for the Count." For once Mrs Shere looked every year of her age.

"Infatuation, ma'am," Miranda told her crisply. "It has happened before."

"But Count Toumanov? Has he led her to believe…?"

"No, that is all in my sister's mind."

"Then I must wonder how your mama puts up with all this nonsense. I would suggest that she goes home, but your marriage is so close, and she must return for that."

"Aunt, if you will allow me, I will speak to her alone."

"Very well, my dear. You may succeed in bringing her to her senses where I could not." Her manner was unusually stern as she left the twins together.

Miranda walked over to the bed and looked at the weeping figure of her twin.

"You may stop that!" she said coldly. "It will not wear with me."

"How could it? You can have no idea of how I feel. Oh, how could he be so cold? I tried to see him alone, but he did not support me."

"Fanny, your behaviour was the outside of enough. That blatant attempt to persuade the Count into the garden! I thought I must have died of shame."

Fanny's sobs ceased. "That is all you care about," she accused. "I declare you are become as stuffy as Heston himself. You should deal well together."

"Don't try to change the subject. We are not discussing Heston. Surely you must realise now that Count Toumanov had no intention of offering for you?"

Fanny began to wail again. "I shall become a dried-up spinster," she declared. "Lakenham has deserted me, and now the Count. I hope you are satisfied."

"None of it was of my doing," Miranda declared with some asperity. "Now wash your face. You must apologise to Aunt Emma. She had almost decided to send you home."

"I should not care," her twin said in a sullen tone. "I am beginning to hate London. Nothing pleasant ever happens here." She turned her head away and buried her face in the pillow.

Miranda left her to her sulks.

* * *

By the evening of the following day she was growing worried. No food had passed he sister's lips, and Fanny replied to questions only in monosyllables.

"Perhaps we were too hard on her. You do not think that she will fall into a decline?" Mrs Shere was clearly anxious.

"No, I don't." Miranda gave her aunt a reassuring smile. "I'll speak to her. She may be feeling better now."

As she made her way upstairs she felt perplexed. It was difficult to know exactly what to do. Fanny might be genuinely ill, in which case they should summon the doctor without delay. On the other hand, this refusal to eat could be her way of punishing her sister and her aunt for the lectures which she had suffered.

She opened the door to the bedchamber as quietly as possible, in case her twin was sleeping. The blinds were drawn against the evening sunlight, but Fanny was sitting up in bed. She looked up startled as Miranda entered and pulled the bedcover up to her chin.

"Are you cold? Will you have a hot brick for your feet?"

"No!" Fanny mumbled. Her guilty expression

aroused Miranda's suspicions. She crossed over to the bed and threw back the coverlet to reveal a plate of cakes.

"I see! Ellen has been smuggling food to you. You have not been starving, have you?" The contempt in her voice made her sister blush. She did not reply.

"How could you, Fanny? Aunt has been so worried and so have I."

There was still no answer.

"You can't hide up here for ever," Miranda continued. "You must come downstairs and speak to Aunt."

"I won't! I'm tired of being scolded. I wish we had never come here…" Fanny scowled at her.

"It's too late to think of that. We are here and you must make the best of it. Now pray get dressed and do as I ask…"

"Not tonight. I'll come down in the morning. You may tell Aunt Emma that I feel a little better."

Miranda felt dispirited as she returned to the salon, but her anger was mingled with relief. If Fanny might be persuaded into an apology, Mrs Shere would readily accept it. Count Toumanov was gone, so there could be no repetition of Fanny's ill behaviour as far as he was concerned.

"It think we have no further cause to worry,

ma'am," she said. "My sister is much recovered and will come down in the morning. She is distressed to think that she has worried you…"

"That she did!" Mrs Shere replied with feeling. "I cannot like the way that she goes on. If it were not for your wedding, I should send her home."

"Ma'am, pray try to understand…she is so impressionable and she does not always consider…"

Mrs Shere gave Miranda a reluctant smile. "You will always defend her, my dear girl, and I admire your loyalty, but I could wish that she were wed to some sensible man such as Mr Young. With her children about her she might settle down."

"Aunt, I share your hopes, and so does Richard. He is devoted to her."

"Heaven protect him!" Mrs Shere threw her eyes to heaven. "He cannot wish for a quiet life."

"He knows her very well, Aunt Emma, and he does not mind her fits of temperament. When we were children he could always coax her out of them, and was happy to do so."

"He must be a saint."

"I have often thought much the same myself, but she must be loved, you know, and he would give her all the love she needs."

"Your twin is spoilt, my dear, but there, I shall say no more to distress you."

"Or her?" Miranda begged.

"I suppose not. My only comfort is the thought that you are to be wed so soon, and will no longer bear responsibility for her. When does Lord Heston return?"

"I'm not quite sure. He is staying with his god-father. The Count told me that Lord Rudyard is not well."

"Doubtless reports about Harry Lakenham have reached him. I do not understand the young these days. It makes me wonder what the world is coming to."

On this sombre note both ladies retired.

Fanny was on her best behaviour for the next few days. Her apologies were given and received with good grace. Then she exerted all her charm in an effort to restore Mrs Shere's kind opinion.

This was the calm before the storm, Miranda thought with a shudder. When Heston returned and she refused him, they would be plunged into further scenes involving herself.

And with each day that passed she missed him more. Even to endure his anger would be preferable to not seeing him at all. Perhaps if she threw herself upon his mercy he might forgive her? Then the memory of that harsh dark face rose before her eyes. No, he would not forgive deception followed by humiliation. It was alien to his nature, and an offence to any man of honour.

It was in no happy frame of mind that she joined the others in the carriage as they set off to see the mock battle on the Serpentine.

The Park was crowded, but Richard found a place for them beside the water's edge. Fanny was in the highest of spirits, Count Toumanov apparently forgotten. She chattered gaily, begging to be told the names of all the miniature ships upon the lake.

"They are larger than I had expected…I thought they would be toys."

"Not if they are to hold the crews. It is all to be as realistic as possible, you know. The Prince has spared no expense." Richard was eager to explain. "He wished to mark the centenary of the House of Hanover in appropriate style. What better than a re-creation of the Battle of Trafalgar?"

Miranda looked about her. "I wonder if we should not move further back?" she said. "The crowd is pushing from behind and we are so close to the lake…"

"No, no!" Fanny clapped her hands. "We have a splendid view. I won't give up my place."

The Alderman had seen the danger. He took his wife's arm and moved back a pace or two, pushing the jostling mob aside. Other's took their place at once, and soon they were lost to sight.

Miranda heard him call to her to come away. Then his words were drowned in a cannonade of gunfire.

Startled, Fanny screamed and lost her footing as he turned. Then she plunged headlong into the lake.

A roar of laughter ran through the crowd as Richard waded after her.

"Oh, she will drown!" Miranda cried in anguish.

"No, ma'am, it ain't deep enough just here," the man beside her comforted. "See, the young man is only in the water up to his waist."

At that moment Fanny found her footing and flung her arms in a stranglehold about Richard's neck. It took him by surprise and they fell together into deeper water. The crowd grew silent.

"She will drown the pair of them," Miranda's companion murmured. He sat down and began to struggle out of his boots.

Miranda was frozen into silence as she watched

the struggling pair. Then Richard brought both arms up through her sister's grip and broke it. He cupped one hand beneath her chin and forced her head back. Then he slipped behind her and began to tow her to the shore.

A circle formed about them as he lifted Fanny's unconscious figure up onto the bank. Then he turned her over and pressed upon her back. Streams of water flowed from her mouth and then her eyelids fluttered.

Alderman Shere was on his knees beside them. "Well done!" he said in a low voice. "Is she conscious?"

Richard nodded. "It is all my fault, sir. I should not have let her stand so close to the edge."

"You are not to blame. Let us take her home."

Miranda slipped an arm about her aunt's shoulders. The older woman was badly shaken, but with commendable restraint she refrained from any comment upon the accident.

It was only later, when Fanny had been taken to her room and the doctor summoned, that she began to cry.

"Now, Emma, don't give way," the Alderman admonished. "You ladies have held up well in spite of the shock, and there is no harm done." He looked across at Richard. "My dear sir, you showed great presence of mind, for which I thank you."

Clad in the Alderman's coat and breeches, which were too big for him, Richard was a comic figure, but no one smiled.

"She might have drowned!" He buried his face in his hands. "I shall never forgive myself."

"Nonsense!" Miranda told him briskly. "The lake is shallow. She might have walked out of it herself if she had not panicked."

"But she did, and she can't swim."

It took some time to comfort him, but reassured at last by the doctor's hopeful diagnosis he took his leave of them.

Fanny was unharmed, and the ducking had not resulted in an inflammation of the lungs as Mrs Shere had predicted. Once recovered from the shock she took full advantage of the near-tragedy, happy to be the centre of attention.

Richard was now her hero, though he disclaimed the honour.

"The lake was not deep, you know. We might have walked out if…"

"If I had not been so foolish?" Fanny smiled up at him. She was lying upon a sofa in the salon, dressed in one of her most becoming gowns. "Oh, Richard, you saved me from a watery grave. I never was so frightened in my life…"

"It is all over. You must forget it." He took her hand and held it in his own.

"How can I? What should I have done without you?"

He was spared the need to reply when Charlotte Fairfax was announced, and his gaze was rueful as he looked up at Miranda.

She smiled and shook her head. "There will be other opportunities," she assured him. "I believe you have slain the dragon."

After that, Charlotte was a frequent visitor, somewhat to Fanny's surprise.

"I thought her more your friend than mine," she said one day. "Yet she has asked if I will go to stay with her."

"An excellent plan!" Mrs Shere intervened. "It will give you a change of scene."

"But shall you wish to go?" Miranda asked. "It seems a little strange when she does not live above a mile away."

"Oh, I think so." Fanny dismissed the objection. "It will be only for a day or two, and Aunt is right. It will suit both of us. Charlotte is lonely, so she tells me…"

Miranda suspected that Fanny's main reason for agreeing to this plan was to avoid the stricter supervision which her aunt had threatened after the contretemps with Count Toumanov, but she made no comment.

When Fanny had gone, Mrs Shere did not mince her words.

"I cannot but be glad that you are separated for a time," she said. "Sometimes you look positively hagged, my love. Don't tell me that your sister is not a worry to you, for I won't believe it."

"She did not mean to fall into the lake," Miranda murmured.

"I was not referring to that, although the accident was due more to her own folly than to a lack of care upon the part of Mr Young."

"It may be no bad thing," Miranda chuckled. "He is now her hero."

"I know it. That was the only reason why I agreed to let her go to Charlotte. And Sir William Fairfax is a stern papa, you know. The girls will be carefully supervised."

Miranda grew thoughtful. Sir William's reputation as a disciplinarian was well known. She doubted if Fanny would care to stay for long in such a household, but in the meantime it was a relief to be spared the need to fret about her.

In the next few days her life took on an almost dreamlike quality. She wandered about the garden, helping the Alderman where she could, between intervals of playing on the spinet, much to her aunt's delight. Her book was long since finished, but she had managed to obtain a recently published copy of *Waverley,* which had taken the town by storm. It kept her occupied for many hours.

Even an invitation to take tea with Lady Heston did not trouble her as it might have done. The visit passed off without incident, and if she seemed preoccupied neither her aunt nor Lady Heston mentioned it.

Time seemed to have stopped. She was waiting in limbo as the dark cloud at the back of her mind grew ever larger. Heston must soon return and then…? Her face grew sombre. She dreaded the thought of that last interview with him, but it must be final. She would make sure of that.

"My dear, won't you take up your embroidery again? You have neglected it for so long, and it will help to pass the time," Mrs Shere said kindly.

"His lordship cannot be long delayed, and then you will be happy once more."

"I beg your pardon, Aunt Emma. I did not mean to be so gloomy."

"Not gloomy, dearest, just a little sad. It is understandable when Lord Heston has been gone for all this time. I'm sure he would not wish you to give up all your pleasures. We might drive out, you know, or visit the shops in Bond Street…"

Miranda excused herself from the proposed expedition, and Mrs Shere did not argue.

"You fear that he might call when we are out? Very well, but I must go. I shall not be away for long."

Miranda settled herself at her embroidery frame, and began to look through the coloured silks. She threaded her needle, but it was only the striking of the clock which told her that she had not set a stitch for the past hour.

Lost in a reverie, she did not at first attend when the door opened.

"Lord Heston, ma'am," the servant announced.

Miranda looked up to find his lordship advancing towards her. Her smile of welcome vanished when she saw the expression on his face. His eyes were stony with contempt and his jaw was rigid. At that moment he looked capable of murder.

"Where is Fanny?" he said without preamble.

Miranda froze. "My lord, are you not mistaken?" she faltered. Then she heard an ugly laugh.

"Come, madam, let us have done with this charade. It has gone on for long enough."

Miranda made a last attempt to save herself. "I…I don't understand you."

He caught her wrist in an iron grip which made her wince and dragged her to her feet.

"Don't you? Will you deny that you have tricked me from the first? You shall not take me for a fool. Did you think it amusing to take your sister's place?"

Miranda knew that all was over. It would be useless to prevaricate further.

"How long have you known?" she asked in a low tone.

"Does that matter? It did not take long, I assure you. You made a number of mistakes, although I did not need them to convince me. You and Harry Lakenham? It wasn't possible."

"Not even for the money and the title?" Miranda flared. He was entitled to be furious, but his icy disdain was not to be borne.

"Don't trifle with me! There is no time! I ask you again…where is your sister?"

"What concern is that of yours? If you must know, she is staying with Charlotte Fairfax…"

"Is she? You had best read this." He produced a letter from his pocket and thrust it into her hand.

Miranda opened it with shaking fingers. The characters seemed to dance across the page, blurring as she tried to make them out. They began to swim before her eyes.

"Here, let me!" Heston said roughly. As he read the note to her, Miranda's worst fears were realised.

It was from Harry Lakenham, informing Heston that he had eloped. By the time the letter was received, he would be married.

Miranda swayed as the room seemed to spin about her. She sat down suddenly, feeling that her legs would no longer support her.

"I don't believe it!" she whispered. "Fanny would not…she could not…"

"On the contrary, I believe her capable of anything. Was this your idea?"

Miranda felt dumb with misery. She could not answer him.

"Don't play the innocent with me, my dear. It was a clever plan, I'll give you that. Were you to keep me occupied and throw me off the scent until

Lakenham and your sister found a suitable opportunity to disappear?"

"No! I thought she had changed her mind in favour of Count Toumanov."

"Another clever ploy? It will not serve. Both you and she would know that Toumanov would never offer for her."

"I knew it, but she did not, and you yourself threw them together."

"I admit it. I have never trusted her. She was meeting Lakenham after you were supposedly betrothed to me. Don't trouble to deny it, for I have proof."

"Please listen to me," Miranda cried in despair. "Let me explain. I owe you that at least."

"Pray go on," he said in an ironic tone. "It should make an interesting story."

"It is the truth," she said brokenly. "When you first came here, Fanny would not see you. We thought that you had come to offer for her. I was simply to refuse you, and that was to be an end of it."

Heston said nothing, but his eyes never left her face.

"And then...and then you were so insulting that I lost my temper. I said more than I intended. You shall not blame Fanny for that. It was all my fault."

"I lost my temper, too," he admitted in a kinder tone. "I had no right to force you into a betrothal."

"I could not believe that you would go on with it. Each day I hoped that you would release me from my promise. I knew that you wished to punish me, but when everything went so far I could see no way of escape…"

"And did you wish to escape?" There was something in his voice which brought the colour to her cheeks.

She turned her head away. "I had to. I tried to cry off, if you recall, on the day we went to Richmond."

"I remember it well."

"Then why didn't you agree? By then you knew of the deception…"

"By then I had changed my mind."

Miranda did not speak, but a tiny flicker of hope stirred in her heart. She stifled it at once. It would be too cruel to raise expectations which could never be fulfilled.

"Have you nothing more to say to me?" Heston enquired softly.

"I can only apologise, my lord. What you must think of us…of me…I can't imagine."

"Then I must tell you some time."

Miranda looked up at that, and was surprised to see a twinkle in his eyes. She felt confused.

"I wanted to tell you the truth. I was ashamed to do so, especially when I thought about my aunt and uncle, and Lady Heston too. They were all so kind. Oh, sir, if only a scandal might be avoided…!"

"It might be possible." Before she could protest, he took her in his arms. "My love, you are a goose! Can it be that you don't know how much I love you?" He dropped a tender kiss upon her brow.

"But you can't! Not after the way…"

"After the way you have stolen my heart? I have deceived you too, you know, in pretending that I thought that you were Fanny. It is I who should beg for your forgiveness. Will you dash my hopes?"

Miranda found that she hadn't the least desire to release herself from his embrace. She buried her face in his shoulder.

"Why did you go on with it?" she asked in muffled tones.

"Well, you know, I hoped that you had learned to trust me enough to tell me the truth."

"I couldn't. I loved you so, and—" She could not go on as he caught her to him, and his mouth found hers. Miranda clung to him in ecstasy lost in the wonder of his love. Then the door opened.

"I thought I should find you here," said Fanny.

Chapter Sixteen

Two pairs of startled eyes regarded her, and then Miranda sat down suddenly.

"What are you doing here?" she asked in a faint voice.

"I live here, in case you had forgotten." Fanny was clearly in the grip of some powerful emotion. "You won't believe what I have to tell you." She threw herself upon the sofa in a dramatic attitude. "I have been tricked in the most shameful way."

"Who has tricked you?" Miranda feared the worst.

"Why, Charlotte and Harry Lakenham. It is the most deceitful thing. They have eloped!"

Her injured expression was too much for Miranda's composure, but she tried to keep her voice steady.

"Are you quite sure?"

"Of course I am. I suppose I may believe the

evidence of my own eyes. We were shopping in the Emporium in Bond Street when I missed her. I looked about and then I saw her disappearing through the door at the back of the shop. When I followed, Harry was helping her into a closed carriage… I called to them, but they did not answer me."

"And then?"

"Well, I could not make it out. It seemed so strange of them to go for a drive without inviting me, and in a chaise with the blinds pulled down. I could not follow them, so I went back to Charlotte's home to see if they had returned, but they weren't there."

"Oh, Fanny, what a worry for you!"

"You may believe it! I never walked into such a turmoil in my life. Charlotte had left a note beside her bed, so there can be no doubt of the elopement. The worst of it is that Sir William blames me!"

"Astonishing!" Heston murmured. "What could have given him the idea that you would be party to such a plan, I wonder?"

Miranda threw him a reproachful look. "You knew nothing of it?"

"No, I did not. Charlotte may not think herself my friend in future. I shall not speak to her again. To steal off with Harry in that way…? It is beyond anything!"

"But you no longer care for him, I think?"

"No, I don't. He is a fribble. I have had a lucky escape, but that is not the point. I might have eloped with him myself…"

There seemed to be no immediate answer to this remark, but Fanny's expression tried Miranda sorely. Her sister resembled no one so much as a child who had been robbed of a favourite toy. She dared not look at Heston, but she guessed that his feelings were much the same as her own.

Fanny's glance was suspicious as she looked at the faces of her companions.

"You seem to find the situation amusing," she said sharply. "Had you not best go after them, my lord?"

"I think not, my dear Miss Gaysford. I believe I must leave that task to Sir William Fairfax." Heston took Miranda's arm. "Will you not take a turn about the garden with me, dearest, that is, if your sister will excuse us…?"

Fanny flounced out of the room, a thunderous expression on her face.

"Oh dear, I should not laugh," Miranda choked.

"Certainly not in here. Let me beg you to restrain yourself until we reach the summer-house…"

There Miranda laughed until she cried.

"What a wretch I am!" she gasped as she wiped

her streaming eyes. "It is not kind to be so unfeeling, but Fanny looked so…so…"

"Injured?" Heston's own shoulders were shaking. "I thought I had best rescue you before you disgraced yourself in your sister's eyes."

"She must be so hurt."

"Not at all! Your beloved twin is mortified to find that she is not the central figure in this elopement. The injury is to her pride, and I have no doubt that Sir William Fairfax further injured it."

"Fanny was right in one respect, my lord. This elopement will be a sad blow to Harry's grandfather, as well as to Charlotte's parents. Can you do nothing?"

"I wouldn't, even if I could. Sir William is a martinet, as Harry will discover to his cost. He may forget his previous ways. Sir William will have none of them."

"Then you think it may be for the best?"

"I do. I can think of nothing better to bring Harry to his senses."

"If they are already married…"

"Harry won't waste time. He is still under age and would fear pursuit. I imagine he would make for Doctors Commons with a licence in his pocket."

"But Sir William may annul the match."

"I doubt it. Harry bears an ancient name, and he will soon be in possession of his fortune."

"But Lord Rudyard? Oh, dear, he is not well… The shock may be too much for him."

"He knows Sir William, and that will be enough for him."

"You seem so sure?"

"I am, my dearest one. Besides which, I am ready at this moment to consign Charlotte, Harry and even your sister to perdition. We have been parted for a full two weeks, and I have missed you so." He looked down at her with such a tender expression that her heart began to pound.

She lifted her face to his. "I felt the same," she said simply. "Without you, the days seemed endless…"

He bent his head and she surrendered her lips to his. With that kiss the world was lost to both of them. All the heartache of the past few weeks vanished in a rising tide of passion, and Miranda felt a joy which she had not known before. He loved her. Now she could be sure of it, and the knowledge sent her spirit soaring.

When he released her she was breathless. She rested her head against his shoulder and took his hand in hers, absently stroking his fingers.

"My lord…" she began.

"Adam," he corrected. "Or are we not yet well enough acquainted for you to give me my name?"

Miranda blushed as she saw the laughter in his eyes. She could not mistake his meaning. Her overwhelming delight in that kiss had been equal to his own.

"Adam…when did you first know? I mean, when did you decide that I was not the termagant you thought me?"

"It was difficult," he told her gravely. "Those dagger looks quite sunk me. They did serious damage to my self-esteem. At times I considered putting a period to my existence."

"I wish you will be serious," she reproached him. "I asked you a sensible question."

"There was nothing sensible about my feelings, I assure you. I think I must have loved you from the first time that we met."

"Oh, what a fib! You called me a doxy."

"Did I say that? You caught me off balance, my beloved. I had not expected to receive such a severe setdown, though I deserved it."

"You did indeed!" she scolded with a loving smile. "I may tell you that I have never disliked anyone so much. You were a perfect monster, and I wanted to crush you into very small pieces."

Adam began to nibble her ear. "What a fate! When did you change your mind?"

"I don't quite know," she told him in a serious tone. "As I grew to understand you better, I felt that I must have been mistaken in your character and your motives for behaving as you did."

"They were always dastardly," he assured her with a wicked grin. "You have no fear that I shall beat you daily, and lock you in your room for weeks?"

"No!" she said demurely. "I doubt if you would wish to lock me away."

"Minx! What a dance you will lead me!" The prospect did not appear to worry him, for he kissed her again until her head began to spin. "My dearest, I love everything about you, from the tip of your head to those charming little toes. How well I know that enchanting face! It is the mirror of your soul."

"Even when I am looking cross?"

"Especially when you are looking cross. Your chin goes up and your eyes begin to sparkle..."

"At least I do not arch my back and hiss, you will admit. You told me once that I looked like an angry kitten."

"Ah, you remembered that?"

"I think I remember every word you've ever spoken to me." She pressed her lips against his hand.

"Oh, dear, not all of them, I hope? Remember only that I love you more than life, my darling... Will you do that?"

Her answer was in her eyes. He held her to him and then they heard the sound of approaching footsteps.

Alderman Shere was hurrying down the path towards them.

"Ah, there you are, my dear. Your aunt is returned and wishes to speak to you." He bowed to Heston. "There is no immediate hurry, my lord."

"I will come at once." Miranda rose to her feet. "Will you join us, Uncle? We have something to say to you."

"Nothing is amiss, I hope?" He looked at their faces and was satisfied. "No, I see that there is not...but this is a bad business about Charlotte Fairfax."

He turned back to the house, leaving them to follow him.

"I shall have to tell them," Miranda said in a low voice. "I can't go on with this deception, but what on earth am I to say?"

"Will you leave it to me?" Adam slipped an arm about her waist and hugged her. "Don't worry, my dearest. I promise you that all will be well. You must learn to rely on my support, you know."

Miranda threw him a speaking look of gratitude.

It was a comfort to think that she need no longer carry her burdens alone.

They found Mrs Shere alone in the salon and she was looking stern.

"My lord, you will forgive me for speaking out in front of you, but I must know. My dear, did your sister play any part in helping Charlotte to elope? She denies it, but there is no speaking to her…"

"No, ma'am, she did not. Fanny was as shocked as we were ourselves."

"Fanny? But you are Fanny. It was Miranda who went to stay with Charlotte…"

"No, ma'am." Adam sat down beside her and took her hands. "We must beg your forgiveness, Mrs Shere, and yours too, my dear sir. When I first came to you, I asked if I might pay my addresses to Miss Gaysford. I should have asked for Miss Miranda Gaysford. It was she who had my heart. The fault is mine. It was a foolish mistake, but I had thought Miranda the elder of the two."

"But, Lord Heston, you should have spoken when you found out your mistake. We should have understood…"

"You are too kind, ma'am, but I felt an utter fool. My pride was at stake. It is a sad failing in me, I fear. The trouble was that I did not at first realise…fond though I was, I did not know your nieces well."

"Perfectly understandable." The Alderman laughed aloud. "Emma, have I not always wondered how Lord Heston knew one twin from the other?"

Mrs Shere was not so easily satisified. "The girls are not in the least alike in temperament," she said doubtfully. "I confess that it was a puzzle to me to learn that my sister relied so heavily upon Miranda when I found her such a scatterbrain…"

"That was Fanny, ma'am. I feel a perfect wretch. I should have thrown myself upon your mercy long ago."

He was smiling as he spoke and Mrs Shere could not resist his charm. He had always been a favourite with her.

"I should give you a cruel scolding, and Miranda too," she said with mock severity.

"And I should deserve it, ma'am." He bent his head and looked so meek that Mrs Shere began to smile.

"Pray do not add play-acting to your other misdeeds, my lord… Just tell me one thing. Are you convinced that the lady by your side is indeed Miranda?"

"I'm certain of it, ma'am. Aren't you?" He stretched out a hand and drew Miranda to his side.

"Yes, I am, and I wish you happy, sir. You will not find a better wife."

Miranda threw her arms about her aunt and kissed her. Then she went to hug her uncle.

"May I tell Fanny that you know the truth?" she asked.

Mrs Shere reached out for the bell-pull and sent her servant to summon Fanny to the drawing-room.

She entered, looking subdued and in the expectation of another scolding, but Miranda set her mind at rest.

When Heston's apparent folly was explained to her, she looked at him with awe. Then she began to laugh.

Mrs Shere took her to task at once. "This is no laughing matter, Fanny. I am surprised that you should find it so amusing. Pray do not try to convince me that you knew nothing of it."

"No, ma'am, but you see... I was trying to protect Lord Heston's reputation."

"Lord Heston has no need of your protection. He would do nothing dishonourable."

It was clear that Adam was now to be absolved of all blame for his part in the charade.

"Don't look so smug!" Miranda hissed at him. "We have still to face your mother."

"She knows all about it, my love. I had to tell her. She was so worried about you."

"Deceiver!" Miranda threw him a fulminating glance. She might have said more but at that moment Richard was announced.

He seemed unsurprised to discover that a change had taken place and that he might now address his love by her own name.

The conversation now centred upon the arrangements for Miranda's wedding, and for the first time she was able to take part in the discussion with a happy heart.

"And your honeymoon, my lord. Where will you go for that?" Mrs Shere asked.

"Paris, I think, if Miranda agrees." Adam looked a question at her, but before she could reply Fanny intervened.

"Famous!" she cried. "I shall enjoy that above anything…"

Miranda stared at her in stupefaction. Beside her, she sensed that Adam was about to speak, but before he could do so Richard walked over to her sister and took her hand.

"You cannot go with Miranda," he said gently.

"Why not? It is quite the thing, you know, for a bride to have a friend or a relative with her for companionship."

Adam stirred again, but Miranda stilled him with a hand upon his arm.

"I thought you might prefer to go there as a bride yourself, Fanny." Richard stood quite still, but his face was alight with hope.

"How can I? I have no husband."

"You might have, if you will take me?"

He had Fanny's attention then. She stared at him.

"You can't mean it! Are you making me an offer?"

"Hand and heart, dear Fanny. Will you disappoint me?"

Fanny looked about her. The Alderman and Mrs Shere were speechless with astonishment but Adam and her twin were smiling. It was a most public declaration, and she was certainly the focus of all eyes.

"I'd like to marry you," she announced. "But, Richard, I always wanted to elope…"

"Then, of course, we shall elope, but there are arrangements to be made. Your aunt and uncle will wish to know where we are going."

"Is that usual?" she asked doubtfully. "I thought it was always meant to be a secret?"

"Not always!" Richard's face was grave. "I thought we might elope to Yorkshire, and go to Paris later. Then your mother and my father will be able to attend the ceremony…"

Beside her, Miranda felt Adam's shoulders begin to shake. "Hush!" she whispered. "Will you spoil everything?"

"I couldn't if I tried," he moaned in anguish.

Miranda dug her elbow into his ribs. Thankfully, Fanny had not noticed his paroxysms. She bestowed an enchanting smile upon her suitor and allowed him to clasp her in his arms.

Over her head Richard sought Miranda's eyes. His own held a curious mixture of love and rueful amusement but she nodded, happy to think that he had won his heart's desire. Life with Fanny would not be easy, but he loved her dearly and he knew her well. She need have no fears for her sister's future happiness.

"I am about to collapse," Adam whispered in a voice intended only for Miranda's ears. "In a moment I shall disgrace myself…"

He was rewarded with a stern look.

"Don't torture me," he begged. "I rescued you. Won't you do the same for me?"

Her own composure was sorely tried, but she made her excuses after offering the happy pair her good wishes for their future life together. Then she allowed Adam to lead her back into the garden.

This time they did not reach the summer-house. Adam clung to one of the supports of the pergola, unable to speak.

"My lord, I do not take this kindly," she told him with quivering lips. "Richard meant well…"

"I know it," he choked out at last. "The man is braver than Wellington himself. It was the elopement that was too much for me."

"You have a sadly frivolous side to your nature, sir."

"No, you are mistaken. I am the dullest dog in all the world. It did not occur to me to offer you an elopement, although you must have wished it."

"You are behaving very ill, my lord." Her own voice was not quite under her control. "If you go on like this, I shall begin to doubt your sanity."

"Only mine?" The look he gave her destroyed the last vestiges of her self-control, and her peals of laughter rang around the garden.

"Pray don't go on!" she gasped at last. "I feel quite weak…"

"Not weak enough to invite a companion to join us on our honeymoon journey, I hope?"

Miranda studied her fingers. "I had considered it," she announced.

"Really? You do not feel that I shall provide enough companionship for you, both day and night?"

"I don't know," she murmured wickedly.

"I think we had best continue this conversation in the privacy of the summer-house, my love…" He slipped an arm about her waist and led her along the path. Once inside the little wooden building he gripped her shoulders and looked down, still laughing, into her eyes. Then he shook her gently.

"Exasperating creature!" he said fondly. "Haven't I been punished enough? Must you continue to tease me?"

"Why, sir, I can't think what you mean."

"Can't you? Then I had best show you." He sat down and drew her on to his knee.

"Now, fair maiden," he uttered in melodramatic tones. "I have you in my power. To struggle will avail you nothing." He twirled an imaginary moustache.

Miranda found that she had no desire to struggle. Instead she slid her arms about his neck.

"You are behaving very foolishly," she whispered.

"I expect to behave foolishly for the rest of my life, my darling." He pressed his lips into the hollow of her throat. "Shall you mind?"

"I think I shall like it very much." She kissed his

cheek, aware only that his lips were teasing as they travelled upwards. Then his mouth found hers, and all else was forgotten in the wonder of his love.

* * * * *

millsandboon.co.uk Community

Join Us!

The Community is the perfect place to meet and chat to kindred spirits who love books and reading as much as you do, but it's also the place to:

- **Get the inside scoop from authors about their latest books**
- **Learn how to write a romance book with advice from our editors**
- **Help us to continue publishing the best in women's fiction**
- **Share your thoughts on the books we publish**
- **Befriend other users**

Forums: Interact with each other as well as authors, editors and a whole host of other users worldwide.

Blogs: Every registered community member has their own blog to tell the world what they're up to and what's on their mind.

Book Challenge: We're aiming to read 5,000 books and have joined forces with The Reading Agency in our inaugural Book Challenge.

Profile Page: Showcase yourself and keep a record of your recent community activity.

Social Networking: We've added buttons at the end of every post to share via digg, Facebook, Google, Yahoo, technorati and de.licio.us.

www.millsandboon.co.uk